CLEAN TIME

BURROW PRESS | ORLANDO, FL

ADVANCE PRAISE FOR CLEAN TIME

"Ronald Reagan Middleton is a hero for our time! A (sort-of) recovering addict, he finds himself caught up in the gears of a treacherous and all-too-plausible unholy alliance between big pharma and corporate media. *Clean Time* is an exuberant debut from novelist Ben Gwin, a satirical vision of the American nightmare that's a pure joy to read. Like a Nabokovian Eddie and the Cruisers, Gwin's novel goes in search of the missing Ronald Reagan, break-out star of The Recovery Channel's hit reality show *Clean Time*, and finds instead an America gone off its meds. *Clean Time* is a darkly comic odyssey through a land of serial killers, hipster poets, and Bob Seger. Somewhere Nathaneal West is green with envy!"

–KRISTOFER COLLINS, MANAGER, CALIBAN BOOK SHOP

"Read Clean Time. It is many things; dark, inventive, hallucinatory, funny as hell, but above all just hard to put down. And like all journeys worth taking, you won't always know where you're headed, but do so with Gwin and you will be rewarded for it."

–ADLAI YEOMANS, OWNER, WHITE WHALE BOOKSTORE

"There is enough emptiness, money, and heartache in *Clean Time* to make the Jazz Age proud. Ben Gwin knows that every character, like every one of us, is on an endless quest to be loved and he shows us the sadness that kind of desperation brings. It's in his prose. It's in his characters. This novel is outrageous, hilarious, violent, depraved, and, somehow, brilliantly tender. Ben Gwin writes like F. Scott Fitzgerald high on meth and *Clean Time* is *The Great Gatsby* for a generation that thinks fame is the answer to every question. Prepare to have your heart broken by a new and exciting talent."

–LORI JAKIELA, AUTHOR, PORTRAIT OF THE ARTIST
AS A BINGO WORKER

"If Vladimir Nabokov, George Saunders, Denis Johnson, and Hunter S. Thompson were trapped in an elevator for a month they might conceivably come up with a book as funny, frightening, and entertaining as this one. But I wouldn't count on it. Ben Gwin's rollicking vision of us is as sharp and fond as anyone's, and his brilliant tale of Ronald Reagan Middleton's loss and salvation is as profoundly American a novel as I've read in a long time."

–MICHAEL BYERS, AUTHOR, THE COAST OF GOOD INTENTIONS

"Hilarious, horrific, Gwin's *Clean Time* is a self-aware Odyssey for a drug-fueled, media-addled age."

–TOM SWETERLITSCH, AUTHOR, THE GONE WORLD

"*Clean Time* punches a hole in the American Dream with double-fisted prose and a brilliant narrative. This is a meta novel so good it will end all meta novels, a satire so current it reads like a headline in *The New York Times*. Ben Gwin has dumped the prison memoir, the recovery memoir, the academic treatise, and an unscrupulous blast of reality TV into the literary blender and come up with something entirely new and entertaining and horrifying. *Clean Time* is so funny, it will make you cry. You want to know what's happening in America right now? Turn everything off and read Ben Gwin. He is a young writer with a frightening amount of talent."

–DAVE NEWMAN, AUTHOR, PLEASE DON'T SHOOT ANYONE TONIGHT

"*Clean Time* is an eerily timely work of art—a prescient mash-up of the heartland opioid crisis, violent backwoods populism, and the hallucinatory, celebrity-obsessed world of reality television. The story of Ronald Reagan Middleton's struggles with addiction and his rise to fame is a nightmarish dispatch from America in the age of Donald Trump."

–DEREK GREEN, AUTHOR, NEW WORLD ORDER

CLEAN TIME

THE TRUE STORY OF RONALD REAGAN MIDDLETON

A NOVEL

BEN GWIN

BURROW PRESS | ORLANDO, FL

This publication is made possible in part by our Founding Sponsors:

MASTER OF
LIBERAL STUDIES

Burrow Press thrives on the direct support of its subscribers, and generous support from grants, companies, foundations, and individuals.

OF CENTRAL FLORIDA

Published by Burrow Press
PO Box 533709
Orlando, FL 32853
burrowpress.com

ISBN: 978-1-941681-70-1
LCCN: 2017952801

Book Design: Tina Craig
Cover Design: Ryan Rivas
Cover Photo: Nikola Jelenkovic

The poem, "Lonny's Curb Side 1AM," was written
by Celine Roberts and Taylor Grieshober.

Portions of this novel appeared in slightly different forms in the following publications: *IDK Magazine*, *Gulf Stream*, *Word Riot*, and *Burrow Press Review*.

For my family.

TABLE OF CONTENTS

THE GREYHOUND TO ATLANTA

I've been up since yesterday and I'm covered in sweat and pond water. I take off my shirt and try to hang it out the window to dry but it drops and disappears under the bus. My ribs are covered in strange bruises. The bridge rattles as we cross it, heading toward the highway and the promise of a fresh start. Five miles from the interstate we brake so hard my head slams into the seat in front of me. Up ahead there's a roadblock, and the bus falls in line with cars stuttering through the checkpoint. We come to a complete stop. Justin's framed perfectly in my window, cut open and hanging from a tree in his front yard.

I want to puke, but I haven't eaten so it just comes up as stomach acid. I swallow and whisper to myself, "What did you get yourself into?" I can't comprehend all the blood. Not just pooling beneath him, but everywhere. I want to look away, but can't. I watch him float above a ring of police and reporters. He's wearing one red slipper and the jeans Jacky and I gave him for his birthday—thirty or thirty-one. And there's so much blood. Like it couldn't have come from one person.

I bang on the window and scream, "You stupid fuck." I didn't even like Justin all that much, but I start crying and can't stop.

It gets real quiet real quick and everyone stares at me. Face pressed to the window and bawling. My back sticks to the seat when I try to slouch out of sight. The bus jerks ahead and stops again. The driver opens the door, and a cop wearing big sunglasses steps inside. He calls my name. I do nothing and he calls it again.

We can do this the hard way or the easy way. I'm trying to figure out how they know I'm here, what they think I've done. I stand and push my shoulders back.

"What?" I ask and wipe my eyes.

"Need a word with you," the cop says, and I swear he's the tallest human I've ever seen.

The dull cabin sparkles in the light of emergency vehicles. The cop smiles. His mirrored lenses hold my reflection, and I know there's no way I'm getting to Georgia.

FOREWORD

The previous passage was pulled from the memoir of my former student, Ronald Reagan Middleton. For the uninformed, Ronald Reagan Middleton is a man who, on live television, discovered our nation's dreams of redemption and expressed the essence of these dreams in such a manner that he allowed us, the viewing public, a better understanding of the human condition. He took on the national media, escaped a serial killer, and subverted a pharmaceutical conglomerate. During his time in treatment for methamphetamine addiction, he saved the lives of at least two counselors and one patient.

The importance of Ronald Reagan's journey as it relates to present day American storytelling and culture cannot be understated. America desperatly needs a hero, a figure to look to in these tubulent times marred by political strife, class struggles, and rampant drug addiction. A flawed hero who encapsulates what is possible in this great country. One whose tale does more than perpetuate the common anti-hero narrative. A number of academic papers written on reality television and reality television stars, well received inside the academy but inaccessible to the general public, have not touched on any of these parallels. Further, Ronald Reagan has been the subject of several authorized and unauthorized-made-for-TV movies, a novelization of his time in rehab, and countless think pieces and essays. While these renderings of Ronald Reagan's life are not without merit, I feel they have glossed over his spiritual growth and perseverance, as they pertain to his role as a contemporary mythological figure. In response, I have tried to contextualize these feelings in my presentation of his own words, which are published here for the first time.

The following memoir is Ronald Reagan Middleton's chronicle of the many battles he waged against various addictions, compulsions, and institutions. Before he went missing, Ronald Reagan gave his memoir to his writing mentor, Sophia Trent, who in turn, mailed it to Ronald Reagan's younger brother, Robert "Bob" Middleton Jr., with instructions to travel to the town of Booth, North Carolina and locate Dr. Blank to help prepare the memoir for publication.

I am Harold Swanger, MA, three semesters to PhD, Adjunct Professor of Classics and Humanities.[1]

While often misguided, Ronald Reagan was one of my brightest students. His journey encapsulates all that is possible in contemporary storytelling. His is the tale of an addiction laid bare. Recovery rendered through raw narrative power. A triumph of the American spirit. Above all, Ronald Reagan Middleton's story offers hope.

THE ARRIVAL OF THE MANUSCRIPT

I'd recently moved into Dr. Blank's old office and inherited his course load and research assistant, though she was soon fired due to budget cuts. The only good to come of this was the ability to use her desk to hold my first editions, and the box of Ronald Reagan's old term papers, which I'd found while rummaging through Dr. Blank's trash upon his dismissal. That winter, I spent countless hours in my office studying tapes of Ronald Reagan Middleton's time on television. One evening, while engaged in this very activity, I heard a knock on my door in the Guilford State University Classics Department.[2]

After ignoring the knocking for several minutes, it became apparent the caller would not leave. I opened the door. There stood Bob Middleton, Ronald Reagan's younger brother, in the narrow hallway, holding a Brewtown Ice box filled with tattered manila envelopes and composition books. I recognized him immediately. He bore a striking resemblance to Ronald Reagan before he'd dyed his hair and began donning a series of disguises.

"Are you Dr. Blank?" he asked.

"Yes," I said.

Though Dr. Blank had been fired nine months ago, his nameplate still hung from the door. It was a bad habit, impersonating Dr. Blank, which I mainly did out of boredom, but in retrospect, I'm glad I did. Not until later would I reveal my true identity to Bob. Once I realized what he'd brought me, there was too much at stake.

A NOTE ABOUT THE ASSEMBLY OF THE MANUSCRIPT

I must reiterate the incoherent state of the package upon its arrival—not much more than a box of notebooks filled with barely legible scribbling and a set of twelve audiotapes wrapped in a blue rubber band.

As primary editor (with Bob's assistance, of course) I have not altered the content of the original manuscript in any way, though we were at times forced to piece together a linear narrative using a mix of audio and unpolished writing (what appear to be drafts that RR never revised). Any other alterations or deviations have been noted in their respective sections.

Bob and I spent the winter transcribing this work and the spring and summer fact checking. We contacted and met many of the people mentioned or alluded to in Ronald Reagan's memoir. In some cases, names had been changed. In others they had not. This decision seemed arbitrary on Ronald Reagan's part. We've included some of our interviews, as well as relevant excerpts from *Clean Time* scripts, between scenes in the memoir to further contextualize Ronald Reagan's story. Commas and other punctuation have been added, in places, for clarity.

We also reviewed the security footage of his time in jail and spoke with several of his aforementioned associates, many of whom were not directly quoted. Unfortunately, Mr. and Mrs. Middleton were unavailable for comment.

Nearly a year after completing his memoir, Ronald Reagan has not yet surfaced.

PART ONE

THE GHOST AND THE BLUE DRESS

THE GUILFORD COUNTY JAIL:
SECOND NIGHT IN GENERAL POPULATION

I'm huddled in my bunk writing in very low light. Outside, there's an argument over a card game and one of the guards is screaming. The windows in the cell doors are barely the size of a basketball. Last night, through a circle that size, I watched the guy in the cell across the hall die. I swear. Some kind of seizure after a mild heart attack because they wouldn't give him his meds. The dying man and his cellmate, Gator, didn't scream as loud as the guard is screaming now. Someone just threw what sounded like a chair or a table. Cacophony. The echoes bury me in here. I know they're coming, but I jump every time. Late at night it almost sounds like laughter.

Behind me, my cellmate Ace is wearing mustard-colored scrubs and staring out the porthole that overlooks the basketball court and the yard, toward the fence and the barbed wire. He's 63. According to my other cellmates, this is what Ace has been doing every winter for the last thirteen years of his life: he gets out of jail, steals a car, then drives to the police station and turns himself in so he'll have a warm place to sleep.

Now he seeks out windows and stares, occasionally picking at his sideburns or tapping on his prescription goggles. It's like Ace is already thinking about how terrifying it will be when he gets out.

I'm nothing like these people, I swear.

FAMILY

So here's the worst thing I've ever done to my family. I feel terrible about it.

Two Thanksgivings ago, I went back to New Jersey and held my mother hostage with the power washer the landscapers use to clean the marble around the pool.[3] The threat of 3,000 pounds-per-inch of pressurized water pressed into her neck, my dad and little brother screamed and pleaded in the living room. I needed $250.

"Ronald Reagan, goddamn it, it's Mom," my brother Bob kept screaming. "Goddamn it. What is wrong with you? Shit, Jesus. Goddamn it. It's Mom."

Fuck Bob. My parents gave him everything. They bought Bob a car, they sent Bob to Europe, got him his own credit card. It's bullshit.

Dad walked behind the bar in the living room and poured himself a drink. "You've done it," he said. "You have finally destroyed this family."

Dad emptied his glass, and my mouth felt dry. "Go fuck the cleaning lady," I said.

"Honey, you can have the money. Robert, Bobby, one of you just give him the money."

I pressed the nozzle into Mom's neck. If she weren't so emaciated from drinking all the time I think she could have taken me. I'm 6'3", but at the time I only weighed 120, tops.

"Bobby Junior," I said. I called my brother Bobby Jr. because he hated it, fucking hated being named after our dad. "Bobby Junior get the money out of Mom's purse and give me my keys. Right this second, Bobby Junior!"

I needed the money to get back to my apartment in Booth. The idea of spending one more night in my childhood home was horrifying. Bob walked over to Mom's purse, glaring at me. His stare dropped to the floor as he tossed me the keys.

"You're not better than me, Bobby Junior."

The whole thing started earlier that day. It was the night before Thanksgiving, and I was back from Guilford State. I'd flown in to Philly, took Jersey Transit to Princeton Junction, then sat and listened to my mom passive-aggressively bitch at me for twenty minutes on the ride home—my first time back since I'd left for school. After all that, I got home and my bedroom door was locked. My parents had given my old room to Bob. I'd only been away at college for five years. Fifteen credits away from graduation, feeling proud of myself, and I came home to Bob with two bedrooms connected by the bathroom we shared growing up. Bob had turned my old room into a lounge.

Furious, I called around till I found a ride, cashed in my return ticket, and met up with some old friends in Lawrence. My night out ended with me funneling half a bottle of Evan Williams, throwing a bird feeder at a passing motorist, and riding home ten miles on a bike I stole from some hipster.

During the ride I realized I needed to get back to Booth. For that, I needed another $250 and my old car (half of which I paid for myself and which Bob drove around until my parents bought him that SUV). Ever since I left for college it had just been sitting in the driveway collecting dust. On my way inside, I tripped over the power washer and got an idea.

Bob held out a stack of twenties. "It's Thanksgiving," he said. "Just take it easy."

"Take it easy take it easy take it easy. You take it easy, Bobby Junior." I grabbed the money, pocketed my keys, pushed my mom toward Bob and ran through the screen door singing, *Bobby Junior, Bobby Junior, HaHAha, Bobby Junior.*

In the driveway, still singing, I kneeled between our two cars and keyed "FUCK YOU BOBBY JR!" into the passenger-side door when Dad came out and shot me with the pellet gun he'd bought for my eleventh birthday—the kind you have to pump like fifteen times to break the skin.

"You pussy." I felt nothing when I spoke or when the next BB hit me in the arm. Completely dried out, that's what I was. Full of disgust and needing bad to level off, I walked toward him. "I'm just trying to leave," I explained.

I grabbed the pellet gun and hit him in the leg with it.

Dad was over 70 and had had a stroke. "Don't come back," he said and limped back through the garage.

I could hear my mom and brother inside crying. I felt it, saw it through the walls while I fumbled with my keys. Walking back to my battered station wagon, I realized I'd keyed the wrong car in my haste.

I reached into the open window of Bobby's car and grabbed two big binders full of CDs and a half pack of cigarettes. Then I got in my station wagon and took off for West Trenton, where I knew a guy who knew a girl.

After I copped, I headed south with three-quarters of an ounce of coke under the seat. I drove through the night, over four hundred miles. I'd just passed through Greensboro when a cop pulled me over two miles from my apartment in Booth. He gave me a ticket for going 70 in a 65 and let me go.

I got home at dawn feeling lucky. I should have been searched and busted. The whole scene leading up to the ticket replayed itself. Birds started chirping outside. This was the culmination of my first twenty-five years on earth.

After that, I did my best to turn things around in North Carolina. But I couldn't stay clean.

CELLMATES

When I was processed into general population from my holding cell, I traded one of my undershirts for this notebook so I could write Jacky. I got the notebook from my other cellmate, Otto, a bald seventeen-year-old train hopper with tattoos on his face. He confused me with the guy who plays the head detective on *Werewolf Hunter!*, that show that isn't really that great but everyone loves. They're making a movie out of it.

"Did you actually take out the corrupt Deputy Mayor while under the spell of the Lycan of Tilbury?" Otto asked, after we completed the transaction.

"Something like that," I said and flipped through the notebook to make sure it was new.

"That's why you're here," he said, "isn't it?"

I didn't have the heart to tell him I was not who he thought. "Basically," I said, and it got me wondering if I could use this to my advantage. Being famous might give me an easier go of it in here.

Despite his confusion, I don't mind Otto. He may be the only guy in here you can have a conversation with about something other than poker, the food, Jesus, alleged mob ties, or stories of events so outlandish they couldn't have possibly avoided national news coverage. Everyone says they'll be out soon, even Otto.

•

My cell is small and cold. Aside from the doors, there are no seams or creases anywhere. The walls and the floor form one big sheet of lemon-colored linoleum, and the windows just sink into the walls. The toilet sprouts out of the corner like a toadstool. Everything is made of the same pale yellow, even the three sets of bunk beds along the wall that take up half the cell.

•

In here, everyone has a nickname. I write so much everybody calls me Hemingway. Writing helps pass time and keeps my brain limber.

Across the hall, Gator is screaming "HEEEEEMINGWAY!" and banging on his cell door. He's been edgy since his cellmate died. He has a crocodile with a dove in its mouth tattooed across his chest and upper arms and blood dripping down to his fingertips.

Besides Otto and Ace, I have two other cellmates. Magazine Johnny is a 22-year-old heroin dealer who earned his name when he did three-to-five upstate. His girl buys him all these magazine subscriptions. I swear, he has hundreds. "She sells them for her job," he always says. In here they're like gold. Right now he's smearing butter he stole from dinner over a huge cold sore on his mouth.

Then there's Crazy Mike. He's giving Johnny shit for the butter and calling him a faggot. Mike is doing nine months for heroin possession. His white hair looks like fishing line and brushes his shoulders when he doesn't tie it back, which is rare. "Hair can't be in my face if there's a riot," he says. He reminds me of my grandfather and Santa Claus.

One time I asked Mike why he was here. "Can't get away from the needle," he said. "Don't really want to either."

I don't know how long my sentence is, or if I'll even go to trial. This lawyer my parents set me up with won't even take my calls.

•

I get along with my cellmates. I'm scared as shit of Gator. Everyone else just blends together like a living, breathing wallpaper pattern.

At night, Otto scoops the water out of the toilet. He and Johnny and Mike take turns talking to the female inmates through the pipes. Something about the way the plumbing runs makes this possible. Yesterday, I woke up in the middle of the night and saw Crazy Mike jerking off with his head in the toilet.

NORMAL

If I look hard I can see back to when things weren't so fucked, but I can't find the axis, the point when it all went to shit. I know a time exists when I felt and acted normal. I played catch with my brother, did the regular kid stuff like bike riding and tree climbing, collecting rocks and building forts. Family trips to the beach in Georgia. For a while everything was fine. But then it muddles. The tipping point vanishes. All of the sudden I'm a fucking mess. Hiding my wallet and car keys from myself. Writing notes in my phone about which girl I can't call anymore, which one will flip out if I'm on coke and which one will fuck me if I'm holding. Carrying a photo of myself with my name and address written on the back in case I lose my wallet and someone finds me in a blackout. My whole life revolves around getting fucked up and laid.

I don't know exactly what normal is, but I think I saw it once, like a highway exit sign in the distance, and I flew right past it.

WRITING CLASS

I figured it would look good if I presented the appearance of improving my situation, of becoming pro-active in the reformation of my life. So I signed up for the only programming the jail offered: NA meetings on Wednesdays, and a creative writing class run by grad students from my old college. I've been thinking about all the fucked up shit I've been through and that maybe I should write a memoir.[4]

•

When I got to class today, Gator was the only one in the room, on his knees, going through the supply closet and piling magazines on a desk. I sat on the opposite side of the room. A glue stick rolled out of the cabinet and stopped at my foot. Gator grabbed the magazines and sat right next to me. "Gonna write me a story, Hemingway?" he asked.

"No." I picked up the glue stick. "Need this?"

His desk screeched on the floor as he moved closer. Gator's teeth were perfect and his eyes were all pupil. He grabbed the glue stick. His hands were soft.

"Thanks." He tapped the stick on his desk. "So, how about a story?"

"Just trying to keep busy, man," I said. I scanned the room for a weapon and settled on a keyboard within reach. If need be, I could smash him in the face then choke him with the cord. I scooted my desk toward the computer behind me when the door clicked open.

"I hope we have more than two students today," the young woman said. She pushed the door shut with her foot. She carried a three-ring binder that looked like it was about to explode and shower us with paper. "Sorry I'm late. Warden kicked me out of the lot." She wore bright orange sneakers and a matching scarf wrapped around her forehead, black hair damp with perspiration. "Had to park by the pig farm and walk." I smelled citrus and sweat and fresh-cut grass when she passed by. "Got a workout though, for sure." The binder boomed when she dropped it on the big desk by the supply closet. She introduced herself as Sophie and passed out a writing exercise about memory.

Using his hands and the glue stick, Gator ripped out words and pictures from magazines and made a sort of poem-collage that had something to do with leaves and autumn and loss. The poem was heartbreaking.

I started writing my memoir, started from as far back as I could remember. I saved it on the computer in a folder titled "Hemingway." Sophie took home hard copies of my work and said she'd give me written feedback if I could wait a few weeks.

•

Sophie looks so frail, like she might shatter if you touched her wrist. I keep attending her class, and she helps me capture the essence of my childhood on the page. I've written about the days when I played Wiffle ball with my brother. When we melted my action figures in the driveway with magnifying glasses I stole from school. Sophie has this way about her that seems like she understands how pain can just burrow through your chest if you don't find a place for it.

Still no word from my lawyer about what's going on, but by the time I get out of here, I'll have a head start on the complete story of my life. Could be worse. The class is improving my writing. Despite the possibility that my defense attorney is intentionally violating my rights, I'm enjoying my time in class. My goal is to complete the memoir. I've never finished anything.

THE HOUSE IN GEORGIA

Otto's hand just dropped over the side of the bunk above me. The moon and floodlights shine through the window and the shadow of Otto's arm sways on the wall. Everyone's asleep.

If I look into the low light long enough my vision gets that TV pixel-blind feeling, like when I used to put my face right up to the set as a kid to see if I could move through it and into the world of television.

I close my eyes and see my family's vacation home in Georgia. Fragmented, it comes to me, pieces torn from a photograph.

Tucked into the corner of a Georgia beach, my grandfather had named the cottage "Our Atlantis." I don't remember Granddad. My earliest recollections of the house come from a time after his death, but he'd carved a sign out of an ugly piece of driftwood and hung it at the end of the driveway. From the back seat, I used to reach out and touch it when we drove past.

I remember the window above the kitchen didn't close all the way. Mom covered the opening with plastic that rattled in the wind coming off the shore.

The back porch overlooking the Atlantic was a constant project for my dad. Every trip down he spent the first couple mornings replacing rotted sections of two-by-fours and staining the new ones. He never had time to redo the whole thing all at once, or maybe he just liked to leave himself another patch for the next trip so he'd always have something to do.

The last time I went down there I was in elementary school. For most of the first day of our vacation, I stood next to my dad and handed him nails out of a rusty coffee tin while the smell of the ocean and my mom's burnt dinner pulled the two of us in different directions. The oldies station played '60s pop songs by the window that didn't close. Holding those nails felt like the most important job I'd ever have.

There was no TV, but I hardly noticed. Instead I'd go to the back porch, tie fishing line around my army men, and drop them through the knot holes. I bet there's a whole platoon of little green soldiers buried in that sand. Later my parents and me and toddler Bob would play Monopoly and listen to the Braves games fade in and out on the radio while outside the waves lapped and the salty air ate away at the porch. I'd lie on the foldout couch in the living room and fall asleep to the sound of ghosts whapping at the plastic over the window.

JACKY WITH A Y

Here is what I can remember of the series of events leading up to my incarceration.

There was a period of time between the power washer incident and jail that I had it going pretty good. After I got that speeding ticket, I went back to my place and blew the rest of the coke. I locked myself in my apartment and cleaned while I exhausted my stash. I only left for booze. When the coke ran out, my head felt like an aquarium filled with gasoline and predatory fish. I drank myself to sleep and let it run its course. The fish died and the feeling subsided.

Living in a clean but empty apartment and finally through with blow, I was determined to get my shit together. Boredom was a problem, but I was determined. If I could keep it to moderate amounts of alcohol, I'd be okay. Finals came and went. I passed fall semester by .02, and found myself six credits shy of a degree. Over winter break, I took a job doing yard work for an old lady in West Booth for seven dollars an hour. I spent Christmas alone and cleaned my apartment again. I painted the walls dark green with blue trim and replaced my Phish posters with prints by famous-sounding artists. I cut out the booze entirely and started going to the gym. I called home every Sunday but no one ever answered.

Grandma sent me a gift card that arrived five days after Christmas, and instead of trying to sell it, I decided to buy myself some decent clothes. That's how I met Jacky. She worked at the Jordache$Fitch store near campus, folding sweaters.

When I asked her name she said, "Jacky with a Y," in that soft drawl that still haunts me.

Together we weaved through the neatly stacked and color-coded shelves and I let her pick out shirts for me. Emboldened by my ability to stay clean for five weeks, I asked her out, hoping she was the kind of good thing that happened when you quit getting high.

"Sure," she said, "dinner and a movie sounds nice."

"Grand," I said. I'd never used that word before.

She lived with her parents on the edge of the nice part of Booth. When I arrived at her place, her sister met me at the front door and stared at me like I had two heads.[5] Like, where does this white kid in his ridiculously tight shirt and goofy smile think he's taking Jacky in that station wagon with no mirrors and "FUCK YOU BOBBY JR!" keyed into the side?

Jacky's hair coiled like a bouquet of watch springs and bounced when she skipped down her front steps. That Carolina-blue dress was magic rolling past her knees, like she was on her way to church dressed as Alice on leave from Wonderland. After dinner we watched a movie about a kid who could fly.

Without asking, she lit a joint in the car on the way back to her house. Our fingertips touched when she passed it, and the steering wheel grew slick with my sweat as I took the long way back to her house.

Row houses gave way to farmhouses and barns. Streetlights to moonlight and stars. A spark of disappointment burned in my throat, but the feeling got wrapped up in the cloud of smoke curling in front of Jacky's dark eyes and sucked into the winter night. Gone as fast as she could change the music.

"You like country?"

"Old stuff," I said.

"Me too."

After a couple hits I waved it off, feeling like the wind might lift me out of the cracked window.

Jacky fingered the hem of her dress.

On the radio a man sang of whiskey and ruin.

Jacky invited me in. Before I could pretend to get nervous about her parents or how much noise the stairs made when we creaked into her basement bedroom, she pinned me against the wall.

"Why?" she asked. Her nose nudged mine, her lips against my cheek.

"Why what?"

"Why are you making me do this?"

The slippery blue material of her dress swirled between us and made sounds like TV static as she kissed the corner of my mouth. Her leg wrapped around my waist at an angle I still can't comprehend. I whispered *Jesus* when she pushed her foot down my hamstring, over my calf to my Achilles.[6]

•

When Jacky wasn't selling clothes she moved pounds of weed out of her basement room. She got her pot from Tom Canada, a near-mythological figure in Booth. A whack job recluse with his hands in a little bit of everything. Tom was paranoid, but he trusted Jacky, trusted her almost exclusively. He owns a dive bar called Screwdrivers near GSU campus. We drank there all the time but I never saw him.

•

Late January I started my senior project—a screenplay adaptation of *The Odyssey* set in a California high school. It was an independent study with Dr. Blank at Guilford State. I'd taken his World Lit class as a junior. The guy was brilliant, and we shared a similar aesthetic vision.[7]

I graduated in May, but didn't walk. My family still refused to acknowledge my existence. I kept working on the screenplay with Dr. Blank, and I studied *The Odyssey* and all its contemporary adaptations with an ardent academic fervor I'd never displayed while enrolled at the university. Me and Dr. Blank would get stoned and develop our protagonist: a 17-year-old ball player trying to make it to the majors. It was a good way to keep busy while Jacky was at work.

In August, after dating for almost nine months, Jacky and I moved into this great old house on Frederick. The hardwood floors creaked all night and half the windows had been painted shut, but it was as spacious a place as I'd lived in since childhood. Jacky bought it at auction and paid in cash.

Summer started to wane, and I quit working for the lady in West Booth so I could help Jacky with business. She fronted me ounces and I sold eighths and twenty-bags to the college kids and professors she was too sketched out by and busy to deal with herself. A reliable clientele existed among Dr. Blank's associates at State, and small-timers like myself who hung around the bars and coffee shops in town.

"Just be smart," Jacky would tell me. "You're smart."

The sun was finally shining on me.[8]

In September Jacky got me a job in the Jordache$Fitch warehouse as a Blue Jean Vintage Modification Technician. From 9AM to 8PM, I modified new, un-broken-in, acid-washed denim pants. This modification entailed donning the tight, tapered pants, sprinkling on three ounces of acid wash solution, and lunging.

Lunges and squats. Fifty lunges per pair, fifty pairs a day. After this, I'd use a melon-baller and a hammer on each pair to slightly rip and fray the jeans before they got passed on to the Wallet Imprinting Division. I got two free pairs of jeans per quarter (over $1,000 retail) and just over minimum wage. By the time I got off work at night, after doing 2,500 lunges, I was too tired to eat let alone work on the screenplay. I'd crawl into bed reeking of bleach, legs throbbing, and pull Jacky close. I'd lie there and watch her chest rise and fall, terrified of what I might do.

•

I'd been doing well enough on a regimen of weed and beer, but in mid-September an old friend of Jacky's moved to Pittsburgh and set up a meth lab outside the city near Trafford, Pennsylvania. The stuff she cooked had a weird blue tint to it, like Jacky's dress, the exact color actually, and this friend sent us pounds of it in the mail. It arrived in old Lego boxes, and we called it Trafford Dynamite, The Ghost of Trafford, Blue Dynamite, Blue Ghost, or some such variation.

Initially it was perfect. Thanks to Jacky's connection, there was money and glass everywhere. The Ghost solved my too-tired-to-write problem and the screenplay hummed (but it was lost before we finished it).[9] I broke in one hundred and fifty pairs of J$F jeans a day. I was a machine. I was promoted to Shift Supervisor.

By Halloween we were rolling in it. Between the prep school and the college, we were in prime real estate for that kind of operation. But it wasn't just kids from Prep and State. People came from several counties for this stuff. And all with Tom Canada's blessing. I don't know what kind of a kickback Jacky gave him, but he never bothered us. We kept all this up until June. I was arrested in July.

NEMESIS

Jacky's only real enemy was Justin. He was the reason she swore off cell phones. We were almost friends for a while, before he lost it. Meth and molly crippled his brain. Caught up to him all at once. He started sending text messages in stupid slang. Stuff like: "Can we see your blue friend from Trafford later?" and "Let's watch that Ghost movie with Mary Jane tonight."

Justin rolled around with our friend Mooch so we couldn't avoid him entirely. Once in a while we'd wind up at Justin's with Mooch, not knowing exactly why or what for. Or Justin would randomly stop in at the house, or we'd see him at Screwdrivers. He'd give me shit for dating a black girl, and I couldn't do anything about it because Mooch was there and he is fucking enormous. Scrawny-ass Justin would drink and start fights and no one fucked with him because the whole town loved Mooch.[10] Sometimes Justin would get real hammered and start feeling on Mooch, who just sat there disinterested. And I mean, great, if that's your thing, but there was something off about it. Like everyone knew they were a couple but Mooch.[11]

COST OF BUSINESS

Jacky never cut breaks and didn't front anyone. Her only thing was that she would take trade.

I'd be smoking pot with Dr. Blank in the den and we'd watch these hollow-eyed kids, spines all tangled and hunched, carrying armloads of porcelain figurines and music boxes and pocket watches up the front steps. One speed freak antiques dealer basically furnished our house. By Jacky's account, close to thirteen percent of her profit was bartered for, and she kept most of it. What she didn't keep, I fenced through Mooch's buddy. One time some guy traded her a pistol. I don't know shit about guns, but it was small, a .22, with this ornate handle that looked like fish scales. Enough money and drugs passed through Jacky's hands that she figured she'd keep it.

•

The biggest thing Jacky ever acquired was Justin's piano. Maybe six weeks before I got thrown in jail, Justin fucked up a deal with these guys down in Tampa that was supposed to make Tom Canada ten grand.

It was a humid summer morning when Justin showed up at our place begging for Jacky to front him a couple pounds of meth so he could sell it and make back the money he'd lost on the Tampa deal, so Tom Canada wouldn't cut him up into pieces and send them to his mom in the mail. "Don't ruin my plan," he told Jacky. He kept rambling on about something called The Firm, but I had no idea what he was talking about.

Jacky said, "No breaks."

"You're being completely unreasonable," said Justin. "What do you really want?"

"I told you, the piano," Jacky said, and that was it. She charged him street value, less the cost of the piano, for three pounds of meth.

Jacky put up the money for the movers and the truck and everything. Justin and Mooch came back in the afternoon. Justin paid Jacky and cut himself out a taste in the office while we waited for the truck to arrive.

They had to pulley the thing up to the balcony and through the double doors that opened into the master bedroom on the second floor. The room was already crowded with electronics and designer clothes and a collection of lamps we didn't have space for.

One of the movers had a nose ring and a bad tattoo that looked like someone did it with a knife and fork. "Can't get it down the stairs," he said. "It's staying here."

"There's a room next door," Jacky said.

"Door's too small," he said, and mussed his greasy haircut.

Jacky stood and stared at the bed. "Through the wall."

"What?"

"The wall. Go through it."

I helped sledgehammer through the plaster and drywall, and after an hour we rolled the baby grand into our new sitting room.

Jacky lit a cigarette and sat on the piano bench. "It's a shame," she said. "I don't even play."

THE GREATEST TRADE EVER MADE

One time Jacky took a complete set of 1989 Upper Deck baseball cards off a kid for a twenty-bag. She gave me the Ken Griffey Jr. rookie card, the crown jewel. When we first started dating, I'd get drunk and tell her about how much I missed baseball and watching Griffey play outfield as a kid. She gave the rest of the cards to our friend Cindy, who lacquered them all into a set for a marionette performance of *Fences* she put on at Guilford Prep where she teaches twelfth-grade drama.

A few months passed, and I cut back my hours at the warehouse. I started thinking about the future. After we made enough money, I thought we'd get out of Booth. We were fucked up—I know I was anyway—and we both knew it wasn't often you stayed in that line of work for very long and got out unscathed.

This wasn't going to be one of those stories where the anti-hero criminal gets busted on that last big job before they go straight. We were inconspicuous. Jacky kept close track of our finances, and I organized all the bartered goods and sold pot on the side. Our house continued to fill up with other people's memories. But I didn't mind. They were better than most of my own.

AND THEN IT GOT WORSE...

In June, it got worse. Without warning, the Lego boxes stopped arriving every Monday and Jacky couldn't reach her girl in Trafford. With her connection gone, we had to go into the city with Mooch to buy weight.

Mooch always took Justin's Mercedes. To get car permission, Mooch had to tell Justin he was going to drop off the dry cleaning at the twenty-four-hour place outside of town, so we always rode with a pile of Justin's dress shirts.

When we got to the city we'd park in front of this house with the frame of a torched foldout couch on the porch, and a crooked tree pushing up between the fence and a broken brick walkway. Jacky and I would sit in the car while Mooch went around the block to an apartment complex where some kid he played high school football with made cut-rate meth. After an agonizing wait, Mooch would come back with 2-to-4 ounces of shitty, overpriced crank. We had to make two or three trips a week to keep up with Jacky's cash flow projections, and we were still using heavily. Jacky's girl up north wasn't calling any time soon.

It was a Saturday, during a trip to the city, when we decided to leave for Georgia sooner than we'd planned. It wasn't like there was some big, epiphany-causing event that night. No overdose, stick-up, or arrest. No message from God. It was more like the dull repetition of this routine played out in front of us on a loop. The drive. The car full of laundry. The shadow cast by the burned-out couch in front of the projects when hit with a passing car's headlights. The insufferable heat. All the waiting and waiting and waiting. Something about that night made the decision to leave feel inevitable.

When we got home we decided to give ourselves two weeks to get everything in order and then leave town. With my car in no shape for such a trek, we bought bus tickets that night. "In advance," I told Jacky. "So we can't change our minds."

THE NIGHT OF JUSTIN'S DEATH

Cindy wore a pair of thick-rimmed windowpane glasses. "Placebo lenses," she liked to call them. "I can see your thoughts." Her hair was done up in a series of concentric buns.

At the time, I didn't like any of the people we hung out with besides Cindy. Everyone else had an agenda. Along with teaching, Cindy was an activist and playwright. Always writing and organizing and trying to inspire the privileged high school kids at Prep. She was lighting candles and incense when we got to her apartment, which was on the Guilford Prep campus with the rest of the faculty. All the high school students were on summer break, and most of the other teachers had moved out for the renovations, so we had the place to ourselves.

Cindy's sister had died a month earlier. She used to make her own acid. Later that night, a Grateful Dead cover band was playing across town at Guilford State, and Cindy wanted to sell the rest of her dead sister's acid there. This was our last night in Booth. We had our bus tickets and had been talking all week about leaving for Georgia. Things had grown unbearable, but we felt like we had a purpose. Getting down south and gaining some perspective on our whole situation was going to do us some good. Cindy said she'd come visit.

We split two hits of LSD and snorted a couple green pills in Cindy's living room. The Hold Steady shot up on the stereo.

"I'm pretty sure they're E," Cindy said of the pills.

Jacky leaned forward and waved her hand over a stout candle. "Well, it'll be an experiment," she said, letting wax drip and harden on her fingers. "I'm up for it." She buzzed beneath a watery curtain, smiling. She wiped wax on her skirt, leaving faint white smears on the dark red corduroy. "Let's walk," she said, and we left.

Whatever the pills were they felt dopey initially, and we decided we needed a pick-me-up before the show. We took the alley and turned down East St. past Screwdrivers, toward the 7-Eleven. It was Friday night and the town hummed as we moved closer to the big stone buildings on State's campus. The idea of a pick-me-up intensified.

We stopped at the payphone by the 7-Eleven to make arrangements. Cindy and I chain-smoked and watched cars try to park while Jacky made the call. From far off I thought I heard bells ringing. A girl riding her bike across the street swerved to avoid a student passing out flyers. Two kids wearing white t-shirts with magic marker scribbled all over the fronts kicked a hacky sack at each other by the dumpster. Cindy watched them and laughed. It was good she was laughing.

Jacky came back and told us Mooch's guy in the city was a no-go that night. Best Mooch could do was set us up with a kid who could get forged Ritalin scripts. That kid, of course, was Justin.

By the time we got to State, the dreamy, mellow feeling from earlier had faded and I had completely forgotten we were trying to buy Ritalin. But the sight of Mooch sitting on the side of the fountain shifted everything back into perspective. Mooch wore a stupid tie-dyed tank top and a pair of J$F bellbottoms that obscured his feet and swayed off the edge of the fountain. Even sitting, he looked more imposing than the Poseidon statue rising out of the water behind him.

A beach ball bounced over the growing crowd by the stage as the quad flooded with students dressed like hippies. The last cut of orange hung in a sky about to go completely purple.

When we got closer to the statue, Mooch waved, and Justin stepped out of the fountain. Water dripped off him in glassy strips of light.

"Mooch filled me in on your situation," Justin said. "I'm your man." He'd grown a beard since the last time I saw him. It was grey-black and patchy, the side of a mountain after a forest fire.

"Sticking around for the show?" Jacky asked, and lit a cigarette. "These guys have a killer piano player." She picked a piece of dried wax from her skirt.

"Perhaps," Justin said. His pants were bunched above his knees.

"Let's be quick," Jacky said.

"Hold on, Sugar." Justin touched her hip, and Jacky slapped his hand away.

"Don't fucking touch me."

"Watch it," I said. Poseidon's shadow split me in half. I cracked my neck, let my spine swell, and we all stood in a circle.

"Please," Cindy said. "Calm." She pushed down at the air beneath her palms.

A cloud of pot smoke drifted over from the crowd. On stage, a roadie tuned a guitar to the first chords of "I Know You Rider."

Jacky adjusted the strap on her shirt.

"Where's the car?" Justin asked.

Mooch pointed across the street.

"Fuck your car," I said.

"I think we all got off on the wrong foot." Justin kept his jeans rolled up and stepped into a pair of slippers. We all walked across the street.

The car was illegally parked, the windows tinted hearse-black, and Justin had bought new vanity plates that read THE FIRM. I piled in between Cindy and Jacky in the back. The AC blasted and someone turned on the heated seats. We sat freezing and sweating and about to start tripping, hoping to counter the effects of the pills. Justin stared at us in the rearview mirror like he wanted us to melt.

I lit a cigarette and cracked the window. Jacky grabbed a piece of blue lace from her purse and tied her hair back. Mooch gave us some bullshit about having to wait until Justin's prescription got refilled that night at midnight before they could sell us any, but they'd share some of what they had now.

"No problem," Cindy said, adjusting her glasses.

"I've got a grand piano-sized problem," Justin said, and scratched at his beard.

Mooch crunched the pills with a ballpeen hammer he'd grabbed from the glove box and took his goddamn time setting everything out on a Prep cafeteria tray.

It never made any sense to me that these two would be so tight. According to Cindy, when Mooch was a kid named Drew, his dad left and his crack-whore mom put all the utilities and several leases in Mooch's name and never paid bills or rent. When his mom wound up in some shelter, Mooch moved in with Justin and his mom. His credit had gotten so fucked he couldn't get a place of his own. For as long as I've known him he just goes where Justin goes and mooches off him.

"Show starts in five." Cindy banged on the ceiling.

"Justin and I got a place together," Mooch said. "Housewarming party's tonight."

"Grandpa finally died," Justin said.

"Cotton money," I said.

Jacky gave me a look that said *not now* and zigzagged a fingernail over her skirt, making little zipping noises on the corduroy.

Mooch reached an arm the size of a leg across the front seat and rubbed Justin's neck while I blew a line off the smiling Guilford Prep Pirate logo, one eye covered by a patch, the other a giant cartoon eye staring into space. I swear I saw that smug pirate wink at me. My nose burned like it was full of salt, and it got fuzzy in the back seat. Then clear.

Once everyone took their turn Jacky said, "See you after the show," and we flew out of that burning black death machine.

We split up at the quad and sold about half of Cindy's sister's acid. The band started fast and hard with a lineup like 1983. A couple songs in, we met back up, and the band played a rendition of "Candyman" from a time when the real band had just started playing Pigpen stuff again. A cover band covering '83 Dead covering 1970 Dead covering a blues standard.

I was spinning around in circles blown away by the stage lights when, in the middle of the set, Cindy stopped dancing and stared out at the moon rising above the buildings on the edge of campus.

"What's wrong?" Jacky asked.

Cindy said, "I want to go to Nancy's." Nancy was her dead sister. She'd lived near the Park 'N Ride, a fifteen-minute walk.

So we walked. We drifted around each other in figure eights like we were ice skating across the Park 'N Ride, toward the woods leading to Nancy's backyard.

"Use the street lights," I said. I remember I went on at length about the lights: "Keep them behind us at an angle so they shine to the starboard side of the yard, which is northerly." I thought I figured out such groundbreaking shit while tripping. I made the decision to walk in a straight line and try not to get knocked down by branches.

Tucked between a forest and a field, the two-story house looked down at the valley all lit up and sprawling. I watched Cindy's sister's place shiver and fade into a gingerbread house covered in giant gumdrops. I couldn't shake this visual.

"I wish I could live here," Cindy said.

"Nancy was a good woman," Jacky said.

Cindy said, "I can almost feel her presence, like she's upstairs or something."

Jacky put her arm around Cindy and they walked like that around the front of the house to the back patio. All the stars overhead shot across the sky simultaneously and blinked different colors I didn't know existed. My senses felt exponentially clarified and distorted at the same time.

Cindy sat on a plastic chair and stared at a charcoal grill. A cat meowed by the steps, looking up at the sliding door as if someone would let it in any minute. Nancy's Pontiac was parked next to the house, half in the side yard, half in the driveway. It looked like its wheels were spinning in place.[12]

"She made great hotdogs," Cindy said, and moved her hand along a crack in the plastic armrest. "We'd all come over before football games on Saturdays and have cocktails and grill out. It was so nice."

Jacky and I sat on either side of Cindy and the three of us shared a joint. I stared at the lights in the valley, thrilled I'd guided us here safely.

Jacky's pager buzzed. "Can I get inside?"

Cindy got up without saying a word and grabbed a hidden key from under a flowerpot.

When she slid open the door, something cold washed over me. Wind poured out around the sugar-frosted glass, over the graham cracker porch. The frosting on the roof melted and dripped onto the chairs. I tried to catch some, but when I licked my hand I tasted dirt and sweat.

Cindy and Jacky disappeared inside.

Thoughts fell through my head like snow past a streetlight. I fought against the chemicals creeping in the base of my skull telling me I'd spiral into nothing and wind up friendless and alone, sleeping in abandoned houses. I'll quit all this shit soon enough, I thought. It's our last night in town. Relax. I'm fine. Things are looking up. I can't un-eat the acid. Enjoy it.

My teeth were throbbing. Jacky and Cindy had been standing there for a while before I noticed them. Apparently, it was time for Justin to pick up his prescription, and he was too fucked up to drive to the pharmacy. He needed a ride, but we needed a car to get all the way to Justin's.

"We can't use Nancy's," Cindy said. "She never lets anyone use her car without her."

Jacky gave me a look.

"Our place is pretty close," I said. "We can take my car."

•

We took the back roads to Justin's place on Rural Route 404. Since the construction, it was the only road out of town and traffic was heavier than normal. The party was just getting started when we showed up. A few early guests parked on one side of the drive facing away from the house. The right side of my station wagon flirted with the trees. Branches clawed at the roof. "It's fucking Apollo," I said, pulling up in front of the house. The hedges looked like they'd been carved into Greek Gods.

Jacky squeezed my thigh, leaving a faint imprint on my jeans. "Wonder what the Oracle sees?"

Cindy leaned between the front seats. "I bet they have a maze around back. With a minotaur."[13]

The house was the kind you could get lost in, bigger than any in my development back in Jersey. Inside, Mooch and Justin had been snorting Ritalin and chasing it with Heineken. A DJ wearing a backward Tigers hat spun hip-hop on real turntables. The door shut behind us.

Justin collected crystals and polished rocks. Quartz and amethyst glistened on end tables and bookshelves, everywhere. Aside from a few unopened boxes, the house was spotless.

"Beers?" Mooch pointed at the kitchen.

I made my way to the fridge through a crowd of college-aged kids I'd never seen before, but who seemed to recognize Jacky and Cindy. I opened a beer and chugged it, pocketed one, and cracked another to drink back in the living room.

Christmas lights looped around the room, stapled in butchered crescents where the wall met the ceiling. The dim colored bulbs played with the angles on the rocks. Bass from a sub-woofer thumped and reverberated through my extremities.

"Where's my driver?" Justin said.

"Ready when you are, Hoss." I'd agreed to drive Justin on the condition we took the Mercedes. It was just me and Justin going, unfortunately.

I drove several miles in the wrong direction before Justin corrected me, then spent ten frustrating minutes finding my bearings when, on Justin's advice, I cut through Guilford Prep's campus on a road the size of a sidewalk. We were surrounded by empty gothic buildings and shadows and moonlight. Prep's campus always put me on edge. It was creepier and more extravagant than any high school I'd ever known. The throughway circled the football stadium and emptied us onto a dark road that Justin swore would lead us back in the right direction. "Shortcut," he said. Poorly lit dirt roads wound beneath us like we were driving on yarn woven into a quilt.

"Quit being a pussy," Justin said. "Drive!"

"Easy, Hoss," I said. "I'm not in the mood for a ticket."

"You're doing fine. Sorry," he said.

Maybe a sweater, the yarn road moved through a sweater. It seemed soft. The car almost buoyant. Justin flipped through the satellite radio, settled on something electronic. The interior lights changed color in time with the music. It was like being at a rave inside the Batmobile.

Out of nowhere, Justin said, "What's it like fucking a black girl?"

"What's it like fucking Mooch?"

"Fuck off."

"Fuck you."

Justin put his feet up on the dash and I pictured the air bag deploying and folding him in half. "I fucked a homeless girl once," he said. "For a tenth of Ghost. She was white. Ghost-white."

"That's terrible." I focused on my side of the unlined road, gave it a little gas.

"I can't stand this goddamn town," he said. "I'm getting the fuck out. Selling the house. I'm in a great place with The Firm."

"What?" Justin was unemployed and lived off a trust fund and money he made selling pain killers to the high school football team.

"The Firm," he said, "Tom Canada is after me. The Firm is about to take control. I'm getting too big for him."

"Jimmy Page's band was called The Firm. In the '80s."

This conversation was shit. I was glad when we finally pulled up to the pharmacy, which was part of the new three-story Harris Teeter. Pulling into the lot, Justin's face looked pasty and flush at the same time. Out of the corner of my eye I could see every blackhead and clogged pore. I expected him to vanish if I looked over. Hoped he would. But Justin didn't vanish, so I talked to him.

"Your place is great," I said. "Lots of pillars and arches. Plus you just fucking bought it."

"Perhaps you're right," he said. "No reason to leave. Let's not go crazy."

I parked. "Rare to see both pillars and arches."

Justin hopped out. "Back in a second."

The parking lot was empty except for an elderly employee corralling stray shopping carts. It's hard to say if it took five minutes or two months for Justin to fill his script and buy cigarettes. When he came back out the automatic doors, he knocked over the carts the old man was pushing and yelled something about The Firm.

It was after one when we got back to the party. The door hung open, leaking music and laughter. Jacky smiled and my legs tingled as I took her hand and we followed Justin to his room. We walked past a bunch of young kids in white t-shirts shotgunning beers. Cindy was collecting a stack of tens from a group of crustpunks hitting a gravity bong with Mooch in the dining room. Someone fell down the steps. Everything was going to be fine.

Justin, Jacky and I went upstairs to complete the transaction. From the landing, I saw a middle-aged man in a blue sport coat pissing into the fireplace downstairs.

"Quite a turnout," Justin said. He closed the door. A poster of a big-boobed blonde holding a chemistry book hung behind a bookshelf holding a rock tumbler and a few polished gems. The poster said "Study Hard."

"Here's fifty-five." Jacky handed Justin the bills.

Below us we heard stomping followed by a raucous cheer that shook the bedroom. There was a knock on the door and Cindy poked her head into the room.

"Let's get out of here," Cindy said.

"Shut the door," Justin said.

Cindy picked up a purple stone from the shelf and sat on the floor.

The busty student in the poster was melting. I blinked hard and laughed while Justin counted the money and handed Jacky a half-full bottle of the pills. Cindy rubbed the stone like she was nervous. I smiled at her when she slipped it into her pocket.

Justin stared at Jacky, then at me. "Now I want you two to kiss," he said.

"What?" Jacky said. She held the bottle at eye level, shook it and put it in her purse.

"Fucking make out right now," he said. "I want to watch." He adjusted himself and clapped when he was done, as if to say, "Let's go!"

"Get fucked," I laughed.

"Right," Cindy said. "Time to go."

Justin stood up. "Fucking kiss her," he insisted.

"Get the fuck out of here," Jacky said.

"I don't believe you're attracted to each other. It's unnatural."

Jacky ran her thumb under her shirt strap.

Cindy walked to the door and waved us over. "Guys, let's go."

The walls wilted like ferns, felt like sponges.

"Shove your tongue down her fucking throat!"

Out came the gun. Jacky leveled it at Justin.

"Give me my money back," Jacky said. "Your wallet. All of it." The blue lace in her hair floated as she circled Justin.

Justin tossed his wallet on the bed.

"Don't shoot him," I said.

"Convince me."

Justin flattened himself against the wall.

"I'm leaving." Cindy opened the door. The man in the sport coat who'd been pissing from the top of the stairs was wandering aimlessly down the hall, clearly in a blackout, and asked her where the bathroom was. Jacky put the gun away. With a thud, sport-coat guy passed out where he stood.

Then Justin charged and tackled me into the shelf, knocking the rock tumbler onto the carpet. I picked it up and slammed it into Justin's face. My jaw clenched. I saw every color but red. I beat on him until Cindy and Jacky pulled me off. I grabbed the rest of the pills from Justin's pocket and we got the fuck out of there.

Outside, cold air hit the coat of sweat running down my face.

Jacky stopped by Justin's car. The pounding hip-hop pouring out of the house swallowed the sound of the six shots Jacky emptied into the side of the Mercedes. Three holes in the back door, the rear windshield imploded, a popped tire. I kicked the bumper.

Justin appeared in the doorway, face scraped and swollen. Blood covered his Polo shirt. "You can't outrun The Firm!"

He slipped coming down the stairs and dropped his phone. He mulled around on his hands and knees in the yard, talking to himself.

We scrambled around in the hedges until we found our way to the driveway and my car. As we pulled out we saw Mooch holding one of Justin's slippers, standing over him. Justin stood up and fell again, puked on the lawn. A random partygoer walked past and threw a cigarette at him.

From the back seat, Cindy reached up and turned on the stereo. We listened to the Dead, which was all we'd wanted to do in the first place.

Wind through the open window pulled Jacky's hair toward the night, dark springs unwound into loose coils. Cindy spread out across the back seat and put her feet up. I drank the beer I still had in my pocket, and my hands steadied. Lights from distant houses glared at us.

"What was that?" I asked. The gun twinkled when Jacky pulled it from her purse.

Jacky said, "I don't like how he does business." She wiped the sparkle off the pistol with her shirt, and put it back in her bag. "You beat his face in."

"You shot his car," I said.

"Quit trying to save me." Jacky handed me a couple Ritalin, dumped the rest in an empty cigarette pack and threw the bottle out into the night. "And fuck his car."

Closer to town the houses turned into the closed storefronts of main-street Booth. The lights condensed into a levitating string of white puddles.

We got back to Cindy's place, gave our hugs and said our goodbyes. Promises to visit were exchanged. I gave Cindy the phone number and address of the house in Georgia. "We're going off the grid," I said. "Landline's the only way to get ahold of us."

Cindy folded the paper and put it in her pocket, and Jacky and I left.

●

The plan was to stop at home and grab our stuff. Then we'd ditch the car at the J$F warehouse with my co-worker White Reggie and walk the rest of the way to the bus station. But when we got to our place, Mooch was banging on the front door with his hammer. Faint banners of gold and purple stretched behind the tiny steel head as it buried itself into the paint.

I walked ahead of Jacky. I could smell the grain alcohol on Mooch from ten feet away. "Mooch, what the fuck?"

"Need the money you stole from Justin."

"Fuck that guy, Mooch. He's a scumbag."

"You don't get it."

"You're right. I don't."

"Fucker!" Mooch turned and swung the hammer at me, but he missed and collapsed to the pavement. I kicked him in the ribs. Then in the face. I stepped on his hand, grabbed the hammer and threw it into the dark. He tried to get up and fell again. I could have never done this to a sober Mooch, and I hoped he wouldn't remember it. I kicked him a few more times to make sure he was out and so we could go inside and pack.

Before we took off, I dragged Mooch onto our front lawn. His nose was bleeding and he was bruised, but mostly he was drunk. I rolled him on his side. He'd be fine.

The Greyhound station was on the west end, near the J$F warehouse and a bunch of Section 8 houses. We ditched the car behind the warehouse. White Reggie was more than happy to play a part in our escape. He said he'd keep an eye on it while we were away. I didn't care if I ever saw that car or Reggie again. From the warehouse it was about a ten-minute walk to the bus, over the creek, through the forest and across the train tracks. In the thick of the woods, Jacky pulled the gun from her purse and tossed it into the deepest part of the creek.

Sunrise crept up our backs as we crossed the tracks toward the station. Covered in sweat and muck, the two of us lit cigarettes and sat on the curb outside the Greyhound station and stared at our tickets to Atlanta through rolls of tin-colored smoke.

THE GREYHOUND TO ATLANTA[14]

WITHDRAWAL

Coming off acid in a holding cell is like having your insides replaced with broken glass and your head wrapped in sandpaper. You want a joint or a beer, anything to take the edge off, but you can't even get half a cigarette. Once in a while, for a brief second, you forget exactly where you are. Then you're hit with the why of it, and it hurts even worse.

•

We were so close. If it wasn't for the construction, we'd have taken the busway out onto the interstate and been gone. But the police set up a roadblock right in front of the crime scene. Fish in a fucking barrel. When the cop got on the bus and started yelling for us, Jacky kissed me. As we walked toward him, past all the groggy passengers on their way south, I held her hand for as long as I could. The whole night hurts to think about. One different decision, one good break, and right now she and I are sitting by the water in Georgia, free from all this. Together.

•

I don't know what happened to Jacky after they cuffed her and put her in the back of a cop car. She doesn't have a record, so she's probably not in jail. We both had Ritalin on us, though, and Jacky had a whole cigarette pack full of it. Plus the pot and all that cash.

Whenever I get phone time, I call the landline at our old house, but it just rings and rings. I try her parents' house, her sister, Cindy, even Mooch, but no one will take a collect call. Cindy doesn't visit.

•

I resent Justin for dying because I can't blame the night on him without feeling like an even bigger piece of shit. Maybe I'm lucky to be alive. For all I know, if things went another way that night, it could've been me or Jacky bleeding out on that lawn. There's a killer in Booth, but we are alive. I tell myself this, anyway. I tell myself this and remember Jacky's fingers sliding down my wrist as we were pulled apart and questioned on the side of the road while the bus pulled away.

•

I'll see Jacky again. I write her at least one letter a day, trying to better explain all these feelings, all the guilt I have about how everything happened, but I have nowhere to send them. I don't know where she is.

•

I keep going back to that night. For twelve hours I sat in the holding cell till a CO came in with a skinny, tanned officer whose face was pulled back too tight, and the tall cop from the bus, who loved his stupid cop sunglasses so much he wore them inside.

Sunglasses did the talking. Skinny wrote in a small pad.

I was charged with possession. They asked me about the Ritalin and the pot in my backpack. Alleged backpack. They asked about Mooch, and I hoped he stumbled away from our house before anyone found him. And they asked about Justin, as if I was the kind of fuckup to get wrapped up in that kind of shit. Maybe I was, but fuck them for thinking so. I didn't respond to any of it. All their questions were bullshit.

"Where's Jacky?" I asked.

"We're not at liberty to say," Sunglasses said. "She's facing drug charges." Then he asked, "Does this poem mean anything to you?"

He slid a photo across the table. It was a picture of one of the pillars outside Justin's, a haiku written in blood: *The Firm's corpse planted / rots below history, smiles / the first time blood spills.*

"That's not even good," I said. "It doesn't mean a fucking thing. Do I get a lawyer?"

Skinny put the picture away and told me my lawyer was on the way. This was a surprise.

LEGAL COUNSEL

Before being interrogated, I used my one phone call on my parents and they didn't even accept it. They must have heard "collect call from Guilford County Jail," put two and two together, and sent a lawyer. Dad's a higher-up at a massive pharmaceutical conglomerate. He likes to be this big swinging dick who can pull strings. Probably could've gotten me out if he wanted, but he's a cock. This lawyer my dad set me up with got there quick. I'm grateful and all, but it's one more thing for my parents to hold over me.

My attorney and I met in the interrogation room next to the holding cell, which looked just like the holding cell but with a table welded into the center of the floor. Two guards shuffled me in, shackled at the wrists and ankles. They hooked my foot cuffs to a heavy yellow chair, and clipped another restraint around my chest. Staring at the tabletop, I counted to one hundred twice before the lawyer showed up and sat down across from me. He introduced himself as Peter Dewey, Esquire, and seemed confused when he tried to shake my shackled hands.

"Listen, Ronald Reagan." His suit cost more than my car, and he looked like a cologne ad. "Your folks want you to stay in here for a while."

"Of course they do. Shit," I said. "Addiction is a disease, you know."

"Let's hope the judge sees it that way."

"Is this chain across my chest necessary?"

"Probably not."

"Addiction is a disease," I continued, "and I need help." My wrists swelled against the cuffs. "Can I get these loosened?"

"No. We're almost finished," he said. "You won't get bail, but as soon as we can get you in front of a judge, we can plea you out. Also, don't answer any questions about Justin Haas. You're not charged with anything involving him. And that football star you kicked the shit out of, he's not pressing charges." He looked through a folder full of multicolored documents.

"I'm an addict. I need help."

"Right. As per your parents' request, we will stay in a holding pattern until I can talk to the judge, at which point we make a plea to get you into rehab." He flipped again through the papers, pausing occasionally to look past me. "Your father knows some folks who can get you into a facility." He made eye contact, held it, and said, "You're lucky. You're white and come from money." He stuffed the folder back into his briefcase.

I said, "Can you do me a favor?"

He said, "Maybe."

"Find out what happened to my girlfriend."

I gave him Jacky's full name and last known contact info, the names of a few known associates (legal ones) and family members. Pete wrote them down and said he'd do what he could.

"Pete, one more thing," I said. I didn't want to go back to my cell. "Are the portrayals of the legal system in *Werewolf Hunter!* accurate? I mean it seems really intense and loud all the time. Lots of gavel." I tried to look behind me, at whatever Pete was staring at, but I couldn't turn far enough.

"They take some liberties. Listen, do anything you can to make it look like you're trying to improve your situation. It will help." He looked at his watch. "I know they have Twelve-Step meetings."

"I can do that," I said.

"Good."

"What's behind me?" I assumed Sunglasses and Skinny were eyeballing us behind a two-way mirror. I tried again to twist and look, but I fell. It was all I could do to keep from crying while staring at Pete's wingtips before he walked out of the room.

I haven't heard from Pete or anybody about a plea or rehab in weeks. I'm convinced my parents want me to rot here.

STILL WRITING

There's something in the bags beneath Sophie's eyes that reminds me of Jacky when we'd wake up holding each other, unsure if it was dusk or daybreak.

On the way to class, we passed the room where they hold chapel services. The windows in there might as well be the size of football fields. You can see all the way out to the pig farm and the access road that leads back to Rural Route 404.

Thankfully there were more students besides Gator and me this time. All my cellmates signed up when they heard a woman was teaching and now there's a waiting list. Everyone keeps talking about her orange shoes and stringy black hair.

I'm still writing the memoir. Writing scenes through my high school years and revising some of the old scenes based on Sophie's edits. My whole childhood is on the jail computer in my Hemingway file, but I have no other choice. I don't want to keep a copy in my cell and have the guards take it. I already have to hide my journal. So I asked Sophie to print out a hard copy at the end of each class and take it home with her. She sees some kind of promise in my writing, I think, which must be why she humors me.

I told Sophie everyone calls me Hemingway, and she smiled. She still calls me Ronald Reagan.

ROUTINE

I have a routine. It's like being stuck on a haunted Ferris wheel.[15]

My day is this: breakfast, pushups, yard time, write, lunch, pushups, write, play spades/optional programming, dinner, TV hour, read, write, lights out at ten (cell doors lock at midnight), try not to wake up and look at the toilet.

Highlights of my week: Monday it's *Werewolf Hunter!* reruns. Tuesdays I have class. Wednesday is the NA meeting. We watch replayed Atlanta Braves games from the '80s on Thursdays, Roller Derby on Fridays, and the Animated Video Bible on Saturdays. Sunday nights at nine, Otto and I stand by the window and listen to the Grateful Dead Hour on his mini radio.

We've been saving our apple juice from meal times, pouring it into a trash bag between the bunks and letting it ferment. Tonight, Mike's gonna use it to make moonshine with the water Otto scoops out of the toilet.

DRUNK

Six days ago Mike made moonshine, and every night since I've been drunk. I am drunk right now.

I have to go to rehab when I get out of here, so I might as well get it in while I can. My dad's rehab connection better work out soon. Fuck him for making me wait in here.

In the meantime I've embraced the moonshine and added drinking to my routine; at lights out I drink until I have a decent buzz, and then I try to read/write in the dark until I pass out. I still go to my NA meetings. They say relapse is part of the process, and really I'm in those meetings for narcotics, not alcohol. AA is for pussies.

THE EMPTY BUNK

Day before yesterday we got another cellmate. Now I have to sleep below this tattooed crustpunk kid from Pittsburgh who cries all night about having had his dreads shaved off.

"Fuck your dreads, Pittsburgh," I told him. "I bet you're from the suburbs."

He still won't tell us his name. He just stammers and whines, hardly talks and can barely form a sentence when he does. You can tell he's a speed freak by the black space around his gums. We don't give him any moonshine.

When Otto drains the toilet, Pittsburgh shouts into the bowl,

"Where's my baby girl?" It's all I've heard him say that doesn't sound like a scratched CD. He'll scream into the shitter for her for five minutes at a time until Mike shoves him out of the way.

•

One night Mike and Pittsburgh went at it. Mike said something like, "We'll find you a new partner, Pittsburgh." And Pittsburgh walked around rubbing his head for a minute before he jumped on Mike and tried to strangle him with a pair of briefs. The elastic broke and Mike slammed Pittsburgh's head into the floor and tied him to his bunk with a sheet for the night. The COs don't get paid enough to give a shit.

After a few days of near-silence, now we can't get Pittsburgh to shut up. All day he rambles to Ace about the big Rust Belt crime initiative, and all the kids overdosing from Fentanyl-laced dope up there in that dying fucking city, how he grabbed his shit one day, headed south and made it as far as Guilford County, where he got caught shoplifting from a 7-Eleven while his girlfriend sat outside in a stolen car with an ounce of Ghost in the glove box.

Last night around 2AM, Pittsburgh told me to call him Foster. When I said my name was Ronald Reagan, he laughed in my face.[16] I told him I didn't choose it and to enjoy getting ass fucked upstate. Then Pittsburgh started bawling all over again. Gator heard him wailing and serenaded him with "Cry Baby Cry" from across the hall. He's got a great voice.

PLEA DEAL

I finally talked to my lawyer again today, and he said we're officially a go for rehab. An associate of my father's owns a facility in North Jersey. I will, apparently, repay my debt to society there.

The only thing my parents hate more than me is being embarrassed. They especially hate being embarrassed by me.

At least half my mom's friends have been to rehab, the psych ward, or a shrink of some kind. Now Mom will have a talking point at the country club about how I'm taking care of my problem.

Five days and one writing class and I'm out of this shithole.

LOCKDOWN

What a shitty fucking week. Our last class was bullshit. We filed into the room like we always do, but Sophie never showed up. There was some dude there who tried to get us to write flash fiction. All the hard drives had been wiped clean, so I couldn't even work on my memoir. I bet Sophie had a good reason for missing class, but this blows. I couldn't concentrate on the new guy's prompt, and he wouldn't say anything about Sophie or where my work went.

Then, at lunch, Pittsburgh jumped Gator and we all got put on lockdown for the rest of the day.

If I ever see Sophie again, it won't be in here. I'm out the day before the next class and I have no idea how to get the beginning of my memoir off the jail computer, or how to get the hard copy from Sophie. I'm worried I'll never write as well as I did in class. Those first years of my life. I need those pages.

I hate the whole city of Pittsburgh.

LETTER FROM HOME

It's hard to write while worrying about the fate of my memoir and being hammered off toilet moonshine all day to cope with said worry. But with forty-eight hours left, I finally got some mail. From my parents: "You are not welcome in our home unless you go to rehab and get your act together. We have made arrangements to get you into a suitable facility. No more money. Ever. Love, Mom and Dad."

CONDITIONS

The conditions of my probation dictate I attend and complete mandatory in-patient rehab at Rose-Thorn Recovery Center, followed by 12-Step meetings upon my release. They didn't say how long I'll have to stay in rehab though.

Pete came through and told me Jacky had been stuck in rehab and was recently sent to a sober living facility, where she was supposed to stay for another few weeks. He wasn't allowed to tell me which one. I took all the letters I wrote her, gave them to Pete, and asked him to make sure Jacky got them.

RELEASE

I was released earlier today, the morning of August 24. Now I'm sitting downwind from the pig farm on a patch of grass by the access road connecting Rural Route 404 and the jail. The last few days inside, I got caught on this idea: What if cops were actual pigs, like the kind that live on farms?[17]

These last nights have felt awful. I couldn't get more than three hours sleep at a time. I operated in a constant state of crusty-eyed psychosis. If I concentrated hard enough, the guards became walking pig creatures, trotting around the pod in uniform but with black-eyed boar faces.

This morning before breakfast, a guard with a big moustache came to my cell. "Middleton. Time to go," he said, and I smiled for the first time in six weeks. While he led me through the maze of electronically locked doors and slick, rounded hallways, I imagined how I might manifest a lifestyle I could at least pretend was normal without going to rehab and meetings. But every idea involved changing my identity.

I followed the guard past the interrogation room and into an office. Framed and hanging on the wall behind the desk of a sallow officer was the front page of the *Booth Picayune* from ten years ago: Mooch and the Prep Pirate embracing after their fourth consecutive state title. As if nothing else worth framing had happened in the last decade. It gave me the creeps.

On the desk was a plastic bag containing the clothes I'd been wearing when I was arrested, and a GSU football t-shirt that was three sizes too big. They said my backpack was in evidence. Someone was in the bathroom, so I changed in the middle of the office while the guard talked on the numberless phone.

The cops had taken all the money from my wallet, but not the $50 I had hidden in my jeans. My feet throbbed with relief inside my old sneakers. I put my jail yellows on the officer's desk and stood there in the too-cold AC, listening to half a conversation about high school football.

I wondered where Jacky was. Her absence hurts even more now that I'm out.

I was about to yell "Get off the fucking phone, fucker" when the guard hung up. He turned around in his chair and looked at the picture of Mooch. "If it were up to me, boy, you'd rot in here." Gray hair sprouted from his ears. "Drew means a lot to this town," he said.

In Guilford County, everyone is on a first name basis with Mooch. Fuck Mooch. Fuck high school sports.

On my way out of the office, I pulled the fifty from the pocket inside the waist of my jeans and slid it into my wallet behind the Griffey rookie card. At least they hadn't taken that. Finally, I left the ring of cement and barbed wire behind me.

My face itches where my eyebrow was and my body still aches all over. It smells like pig shit and pigs fucking and rotten dead pigs out here, and I will always associate this smell with freedom.

THE COWBOY

I was sitting on Pig Shit Road waiting for my ride when, finally, a cloud of dust turned into an ugly green Prius. It almost hit me when it pulled up. A man in a purple tracksuit and a cowboy hat like a satellite dish got out and helped me up off the ground.

"You must be Middleton's boy," he said. "We've got a nice place for you to stay, son." He removed a wad of tobacco from his cheek and tossed it onto the pavement. He opened the back door and offered me a seat.

Fuck it, I thought, and got in.

The Prius smelled like tobacco and Armor All. The Cowboy was an associate of my father and said he lived in the Poconos, in the mountains outside Reading. I'm sure in some one-streetlight, middle-of-nowhere town full of meth labs.

"Where are we going?" I asked.

"Airport," he said. He sounded like Doc Holliday. "Then a plane to Montclair. You're from New Jersey, right?"

"Further south though. Hope County. Central Jersey."

He handed me three green triangles, a bottle of water, and smiled a cowboy grin. "To take the edge off," he said. "Ronald Reagan. What a name."

I didn't tell him how much I hate my name. My chin dipped to my chest and I hiccupped. The pills tasted like artificial sweetener and sand.

"There'll be more on the plane," he said, and gave me a pat on the chest.

Once we hit Rural Route 404, I stuck my head out the window like a dog. The air tasted damp and beautiful. Road signs zoomed by. We passed Justin's house, held together by yellow police tape. Overgrown lawn burnt to a crisp. The Gods carved into the hedges looked beaten and drunk.

·

There's something about watching a baseball field fall away after takeoff that makes me nostalgic.

I'm writing from the comfort of a private jet. Just the Cowboy and me, heading to a private airfield in North Jersey.

He says, "Call me Bruce," and I realize I've been talking out loud intermittently since we left the jail.

"How about I call you Doc?"

"Bruce will be just fine."

He gives me another handful of green triangles, and the edges of everything start to soften. Goodnight.

RONALD REAGAN MIDDLETON'S LAST NIGHT IN JAIL

During the investigation of the death of Gator's cellmate, [name redacted], several weeks of security footage from Guilford County Jail was leaked to a local news affiliate by a source close to the jail. Under the condition of anonymity, the source agreed to speak with us and share portions of the tape not related to the criminal investigation. We used information gathered during the interview and from the security footage to construct the following account of Ronald Reagan Middleton's last night in Guilford County Jail.

•

Five minutes before dinner ended, Ronald Reagan stood on a table in the corner of the cafeteria and announced, "Everyone, it's my last night. I leave you with this warning. Heed my words: Don't let the pig creatures take your heart. And beware their heightened sense of smell."

The room fell silent before a small torrent of profanity, half-eaten food, and yellow plastic trays flew at Ronald Reagan, who then jumped from his perch and hid beneath the table. A guard pried him out and led him back to his cell where, for two hours, he paced in complete silence. Had Otto not produced his radio at 9PM and tuned in to the Grateful Dead Hour, the pacing would likely have continued indefinitely. Instead, Ronald Reagan joined him at the window and held aloft a frayed radio wire attached to a paperclip, enhancing reception.

With the water already vacuumed from the toilet, the "shine" began to flow at 11:30PM, shift change for the guards. A game of spades spread across the cell floor. The small radio crackled near the even smaller window. It was completely black outside.

Thirteen minutes before lockdown, at precisely 11:47, "Crazy" Mike got up and left. He came back carrying a piece of pink construction paper folded in half lengthwise. "You got an invitation," he said, "must be a party." He handed Ronald Reagan the paper. The invitation read, "GAY BUTT FUCKING PARTY IN CELL 107! GUEST OF HONOR: HEMINGWAY!!!" The words appeared to have been cut from magazines with great precision and were arranged between pictures of homosexual celebrities and professional wrestlers, adhered with, we assume, a contraband glue stick.

The invitation was signed, "Love, Gator."

The craftsmanship implied the time and attention one might only be afforded in such an institution. Ronald Reagan stared at the paper, then handed it to Mike and said, "Send that shit back. Not happening. No."

Mike left with the invitation, and the mood seemed to lighten. However, upon Mike's return, Ronald Reagan's cellmates hogtied him. Otto watched Mike, Johnny, Ace and Foster beat Ronald Reagan with rolled up magazines and tube socks filled with bars of soap. When Ace punched him in the spine, Ronald Reagan stopped struggling and Otto shaved off his right eyebrow with a disposable razor.

The space where Ronald Reagan's eyebrow once grew began to bleed and he tried to wipe his head with his shoulder for ninety seconds before giving up and emitting and uneasy laugh followed by a request: "Guys. Untie me. Not funny. Please. Guys?"

Amidst his pleading, Gator appeared in the doorway and shouted, "Where's my bitch?"

Ronald Reagan tried to roll under his bunk, but Gator grabbed an arm and a leg and pulled him toward the toilet.

With Ronald Reagan trapped in the crevasse between wall and toilet, Gator dropped his pants and slapped Ronald Reagan in the face with his penis, taunting, "Hemingway write me a love story. Hemingway, write me a love story." He repeated the phrase several times.

Gator climaxed and semen spurted into Ronald Reagan's eyes.

Immediately, Ronald Reagan raised his chin and vomited, covering the empty steel bowl with what we presume was shreds of jail pork soaked in fermented apple drink. One can only imagine the smell that filled the sweltering cell.

Gator slapped his phallus against Ronald Reagan's face a final time, and Mike ushered him back to his cell. On his way out, Gator laughed, and announced, "I'll miss you, Hemingway!"

Otto gave Ronald Reagan a shirt to clean up with.

The next morning Ronald Reagan was released.

PART TWO

THE FLAMINGO INCIDENT

A STAR IS BORN

It struck me, while reviewing the jail security footage, that the tape I was watching was quite possibly the first record of Ronald Reagan put to film. Upon a third and fourth viewing of the footage, it is apparent that Ronald Reagan appeals directly to the camera, a plea for help to whomever might be watching. No help came. This would prove to be an ongoing theme in Ronald Reagan's life, beginning with his appearance on the debut season of the breakout reality television show *Clean Time*.

Clean Time is produced by Jackson Entertainment, a subsidiary of Philson & Jackson Co., a multinational corporation that holds majority ownership of the pharmaceutical company that employs Ronald Reagan's father. With help from Guilford State College and Guilford County Jail, Jackson Entertainment filled their rehab facility with addicts who would compete for the right to stay in treatment based on their popularity. Audience members could vote by text or online poll at the end of each episode to keep their favorite "characters." To add some spice to the proceedings, the contestants that were voted off were given a chance to fight their way back into recovery. Out of the six contestants featured on the show, the two least popular addicts were pitted against each other in a makeshift ring with weapons designed, according to the producers, "to injure but not kill." This made for exciting television.

The show was created by Margaret Turner, a Guilford State Alumnus with ties to the county jail via Guilford State's creative writing outreach program. She worked tirelessly to pull the right strings to bring *Clean Time* to the people. These connections were only made public recently and did not cause nearly the uproar I had hoped.

As a condition of his rehabilitation, Ronald Reagan appeared on the inaugural season of *Clean Time*, and his journey to self-realization became fodder for public discourse. His most intimate and painful experiences were available to anyone with a cable subscription or internet connection. In a stunningly short period of treatment and screen time, Ronald Reagan became the most popular reality TV star this country has ever seen. His rise to fame has been well documented and produced many conflicting theories as to why he became so magnanimously ensconced in the eye of the public.

One theory cites name recognition as the driving force behind Ronald Reagan's popularity. Viewers voted with their gut, and their guts told them to vote Reagan. I feel this theory is oversimplified, as it does not account for the sheer goodness that clearly drove Ronald Reagan's actions. He tried to get clean. He spoke the truth. If anything, the American people want the truth, and when it was delivered to them by a meth addict from Central Jersey with perfect teeth, they were receptive.

One must also take into account the love story. As *Clean Time: Season One* progressed, the authenticity of Ronald Reagan's complex relationship with addict Althea Blake became the subject of internet think pieces, tabloid journalism, and critical essays published in a number of highly respected academic journals. Those familiar with *Clean Time* may be surprised to read about Jacky. Upon reading Ronald Reagan's journals, I found myself siding with Jacky, and torn by Ronald Reagan's relationship with Ms. Blake, as it retroactively muddles the pleasure of my initial viewing experience. As those unfamiliar with *Clean Time* will come to see, Ronald Reagan clearly found comfort in Althea's arms. But had he been better able to communicate with Jacky, perhaps he would not have run into those arms at all. Perhaps he was doing what he felt was necessary at the time to get through a difficult situation. Sometimes, there are no right answers. (Althea Blake was not available for comment.)

Initially, Ronald Reagan was unconcerned with his rise to fame. He saw it more as a means to improve his time in rehab. Much of his writing about this time is, naturally, quite raw. Ronald Reagan's memoir package included writing from this time period that is mostly unedited (perhaps to be edited later), which is why I've included, in this section of the book, various source materials such as interviews and select excerpts from the script of *Clean Time: Season One*. My intention is to capture the context of the moment, to heighten the disparate and complex feelings of a recovering addict. Think of the inserted media as the scrambled, sometimes disjointed, moments in our own lives that don't fit together as nicely as we'd all like them to. Now multiply that feeling by a factor of ten thousand.

AN INTERVIEW WITH SOPHIA TRENT

Bob and I recognized Sophie immediately from Ronald Reagan's descriptions. Sitting behind a desk at the Guilford State Writing Center, she looked weary and exhausted, but her pale eyes spoke of resolve. She smiled and rose to meet us, clad in orange sneakers, bright blue pants, and a flower-patterned shirt that whistled when she motioned with her hands. Implied by this motion: the walls have ears. I suggested the café a few blocks away.

At the café, we took a table outside. Our discussion touched upon such subjects as the state of the university system, Ronald Reagan's memoir, and Sophie's participation in the jail writing program, which has since been renamed Words And Feelings For Life Enrichment, or WAFFLE.

Harold Swanger: Let's discuss your work in the jail. I remember the *Picayune* article detailing WAFFLE's resounding success.

Sophia Trent: WAFFLE started with good intentions, two years ago, as a way to get Guilford State students involved in the community. Initially it was entirely operated by student volunteers. Work in the jail seemed so important and fulfilling for everyone. The program took off. Then the MFA director [whom we shall call "X" for legal reasons] stepped in, put his name on it, and took control once all the grunt work was done. As the program grew with grants and some private funding, X started using it as a marketing tool. He gives a WAFFLE Fellowship every year to some privileged white kid who wants to feel good about themselves for spending two hours a week

71

working with mostly black inmates. It's all anyone at the school talks about. The creator of *Clean Time* is an alumnus. She heard about the program on the news, and then reached out to X. And you know how that turned out.

HS: Can you speak about Ronald Reagan's work?

ST: The course is not always impactful, but in Ronald Reagan's case, it's clear he needed and wanted to explore his troubled past. I told him to remain vigilant of his recidivist tendencies and let him know he had options, and that he could find freedom in his work.

HS: So his effort was surprisingly impactful to you as well.

[Sophie nods in agreement.]

HS: He turned over most of his memoir, all of it except the section in which he details his youth. We understand that these are the scenes from his childhood he wrote in your class. Would he not want a complete story of his life told? I'm not sure I understand the reticence.

ST: I don't know. It's his life.

[I show her the journal entry in which RR expresses his dismay at the unprompted cancellation of his last class.]

ST: I feel terrible I bailed on my students. This might help explain it.

[Sophie lights her cigarette and hands me the following document, which we've reproduced below.]

•

To: mturner@jacksonentertainment.org
From: x@gsu.edu
CC: sophia.trent@gsu.edu
Subject: re: Proposal

Maggie,

My reply to your offer is an enthusiastic YES! I'm sorry the jail has been so difficult with you. I will fax you our class rosters and all the drug and alcohol related writing I can get my hands on. In fact I will personally attend classes and take notes on the lives of these people in order to best assist you with casting. It's a shame you've already found your cast for season one.

As our program grows and we gain exposure through The Recovery Channel, we will continue to supply student work from Words And Feelings For Life Enrichment in order to keep our relationship sustainable and to promote the importance of creative writing as a means of cathartic self-expression.

All Best,
X

Original Message --
From: mturner@jacksonentertainment.org
To: x@gsu.edu
Subject: Proposal

Dear X,

One of our current cast members was referred to us by a business partner of mine, and according to our preliminary research and background check, we discovered he was a participant in the university's WAFFLE program. We think this one may be star material.

The Guilford County Jail is asking for an incredibly steep sum of money in return for the necessary information regarding Drug Offenders Most Susceptible to Relapse or Exhibiting Relapse-like Symptoms. We feel the writing of these criminals will allow us to pinpoint their greatest fears and triggers.

As discussed in our previous correspondence, we wish to put these individuals in situations that will elicit organic, spontaneous responses to stimuli and produce exciting television and web content while we work to heal them of their addictive tendencies. We are hoping you can help us secure this information and help move forward with the production of our new series, Clean Time. We understand your MFA program is under scrutiny by the university and you are having difficulty maintaining funding. In addition to a monthly payment, The Recovery Channel and Jackson Entertainment can make Guilford State University the unofficial Official University of The Recovery Channel, the benefits of which would include free advertising during the first and fourth commercial breaks of Werewolf Hunter!, and product placement during Clean Time and any forthcoming spin-offs. Unfortunately, most of our season one cast has been chosen, but we see our show as having an amorphous cast of characters that will keep our viewers engaged with a variety of ever-changing personalities. I hope you will accept our offer.

Have a great day!

-Maggie

•

ST: That was sent on a Monday morning. I went in that day, cleared all the existing files from the jail computer and told X I quit WAFFLE. My hope is to leave State and start an independent non-profit group that will teach in nontraditional settings. Academia fucks everything up.

[Sophie rubs her eyes, refills her glass, and shakes the empty bottle.]

Bob Middleton Jr.: Are you still in the loop with what goes on in the jail?

ST: My classmate and friend Jim took my place. He says X shows up toward the end of each class and tells the students he needs copies of their work so the university can evaluate the teachers. So after Jim encourages our students to be forthright in their writing and to risk emotional exposure, X photocopies all their work and faxes it to the network so they can more easily choose the most damaged addicts to put on their show. I'm glad I'm out. I cancelled my cable and boycott all subsidiaries of Philson & Jackson. [She looks at her watch.] I have to get back to work.

•

We agreed to meet for dinner. Sophie returned to the writing center, leaving her cigarette burning in the ashtray and a half empty glass of wine cresting the edge of the table, which Bob quietly drank as the waiter set down a new bottle.

I probed Bob for childhood memories of his older brother. Bob described a fairly typical upper-middle-class existence, lacking traumatic incidents. I felt he was holding back, but decided not to press the issue. While we waited outside for Sophie to return, we studied the information gathered from our meeting earlier that week with Margaret Turner, Executive Producer of *Clean Time*.

AN INTERVIEW WITH MARGARET TURNER

Margaret Turner produces the hit television show *Clean Time* and counsels chemically dependent patients at the Rose-Thorn Recovery Center in Montclair, NJ. The New Jersey native holds Masters degrees in Communications and Counseling Psychology from Guilford State University.

The Rose-Thorn complex rests on the top of a hill surrounded by pine trees and a complicated system of gravel driveways with no discernable pattern. The forest surrounding the institution has been renamed Ronald Reagan Middleton Wood, and a plaque commemorating his stay last summer has been erected near the main entrance.

Bob joined me for the trip. Though I assured him I could manage on my own, I was grateful for the company and the further insight into his brother's life he could provide. We got out of the car, and Bob stood and marveled at the surroundings for a moment before following me across the parking lot. His pace was deliberate, his movements carefully measured. A look of consternation settled on Bob's face, as if he was getting a view behind the curtain and didn't know what to make of it.

We spotted Ms. Turner rummaging through a box of papers resting in the open trunk of a green Prius. Despite her expensive turtleneck and slacks, she appeared harried. Weathered by ambition, or perhaps a lack of sleep. In her early forties, her black hair was streaked with white.

When I called to her, she looked startled. She put out her cigarette, shut the trunk of the car, and approached us holding a tablet and a small stack of folders alternately stamped with Guilford State University and Guilford County Jail insignias.

I inquired about Ronald Reagan's time at Rose-Thorn and his impact on *Clean Time: Season One*. She instructed me to call her Maggie, and proceeded to go on at length.

Margaret Turner: Even after all this time, Ronald Reagan Middleton remains the fourth most popular character in the history of reality television. Online polls show he and Althea passed the couple from *Road House IV: Alabama* as the most desirable partners on a cable television reality series featuring the use of controlled substances. They won a Reality TV Emmy. You've heard of the Emmy's, haven't you?

Please understand, writing for reality television is difficult; a star like Ronald Reagan is a godsend in this business. In addition to around-the-clock streaming for the website and scripting out and editing web extras, we cut a week's worth of footage down to forty-four minutes and arrange it in a manner that conveys our positive message and keeps viewers and advertisers happy. From this footage we compose a script for reference. A means of reverse engineering, if you will. Similar to how we help our addicts reverse engineer their disease by providing them the means to get to the root causes of their addiction. See how that works?

[I nod in a manner that shows I'm interested, but would rather she cut to the chase about Ronald Reagan and his whereabouts. Ms. Turner has a remarkable way of controlling the conversation.]

MT: At *Clean Time*, we are fortunate. Our program helps society, and our actors come from a traditionally action-packed and unpredictable demographic, i.e., drug addicted and mentally ill populations. Research shows viewers between the ages of 18 and 44 with disposable incomes in the top thirty-three percent are disproportionately interested in these people.

We promote a good cause. A good cause that happens to be profitable. We have 2.5 million Twitter followers. We've been extended for another five seasons. Frankly, I'm writing my own checks at this point and I owe it all to Ronald Reagan.

[A bird swoops between us and landed on the Prius.]

HS: I see you still have a rather wide assortment of animals and birds on the premises, even after the incident with the flamingo. Why is that?

MT: That was Bruce's idea. Before he joined our team, he collected exotic birds. He donated them to *Clean Time* and we keep them in honor of Bruce's contribution to our inaugural season. According to our preliminary research, addicts find nature uplifting. We desire to show them a way of life in which the term "addict" doesn't exist. Similar to the way it doesn't exist among exotic waterfowl. Nature is a means through which our patients can find solace in a higher power. Peacocks and swans don't need drugs to exist happily. They set an example. Currently, Bruce is in North Carolina working on one of our spinoff programs. Here, have a look.

[Maggie opens the *Clean Time* app on her tablet and shows us a brief trailer of Bruce in his cowboy hat, trying to revive an overdosed addict with Narcan. She had successfully detoured our conversation and I was beginning to become annoyed.]

Bob Middleton Jr.: What about the sex?

[I nudge Bob, and give him a sideways glance, urging him to not push too hard.]

HS: He's been missing for over a year now. You two were… intimate. You don't have any idea where he might have gone?

[Maggie looks at Bob and carefully chooses her words.]

MT: He was my patient. And yes, we consummated our relationship. It was the only way to work through his intimacy issues and the distress he still felt about his family. Oedipus complex. I've never seen a young man so clearly afflicted. To be honest, I feel I was seduced.

HS: Yes, but there are certainly regulations…

MT: Regulations addressed in his contract. If you're insinuating improper conduct, then I have to say you're barking down the wrong rabbit hole.

HS: I don't think I was suggesting such an insinuation, however, given your tryst, it doesn't seem out of the question that Ronald Reagan might remain in contact with you. Is this the case? Do you know where he went?

MT: Even if I weren't bound by confidentiality, I wouldn't tell you. We still have a team dedicated to pinpointing his whereabouts, and when they find him it will be national news. He was my star. I miss him. His disappearance is so unfortunate. Very sad, and yet, uplifting. Don't you agree?

•

From within the main house we heard a thunderous crash. Maggie suggested we meet in the cafeteria in thirty minutes, then hurried inside, leaving Bob and I alone in the parking lot surrounded by birds.

Later that day, after strenuous but amicable negotiations, Ms. Turner agreed to provide us with copies of the transcribed script from the pilot episode of *Clean Time*. We have included portions of the script (courtesy of The Recovery Channel and Jackson Entertainment) spliced together with Ronald Reagan's journal entries from his time in the facility. This editorial decision was made to better illuminate the contrast between Ronald Reagan's public experience on the show and his private thoughts and experiences as he progressed through treatment.

CLEAN TIME — SEASON ONE, EPISODE ONE

TITLES: IDENTITIES OF NON-CONSENTING PARTIES HAVE
BEEN CONCEALED. PORTIONS OF THE SHOW HAVE BEEN
RE-ENACTED FOR DRAMATIC EFFECT.

                                    FADE TO BLACK:

COLD OPENING:
Black Screen
                    CONFIDENT MALE (V.O.)
                (Assertive but somber)
            Crack-cocaine.

                                         CUT TO:

INT. CRACK HOUSE, GREENSBORO, NORTH CAROLINA — NIGHT

Moon shines through broken window.

Wearing acid-washed J$F jeans and hot pink tank
top, SHELLY crouches beneath window smoking
crack. She stands, looks out window, and picks
at a scab on her cheek.

A shadowy figure approaches, Shelly turns, drops
crack pipe and SCREAMS.

                                    FADE TO BLACK:

                    CONFIDENT MALE (V.O.)
            Alcohol.

                                         CUT TO:

INT. SUBURBAN HOME, KITCHEN, NORTH CAROLINA — DAY

A framed picture of footprints on a beach hangs
above the counter. Toast pops in toaster.

DOLPH, wearing a wrinkled suit, takes a long

drink from a bottle of whiskey and steadies himself on the counter.

> DOLPH'S WIFE (O.S.)
> Where have you been all week?

Small bag of white powder falls from Dolph's front pocket, lands next to toaster. Dolph collapses.

FADE TO BLACK:

> CONFIDENT MALE (V.O.)
> Heroin.

CUT TO:

INT. MOBILE HOME, BATHROOM, RURAL NORTH CAROLINA — DAY

The mirror above the sink is covered in grime. Dirty toilet sits adjacent to dirtier tub. Shower curtain hangs behind a collection of rubber ducks and assorted bath toys.

HALEY, wearing J$F denim shorts and stained GSU polo shirt, sits on toilet, her right foot resting on her left knee. FEMALE ROOMMATE sits on the edge of bath tub, inadvertently burning her thigh with a cigarette. Haley shoots heroin into her foot.

Female Roommate falls into shower curtain, scatters bath toys with foot. Haley blinks and passes out on the toilet.

CARTOONS audible in background.

FADE TO BLACK:

> CONFIDENT MALE (V.O.)
> Gasoline!

CUT TO:

INT. SUBURBAN HOME, REC ROOM, NORTH CAROLINA –
EVENING

Plasma television plays *Werewolf Hunter! The
Movie!!* trailer.

P&J logo visible offset right corner of screen.
Framed pictures of Paris, France adorn walls.
Intricate model of Eifel Tower sits on coffee
table.

HENRY (GASMAN), wearing purple and gold Guilford
State tracksuit, sits on love seat, dips rag into
coffee can filled with petrol, puts rag to face
and inhales. Henry tries to stand and falls on
model, crushing the coffee table.

CLOSE UP: TV IN BACKGROUND

                                    FADE TO BLACK:

          CONFIDENT MALE (V.O.)
     Amphetamines.

                                         CUT TO:

EXT. SWAMP, NORTH CAROLINA FOOTHILLS – NIGHT

RONALD REAGAN MIDDLETON runs through marsh,
hurdles fallen tree. Police dogs BARK.
Flashlights cut through darkness. Ronald Reagan
dives behind bushes. POLICE OFFICERS approach.
Ronald Reagan pulls bag of drugs from pants,
swallows drugs.

                                    FADE TO BLACK:

          CONFIDENT MALE (V.O.)
     Speedballs.

                                         CUT TO:

INT. UNC GREENSBORO CAMPUS, OFFICE – DAY

Bookshelves and blues posters cover the walls.
Blinds are drawn over a single window.

ALTHEA, wearing tight brown sweater by J$F
and J$F Denim Capris, sits across from TENURED
PROFFESSOR OF BLUES MUSIC. Althea's leg twitches;
she snaps the rubber band around her wrist.

                  TENURED PROFESSOR OF BLUES MUSIC
                        (exasperated)
        This can't continue. You have one
        chance to get help.

Althea stammers, leaves the office crying.

Professor rises, opens the blinds, and watches
Althea stumble across the parking lot toward her
car. Althea fumbles with her keys, gets in and
speeds off.

                                  FADE TO PURPLE:

CREDITS: (Lavender screen with scrolling script)
('Clean Time' Header – 36 font)

                        MAGGIE (V.O.)
     (Reads slightly ahead of scrolling script)
        Substance abuse has ripped a vast
        tear in the fabric of society. To
        help mend this tear, our team of
        psychoanalysts and talent scouts
        has searched North Carolina for
        six addictive personalities who
        want to change and brought them
        to the Rose-Thorn Recovery Center
        in Montclair, New Jersey. Our
        goal is to help exorcise this
        social demon via observation of
        the recovery process. For the
        next six weeks, we'll watch these
        addicts compete for God's grace.

BACK TO SCENE:

EXT. ROSE-THORN RECOVERY CENTER - DAY

Beneath the bright sun and cloudless sky stands
a sprawling Antebellum-style mansion. Chirping
birds, frisky rabbits and squirrels mingle with
R-TRC FLAMINGOS and peacocks in front of arching
double doors.

Holding a clipboard, MAGGIE stands stoically,
wearing pastel turtleneck and corduroy vest
with Guilford State pin on left breast. Lavender
beret casts tufts of shadow over bridge of
Maggie's nose.

                    MAGGIE
          Welcome to Clean Time. We are
          about to see who's serious about
          their recovery.

                                        CUT TO:

SIX WAY SPLIT SCREEN:

(HEAD SHOTS, CLOCKWISE FROM TOP LEFT RONALD
REAGAN, HALEY, HENRY, SHELLY, DOLPH, ALTHEA)

REHAB: DAY ONE

The shuttle dropped me off out front. The first thing I noticed were the brightly colored birds. Second, I noticed the cameras.

Counselor Bruce led me inside the cavernous Victorian house, his tracksuit swishing down the hallway. There were locks on the outside of all the doors and I wondered where the fuck this guy was taking me. We stopped at the med station, where I stared into a camera above the half-door while Bruce wrote me a prescription for a drug I've never heard of: *Nedvedol. 50mg, 3X daily.*

"This will take the edge off," he said, and handed me another triangular green pill in a Dixie cup.

I thanked him and swallowed the pill.

Bruce took my belt and shoelaces. He gave me a clear trash bag with pair of sweatpants and a sweatshirt in it, and I followed him into his office—a sterile room with a desk and a filing cabinet that screeched when he opened it. I leaned in the doorway, holding up my pants by the back belt loop before Bruce asked me to sit.

"You'll need this bad boy," he said, and handed me a recovery workbook.[18] Then he handed me a pile of forms with lots of small print.

"Just give me the gist." I figured I was fucked whether I signed them or not.

"Sign them or you go back to jail, basically."

While I filled out the forms, Bruce went over the terms of my probation. First, complete treatment at Rose-Thorn and get a Wellness Certificate signed by Counselor Maggie. After I'm discharged, I'll have to go to a couple meetings a week, get these slips signed by the chairperson as proof of attendance, and fax the signed slips to the Guilford County Magistrate.

I've been to meetings. 12-Step culture freaks me out. Too cult-y. Better than jail, though, and at least there's free coffee. I just want to get the fuck out of here as quickly and painlessly as possible. Find

Jacky and leave for Georgia.

I finished the paperwork and slid it back to Bruce, who filed it away in the cabinet. "After intake," he said, "don't forget your dentist appointment." He pointed out Counselor Maggie's office and the dentist's office on a map of the grounds tacked between the window and a framed picture of the words "...Think, Think, Think..." that was hung upside down and confused me terribly.

Bruce slid a pencil from the mug on his desk and waved it between his thumb and forefinger, giving the appearance of the pencil being made of rubber. "Listen, I want you to know you can talk to me about anything. I'm in recovery too. I'm not just some guy with a counseling degree who doesn't know what it's like out on the set."

I nodded and picked at the corner of my workbook.

"I have a good feeling about you, Ronald Reagan." Bruce tapped his chin with the pencil, tossed it in the air and caught it without looking.

I didn't know if I wanted to stab him in the eye with that pencil, or hug him and thank him for showing interest in my wellbeing. Bury my face in his purple windbreaker and bawl my eyes out. "That sign is upside down," I said as I got up to leave.

"Is it?" he asked and winked.

It seemed like Bruce had something to add, but I closed the door before I could find out. I carried the trash bag full of my stuff back down the hallway to intake in Counselor Maggie's office.

Maggie's office is cramped but the chairs are comfortable. There's a poster of kittens and another titled "Drugs of Our Times," which is like the periodic table of narcotics, complete with a list of side effects. When I walked in this afternoon, Maggie was flipping through a manila folder at her desk. A pack of cigarettes sat next to the open window behind her and it smelled like she'd just snuck a smoke before I got in there. She had on too much perfume and her makeup gave her face a glossy shine. When she looked up, her lashes seemed fake, but she had pretty, eager eyes. She talked like a real estate agent trying to make a sale, which immediately put me on the defensive. At least there were no cameras.

"Have a seat. Let's go over the rules, shall we?" Maggie said.

"Go for it," I said, thinking she'd tell me normal rehab rules. No fucking, no drugs, no fighting, that kind of thing. I was wrong.

Maggie continued, "Every week one addict is eliminated. The loser gets a bus ticket and seventy-six dollars. Someone from the waiting list replaces them."

"What the fuck?"

"You have a dirty mouth."

"Sorry, I don't understand what you mean by eliminated?"

Maggie explained that my rehab was part of a contest for a new TV show called *Clean Time*. Me and the other addicts will be filmed around the clock. New episodes will air each week, with bonus footage streamed online every day. Apparently viewers can watch web clips and start voting before the first episode even airs.

"You never know what the audience will see," Maggie said, "so it's best to assume they're always watching. It's all in the contract you just signed, but I want to make sure you feel comfortable."

"I feel great," I said, and thought about how I could break out of here and where I'd run to and how I'd get high.

She said viewers will choose their favorite addict each week by casting votes online or using some mobile app, and the two least popular addicts will have to fight each other to stay at the end of the week. She said all this like it was totally normal and handed me a pamphlet laying out all the rules.

"Sounds like a lot of pressure," I said, and stuffed the pamphlet in my notebook. At least it's not jail, I told myself.

"It's best to avoid the Relapse Challenge altogether," Maggie said. "Although, you do seem rather fit. I suspect you'd do quite well." Maggie reached across the desk and squeezed my bicep. "Very fit."

"Thanks," I said. "When I was in jail, I worked out a lot. Pushups, dips. That kind of stuff."

"I bet you did."

I shifted in my chair, trying to sort all this out, when I saw the stationary on Maggie's desk was marked with a Philson & Jackson logo. Then I noticed the logo was printed on all the pens and folders too, even the stress ball sitting on the filing cabinet.

"My dad works for Philson and Jackson.[19] Is that how I wound up here? Is he making money off me?"

Maggie touched my hand. "Let's focus on the present, Ronald Reagan. Is it important how you got here? Not really. You're here. Let's just make the best of it. You want help, right?"

I told her, "Of course I do."

"Good," Maggie said. "Let's start by getting those teeth looked at."

After my meeting with Maggie, I walked around looking for the exit so I could go to the dentist. New Age music piped through hidden speakers in the hallway. The big old house had been gutted and manically carpeted—even the walls and ceiling. The rug changed color every time I passed a door. It took ten steps to get from one door to the next. Each door I passed I changed my mind: make a break for it, or stay and try to win the most popular drug addict contest, maybe get clean. I ran my hand along the grooves in the carpeted wall and thought about how bad my dad had fucked me over and why Jacky still hadn't written back.

Around every corner androgynous people wearing pastel turtle-necks and berets were setting up cameras and wiring microphones. I think the meds started to kick in, and I tried to talk myself into a version of my life in which my parents didn't think I was an embarrassment and my girlfriend wasn't fucking someone else and I felt trapped. Smothered by that fucking carpet. Like if I didn't breathe fresh air, right then, I'd grab a chair and throw it through the big window in the day room and jump into the pool and maybe drown myself, except I didn't know how to get back to the day room.

In the hallway, mounted above a potted fern, was a framed

Wellness Certificate signed by Chaz Dorsey, the drummer from Johnny and the Drivers, and a replica of the gold record they received for their last album before he went solo and started making shitty pop music. Cotton-mouthed and biting the inside of my cheek, I stared at the certificate for what felt like hours, but it couldn't have been more than a minute. Then I remembered I'd already passed Chaz's certificate several times. How had I only made one turn out of Maggie's office and gotten lost? I started to sweat. I thought about being on TV for everyone in America to see. What if Jacky was watching me at that very moment on the internet? She would see me all sweaty and lost in a fucking hallway. I swear, I was about to lose my shit. I started running, screaming at the cameras and all those fucking people, who didn't so much as look up from their work. I sprinted down that fucking rainbow-colored hallway full of weird tech people and motivational posters and plants until I saw daylight through a set of double doors and stumbled outside. The fresh air felt fantastic. I sat in the shade and smoked a cigarette. After a while a bunch of birds gathered around me, and I couldn't even remember what I had been so upset about.

Crossing the parking lot to the dentist's office, I ran into a girl, a redhead who seemed lost. Despite the heat, she wore long black sleeves and her eyes were bloodshot and wide. She struggled, dragging a suitcase the size of a small car.

"Hi," I said, "I'm getting new teeth." Immediately I regretted saying this, but couldn't think of anything else to say that was at all positive. I added, "I used to work for the company that makes your pants."

The redhead looked past me, like she hoped someone else was talking to her.

"Can I help with your luggage?" I asked. This was better. Normal interaction.

She said, "Thanks, but no." Her braces sparkled when she spoke. A blue jay landed between us and pecked at a pink wad of gum on the asphalt. "Poor thing," she said. She stared that bird down like she'd never seen one before.[20] Then a car pulled in and the bird flew away with the gum. Her head snapped up. "I'm Althea," she said.

"Ronald Reagan."

We shook.

"Wait, like the *president*?"

"Yeah." Unsure of where to look, I settled on an acne scar between her eyes.

Althea half smiled and snapped the rubber band hanging loose around her wrist. She said, "See you later," grabbed her suitcase, and headed toward the house.

My hand was still covered in her sweat and the scent of a flower I couldn't name. When she was safely inside, I put my palm to my face and inhaled deep.

The dentist gave me laughing gas, a new set of teeth, and Vicodin, of all things.

They're really big on journaling as therapy here. Supposedly if I write enough about myself, it'll help me figure out why I'm such an asshole. Since I'm already in the process of writing a memoir, it makes sense to keep chronicling my time in treatment. And journaling's a lot easier here, with peace and quiet and no cellmates looking over my shoulder. At least it will allow me to present the appearance of trying to work through my issues, even if I don't really want to. In a place like this the time will be easier if I cooperate.

DAY TWO, ~3AM - PASSING NOTES

I woke up a minute ago to a squirrel banging on my window in the pitch black.

It's after midnight so I have three days clean from booze (forty-five off narcotics, weed, and hallucinogens).

My roommate talks in his sleep about huffing gasoline. He is built like a twelve-year-old, wears bad hair plugs, and his lips are missing. Just a flat blistery nothing around the hole in his face that spits bubbles with every dreamy breath.

I was watching the bubbles float, when Althea slid this letter under my door: "RR, The idiots who watch this kind of shit love couples. The viewers won't vote us off if we provide adequate sexual tension. —Althea"

I see no reason not to go along with this.

We start filming at sunrise.

TITLES: CLEAN TIME: DAY ONE

FADE IN:

INT. ROSE-THORN RECOVERY CENTER - DAY

VIEWER APPROVAL RATINGS GRAPHIC SCROLLS ACROSS
THE SCREEN
VAR: ALTHEA 27%, RONALD REAGAN 23%, HALEY 20%,
GASMAN 11%, SHELLY 10%, DOLPH 9%.[21]

Sun shines through a large bay window flanked
by table holding a rack of pamphlets and a
wide screen TV playing *Werewolf Hunter!* reruns.
Rainbow-colored couches and chairs surround TV
and gas fireplace.

Dolph, Gasman and Shelly sit on couches watching
TV. Dolph throws a pillow at Gasman and gives
him the finger. Shelly snuffs cigarette into
overflowing ashtray.

Lying on the carpet, Althea removes staples from
NA meeting lists and folds paper into origami
cranes. Haley sits with her stuffed rabbit,
stacking wooden blocks with recovery-centered
words carved into them.

Maggie stands in foreground, adjusts turtleneck.

> MAGGIE
> This is the first full day of
> treatment for our addicts. I'm
> outside Counselor Bruce's office
> where Ronald Reagan M. is about
> to finish one-on-one therapy.

Office door opens. Ronald Reagan exits.

> MAGGIE
> Ronald Reagan, tell us about your
> discussion with Bruce.

                    RONALD REAGAN
Get that fucking camera out of my
face!

                        MAGGIE
How do you feel? Why are you
upset? What's on your mind?

Ronald Reagan turns down the hall toward his
room, next to Maggie's office.

                    RONALD REAGAN
I'm exercising my right to
Personal Reflection Time!

                                        CUT TO:

INT. RONALD REAGAN'S ROOM — DAY

Twin beds rest on either side of a communal
nightstand. Branded GSU logo lamp placed on
nightstand.

Ronald Reagan sits on bed near tears.

                    RONALD REAGAN
I can't take this. I thought I
could but I can't. I just want to
stay out of jail. Regain my self-
respect. Now I have a disease?
How is addiction a disease?
Leprosy is a disease. Shit.

Ronald Reagan stands, charges camera.

                    RONALD REAGAN
Get that fucking camera out of
here!

DAY TWO - AFTER TRUST EXERCISES

We watched an infomercial about Nedvedol. Apparently, the drug's effects vary with each individual's neural hardwiring. Nedvedol gives your brain what it tells you it wants, or what you tell your brain it wants. Not sure which exactly. But it works for ADD, depression, and as a detox drug for opiates, benzos, and amphetamines. The fine print at the bottom had a whole litany of side effects that I couldn't read.

Now that I'm used to it, when the Nedvedol kicks in, it's like there's balloon animals twisting in my head and I get a kind of rubbery plastic taste in my mouth. After the initial onset, I'm in an alert state of hyper-calmness. Kind of like doing a speedball after you've been at work lunging for twelve hours, and you're exhausted but you can't sleep. Now that I've been on it for a few days, I don't know how I'd get along without it.

DAY TWO - A FIGHT IN CHURCH

We took the shuttle to a local AA Meeting in the basement at St. Stephen's. AA won't let the crew inside to film, but Maggie secretly recorded the meeting on her phone and streamed it on The Recovery Channel's website. Highlights will wind up on the *Clean Time* social media feeds. I'm hesitant to say anything about Maggie recording everything because I gave a really heartfelt share at the first meeting and my Viewer Approval Ratings got a nice bump. I don't want to mess with that.

So anyway, we're at the meeting and this kid Garret took exception to being interrupted during his share and hit Dolph with a folding chair. Punches were thrown, tables overturned. Althea and I snuck outside and smoked cigarettes while the meeting devolved into a street fight. We went around to the far side of the church, away from the van where the camera crew takes their breaks. We climbed over a short stone wall and sat at the edge of a cemetery.

"Do you think it's working?" she asked.

"According to the website, everyone loves us." I put my hand on hers and whispered in her ear, "Do you think they're watching now?"

"No," Althea said. She took a quick peek over the wall and pulled her hand away.

I sat there until the cigarette in my mouth turned to ash and fell on my lap. I spit out the filter and leaned in to kiss her.

She turned her head. "This is just for TV," she said. "No."

"We should stay in character."

She scooted away from me and picked at a crack in the wall, pulling out a small chunk of rock that she hurled into the graveyard. "I don't even know you," she said.

"What do you want to know?"

"How did they get you on the show?"

"They pulled me out of jail, sent me here. You?"

"I relapsed on meth." Althea lit another cigarette. The graveyard was cramped, full of eroded headstones all covered in moss. I could barely read the names by the lights in the church parking lot. Althea told me she was at UNC Greensboro, and I mentioned I lived near Guilford State. She was offered a spot at Rose-Thorn through the university, so she emptied her bank account and spent it all on meth and dope. "One last run," she said. "Then I drove up here by myself, took the wrong exit and got lost. I'd been living in my car in a boarded up shopping plaza a couple miles from here for almost a week before Bruce found me trying to break into the abandoned movie theater."

"Ever seen a fight in a meeting before?" I asked.

"No, but I've been to meetings and I've been in a fight."

"So, do we know each other well enough yet?"

"False intimacy," she said. "We sit in these meetings with shitty coffee and stale donuts and share all the horrible shit we've done. So you've known someone for five minutes and already know all their worst secrets and it seems like we're close, but it's bullshit. Everyone in that church is in one big fake relationship. Let's just be honest about ours. We know it's fake."

"This seems important to you," I said, and made a mental note to remember the idea.

The fight spilled out into the parking lot. We heard sirens. I lit a cigarette.

"I don't know if I'm saying it right," Althea said, "but you get my point." She looked at ease, smoking in the dim light.

I said, "I think I could date you in the real world."

"You don't even know me."

"Maybe it's better that way."

I thought about Jacky, all my unanswered letters.

Althea stood up. "We should get back."

We hopped the crumbling waist-high wall and walked toward the church. As we approached the edge of the parking lot, we brushed the dirt and leaves off each other's backs and fixed our hair for the cameras.

DAY TWO - DURING EVENING GROUP

Althea started sharing about a terrible experience she had with her stepmother at the Hampton Aviary. I could tell it was hard for her to open up to the group like that, so I shuffled closer on the couch and took her hand for encouragement. "Go ahead," I said. "It's important to be honest. You never know who might benefit from your experience."

She thanked me, but when she started back in with her story, Maggie interrupted. "Ronald Reagan, it's important that we take our own inventory. You don't want to be so focused on Althea's problems that you forget about your own."

"I thought helping another addict was how we get clean?" Althea said.

"I think you're holding the meeting hostage."

Maggie stepped closer.

Haley walked between them. "Counselor Maggie, Althea's helping me, let her share."

Maggie looked around for the orderlies, nervous.

"I need to share too and we're almost out of time," Gasman said. I gave him a look, but he didn't get the hint.

Haley continued, "Bruce says it's a selfless program. You say it's a selfish program. Which is it?"

Althea said, "Thanks, but I can handle this myself."

Haley turned and said, "You don't have to handle this by yourself." Then they embraced. I felt good for Althea's ratings and my own, which would get a boost by proxy.

Then Dolph screamed from the other side of the room about chemtrails. Shelly lit the edge of the table on fire and melted the plastic edge. A team of expressionless orderlies in pastel scrubs appeared out of the shadows, took Shelly's lighter, and shot her and Dolph full of sedative.

Maggie ended group early and we filled out worksheets while she napped in her office.

TITLES: DAY THREE

FADE IN:

EXT. ROSE-THORN RECOVERY CENTER, POOL - DAY

Between the patio and the courtyard, a waterfall
flows from a series of landscaped rocks into a
pool surrounded by six fish statues.

The Outdoor Flamingo Cabin sits on the far side
of the lawn, near the flowerbed and rock garden.

Rabbits hop peacefully through the beach
volleyball court.

Althea wears a long-sleeved GSU shirt cut at
midriff, and bathing suit bottom. Haley wears
mauve bikini with GSU logo on left breast. They
playfully chase a flamingo.

Wearing gender appropriate J$F bathing suits,
Shelly and Dolph sit in reclining chairs playing
dice for cigarettes. Gasman runs alongside the
pool, trips over a fish statue, tumbles into the
water.

Maggie adjusts her beret, smiles.

>   MAGGIE
>   We believe in the importance of
>   Scheduled Unstructured Free Time.
>   The addicts are free to explore
>   the courtyard and immediate
>   outdoor areas as they please
>   while they cycle through their
>   one-on-one sessions. Bruce
>   counsels the male addicts while
>   I work with the females. Despite
>   being clean for less than a
>   week, our addicts have begun to
>   form support groups within the
>   larger group, their own "we," if

you will, and it's wonderful. So
wonderful. Isn't it?

                                        CUT TO:

INT. SERENITY COVE - MIDDAY

Cartoon pictures of happy woodland creatures
reciting motivational, recovery-oriented slogans
cover bulletin board mounted behind plush chair.

Sound of FISH SPLASHING IN RUNNING WATER segues
into "CLEAN TIME INSTRUMENTAL" by Chaz Dorsey.

Ronald Reagan sits in chair, looks curiously at
camera.

                    RONALD REAGAN
          Yesterday, I attacked Steven the
          cameraman. Soon I'll have to make
          amends. I'm not on that step yet,
          but Bruce says I should. I just
          want to do the next right thing.
          I'm really connecting with Bruce.
          He's teaching me accountability.

Ronald Reagan flips unlit Marlboro into his
mouth, clicks lighter several times, grows
visibly frustrated and throws lighter, uses
matches to light cigarette.

                                        CUT TO:

EXT. ROSE-THORN RECOVERY CENTER, POOL - MIDDAY

Haley and Shelly argue over a wet pack of
Newports.

Dolph pins Gasman to the patio, SCREAMS in
Gasman's face.

Althea and Ronald Reagan build sandcastles in
the beach volleyball court. A crumpled pack of

cigarettes lands on their sandcastle. Shelly grabs cigarette pack, smashes castle, walks toward pool.

Maggie stands in the foreground.

                    MAGGIE
          We try to impose the importance
          of filling the void they used to
          fill with drugs with something
          healthy, like prayer and God. It
          is integral to their recovery. We
          also offer volleyball, swimming,
          and Xbox, in addition to Personal
          Reflection Time and access to the
          Serenity Cove.

                                        CUT TO:

INT. SERENITY COVE - EVENING

                    ALTHEA
          Two weeks ago I was about to get
          my doctorate. Now I'm on a rehab
          TV show surrounded by junkies
          and squirrels. Acceptance is key.
          I've been through this before. As
          my stepmother would say, 'It's not
          my first rodeo.'

                                        FADE TO:

FLASHBACK:

INT. ALTHEA'S BEDROOM - NIGHT - FIFTEEN YEARS AGO

TITLES: RE-ENACTMENT: ANY RESEMBLANCE TO ANYONE LIVING OR DEAD IS ENTIRELY COINCIDENTAL.

Beneath an open window, record player spins beside bed covered with blues and psychedelic rock LPs. Black light posters and tapestries decorate walls.

Sitting among albums, YOUNG ALTHEA takes a huge hit from a small bong, blows smoke out window.

"SMOKESTACK LIGHTNIN'" plays.

From downstairs an argument increases in volume and intensity. Young Althea turns up record player, packs bong.

> ALTHEA (V.O.)
> By the time I was a junior in
> high school, I'd shot dope,
> smoked crack, and eaten pills I
> couldn't even pronounce. I got
> clean for the first time when I
> was 17.

CUT TO:

INT. ALTHEA'S APARTMENT - NIGHT - TWELVE YEARS AGO

A lamp with a torn shade burns next to cushion-less couch and table covered in trash. Ancient TV set with coat hanger antenna plays infomercial for Philson Hypodermics.

Young Althea, wearing J$F cutoffs and sweatshirt combo, sits on couch, shoots cocaine into left arm.

Her roommate LEAH, bug-eyed and gaunt, wearing only *Werewolf Hunter!* t-shirt, exits daughter's room. Leah bangs her leg on the table and starts sorting a mound of broken CDs, rags, old shoes, junk mail, and doll parts into piles near the television.

Screen door opens. HOMELESS-LOOKING MAN enters, sits down and puts his arm around Young Althea.

Leah cradles the phone in her shoulder, looks at TV and dials. She continues sorting garbage.

> ALTHEA (V.O.)
> The last seven months of my active addiction were terrifying. I dropped out of high school and got an apartment with a friend who had a two-year-old. We'd wait till her daughter fell asleep and shoot coke all night. I hit her little girl once.

CUT TO:

INT. ALTHEA'S APARTMENT - DAY - TWELVE YEARS AGO

TODDLER spills juice on ratty carpet. Young Althea punches her.

> ALTHEA (V.O.)
> Thank God that kid was with her dad when our power got turned off and we decided to light a fire in the living room of our second story apartment.

CUT TO:

EXT. HARDWARE STORE - NIGHT - TWELVE YEARS AGO

The parking lot is empty save for one car parked near a stack of bricks covered by a tarp. Bushes surround the lot.

HARDWARE STORE CLERK locks up and leaves for the evening.

Young Althea and Leah emerge from bushes, grab bricks, run.

> ALTHEA (V.O.)
> We stole bricks from the hardware store across the street. We

arranged the bricks on the floor
into a makeshift fireplace. For
three days straight we shot coke.

INT. ALTHEA'S APARTMENT - NIGHT - TWELVE YEARS AGO

Young Althea and Leah place bricks in a circle,
throw debris in circle.

> ALTHEA (V.O.)
> We opened the windows and burned
> unopened bills and cedar
> shingles. When the fire started
> to die, we tossed piles of random
> crap onto it.

Young Althea and Leah tend to the fire. Flames
rise and fall.

> ALTHEA (V.O.)
> Someone reported us for stealing
> the bricks. The police walked in
> on me fucking the 50-year-old
> from downstairs who'd helped us
> cop.

Homeless-looking Man and Young Althea fornicate
on couch, genitals obscured by houseplant and
toy bear. POLICE enter just as the floor beneath
the fire pit collapses. Naked, Leah jumps out of
second story kitchen window.

> ALTHEA (V.O.)
> That was the last time I traded
> sex for drugs.

Homeless-looking Man and Young Althea cover
themselves with light blue Guilford State
blanket, shuffle backward against couch. Young
Althea points at hole in floor, SCREAMS.
Apartment fills with smoke.

END FLASHBACK:

BACK TO SCENE:

INT. — SERENITY COVE — EVENING

Althea stares at her hands, looks up abruptly.

> ALTHEA
> After that, I turned it around. I
> finished high school, went to
> college and studied music
> history. I continued my education
> to the level of near-PhD. Then I
> relapsed and put on a one-woman
> show depicting Robert Johnson's
> deal with the devil for my
> freshman class. When I get out
> of here I'm going to finish my
> dissertation. That's my goal.

DAY FOUR[22]

At lunch, Althea talked to Wayne, the head chef and a former patient here before the place was bought by Philson & Jackson. Wayne seems to like us. He gives us extra desserts and cups of regular coffee. Normally we only get decaf. He also told Althea about a couple blind spots in and around the cafeteria and outside by the dumpsters. Althea waved me over to the big fern in the corner and we sat behind it and ate. It was nice, not having to be in full-blown TV couple mode. Althea didn't have to hook me up like that. No one could see it so there was no benefit to her. Unless she's just trying to keep me engaged with the plan. Triangulating against the powers that be. Could go either way. Maybe I'm overthinking it.

The day was going pretty well until Arts and Crafts, when Dolph flipped out again. It started with a story about his brother.

"My brother," he said, "got a citation for smoking pot at a Journey concert, and the judge says 'jail or rehab.' Of course he chooses rehab, but the intense outpatient program made it impossible for him to get to work."

Dolph actually looked shaken. He went on about how his brother was a bricklayer, taking business classes at night. So he lost his job, quit school and started living off his savings. Every day he went to outpatient from noon to 9PM. The only job he could get was the overnight shift at GasLand. Then he figured if he can't get a real job, he might as well sell drugs. Dolph, trying to help, set his brother up with his people and then after maybe a week it went bad. On his way into work one night, his brother got robbed and shot in the neck. Now he's paralyzed.

Dolph punctuated the story by screaming, "That's why all you rehab people can fuck yourselves. You just want government money."

Bruce stepped in. "Dolph, we want to help, we are not affiliated with the people who stabbed your brother in the neck. Let's talk about how you felt when your brother was stabbed in the neck. Did you feel guilty? Totally normal. Don't let those people rent space in your head."

Dolph stood and walked up to the camera. "State mandated rehab kills people!" He screamed until he lost his breath and collapsed. He writhed on the floor, kicking chairs and flailing his arms. At that point the orderlies converged on Dolph and shot him full of sedative.

Shelly attacked the orderlies with a chair and was also shot full of sedative. Maggie propped them up on the couch as the cameras kept rolling.

DAY FOUR - AFTER LIGHTS OUT

I was still having trouble sleeping so I stayed up late reading one of the mystery novels Gasman brought with him. I'd turned the light off finally and was almost asleep when the door creaked open. I could tell by the silhouette it was Maggie. She just stood there in the doorway, silently watching me and Gasman.

I'm pretty sure this happened last night too, but I thought it was a dream.

Now I can't sleep again and I'm too tired to keep writing.

TITLES: DAY FIVE

FADE IN:

INT. MAIN MEETING ROOM — MORNING

Bruce and Maggie stand before the circle of
chairs. Sunlight shines through the bay window
bathing Maggie in white light.

> MAGGIE
> Our addicts, having had some time
> to acclimate themselves to the
> premises, will begin a series of
> contests designed to test their
> willingness to embrace recovery.
> Today's contest was designed by
> the people at Hazelden, but we've
> made a few tweaks to spice things
> up. It's called, "Give Your Fear a
> Face and Slap It!"

Maggie uncovers the white board near the TV,
listing the rules. TV plays *Werewolf Hunter!*
reruns.

> MAGGIE (O.S.)
> Using the craft supplies
> provided, you will break into
> teams and construct a visual
> representation of your most deep-
> seeded fear. The fear that most
> threatens your sobriety. You will
> have twenty minutes. Best visual
> representation wins.

Bruce saunters into the middle of the room,
raises arms.

> BRUCE
> Fuck everything and run, or face
> everything and recover!

PAN GROUP:

Dolph rocks in his chair and pats Shelly's arm. Gasman rubs his lips. Haley bites fingernails and drops them in her lap. Althea twists a pamphlet into a stick and taps her thigh. Ronald Reagan looks concerned, lights a cigarette.

>   BRUCE
>   And here to help me and Maggie
>   judge your projects, a dear
>   friend I worked with when this
>   place was still the Montclair
>   House. Let's have a warm welcome
>   for blues-rock musician, Chaz
>   Dorsey.

CHAZ enters wearing J$F Midnight Magik Skinny Jeans, GSU flat brim baseball cap, and Who t-shirt. Chaz waves, takes a modest bow, and winks at Maggie.

Althea stands.

>   ALTHEA
>   When are you going to put out
>   an album that isn't another
>   over-produced rip-off of early
>   '90s grunge full of faux-ironic
>   choruses?

Maggie and Bruce exchange a worried look. Chaz takes off his hat, scratches his temple.

>   CHAZ
>   Let me guess, you're an academic.

>   ALTHEA
>   How can you call yourself a blues
>   musician?

                        CHAZ
         Can you edit that out? No, well,
         when you're caught in the grips,
         you do things you normally
         wouldn't. But thanks for checking
         out our songs. (smiles) Our
         last album was named comeback
         record of the year. Topped the
         rock, country, and college radio
         charts. Choruses and all.

Althea crosses her arms and is about to speak
when Maggie cuts her off.

                        MAGGIE
         OK, time to break into teams.
         Althea will work with Haley.
         Ronald Reagan, you and Dolph
         are paired together. That leaves
         Shelly and Gasman.

Addicts break into teams. Shelly curses. Gasman
rubs his mouth, looks scared. Haley and Althea
smile and find their seats. Dolph doesn't move
until Bruce walks over and whispers words of
encouragement.

                        MAGGIE
         Let's begin!

TITLES: GIVE YOUR FEAR A FACE AND SLAP IT!
Below Viewer Approval Ratings, TIMER ticks down
from 20 min.

Conversation fills the room. Gasman fumbles with
scissors, Shelly smears paste on a piece of
poster board and covers it with glitter. Haley
and Althea glue popsicle sticks together. Ronald
Reagan spins a crayon between his fingers and
drops it. Dolph leans back in his chair with
hands behind head.

DAY SIX - THE CONTEST

Before the contest Maggie was explaining how important the competitions are to our Viewer Approval Rating, and that this morning's competition was going to be a team activity. Instead of being able to choose our partners like adults, we were assigned teammates. Of course, Maggie paired me with Dolph, and he started giving me shit right away.

"Sellout," he said.

"Fuck off," I said.

"You fuck off, sellout."

A cameraman swooped next to us. I straightened up and smiled, trying to look determined and engaged.

"I don't see how looking at our fears is being a sellout."

"Twelve Steps won't work for me," Dolph said. "I don't believe in God."

"My biggest fear is the unknown." I drew an infinity sign full of question marks with crayon.

"Follow the money, Ronald Reagan. Who profits off this?"

There was a good chance I'd lose the competition if Dolph didn't play along. I'd lost enough already, and I hate losing.

The camera on us turned to Althea's group.

I leaned close to Dolph. "Draw a fucking picture."

"I'm afraid of drones."

The camera came back.

"So, Dolph," I said, "you feel drugs will turn you into a drone. Let's get a visual representation of that down so we can really see how it looks in your mind's eye and further examine how this fear effects your daily life."

"This place profits from the CIA-funded drug trade."

"Try your best. I won't judge you." I handed him a marker, but he threw it at Gasman.

I waited for the camera to drift elsewhere and leaned across the table. "You know, man, you're right. But Bruce is the problem. All his bullshit recovery speak. He's brainwashed." I lowered my voice and drew a few stick figures. "Bruce has to go. Think about it. What would your brother want?"

Dolph nodded and drew a drone of impeccable quality. Dolph is a moron, but all his conspiracy talk gave me an idea. Every good conspiracy needs a patsy.[23]

TITLES: GIVE YOUR FEAR A FACE AND SLAP IT!

FADE IN:

INT. MAIN MEETING ROOM – DAY

Approval ratings scroll across screen. Timer
reads 10 (ten) seconds.

Maggie, Bruce and Chaz sit at folding table with
Chaz's gold record visible on wall behind them.

                    MAGGIE
          Ten seconds!

Time expires, THREE-NOTE PIPE ORGAN CHIME
signals addicts to drop supplies.

                    CHAZ
          Great work everyone. You've all
          done such a super job.

                    BRUCE
          Alright, let's get to it. Group
          one: Althea and Haley. Show us
          something awesome and we'll see
          who can guess what you're really
          afraid of. Remember, everyone, as
          your judges we award points for
          correct guesses, and for accuracy
          of depiction.

Althea and Haley present an intricate diorama of
a house made of popsicle sticks and covered in
star stickers and sparkles. Origami birds folded
out of meeting lists and characters cut from
the covers of anti-drug pamphlets are glued to
a poster board. Miniature clay objects surround
the house.

                    HALEY
          Well, me and Althea talk about
          our fears on a nightly basis, so

the home we're building is a good
example of the two of us, like,
we don't want to let fear inside,
or the accompanying addictive
behaviors, so we started with the
house, and the fears are outside
attacking it. So, OK guys, guess
what's attacking it.

                RONALD REAGAN
I think the clay guy is failure.

                DOLPH
The piece of tinfoil folded into
a boat is the government trying
to trap us by stratifying the
middle and lower classes into
warring factions divided along
racial lines and putting us into
rehabs where we will be broken
down and built up into God-
fearing, right-wing Christians
who can be manipulated into…

                BRUCE
Thank you, Dolph.

Ronald Reagan whispers to Dolph, pats him on the
back.

                SHELLY
How are we supposed to compete
with that? I have to work with
this face-less retard here
drawing a gas station that looks
like a rusty bed frame.

                GASMAN
I did my best.

Haley blushes. Althea looks out at the pool.

116

                    BRUCE
      No more guesses? Then we'll have
      Althea and Haley tell us what
      they fear.

Haley points to her diorama.

                    HALEY
      OK, so, these various monsters
      represent failure, like Ronald
      Reagan said. Also shame and
      disappointment. Then we have the
      birds, which to Althea represent
      caged animals trapped by their
      circumstance for no reason other
      than their beauty, when really
      they are more than just feathers.
      These two here by the boats
      represent commitment and being
      alone, which we're both afraid
      of. The foil is our past.

Haley backs up and looks at the floor, her eyes
shift quickly. She bites her nails and waits for
the judges' response.

                    MAGGIE
      This is nonsense. A total
      failure.

Althea pulls at the rubber band around her
wrist, closes her eyes and mutters to herself.
Haley smiles nervously.

                    CHAZ
      Wonderful. Top notch!

                    BRUCE
      You two did a fantastic job. So
      great! Now Chaz and I will hold
      your piece while you slap it!

Chaz and Bruce each hold one end of the diorama. Althea and Haley attack the project with a series of violent slaps. Everyone in the room chants, SLAP! They destroy the project, hug each other, and take a seat.

> MAGGIE
> Gasman, Shelly, you're up.

> GASMAN
> Please call me Henry.

> BRUCE
> Henry, go ahead pal. Show us what you've got there.

> GASMAN
> It's not very good.

> SHELLY
> Don't qualify it! Our project is strong.

Shelly raises a hand to hit Gasman. Gasman cowers.

> GASMAN
> Shelly, you present it.

Shelly waves her hand in front of their project.

> SHELLY
> This is more literal than
> the last one. We can't all be
> overachievers. But again, I stand
> behind our work. My partner
> didn't do as well as he could
> have. His fear is indecipherable.
> Go for it, give us your guesses.

> RONALD REAGAN
> Gas stations?

                    GASMAN
Exactly! Imagine if your drug of
choice was sold on every
corner for $5.50 a gallon! It's
horrifying.

                    ALTHEA
That piece of cellophane is a
mirror. You're afraid of looking
at yourself. Are the two people
your parents?

                    HALEY
Clouds?

                    MAGGIE
Alright, (makes note on clipboard)
this is another poor effort as
far as I'm concerned. Go ahead,
Shelly, *Henry,* explain yourselves.

Shelly flattens her tube top and J$F cutoffs with
her palms, pushes Gasman aside, and stands next
to the project.

                    SHELLY
We all know Gasman is afraid of
service stations and his ex-wife.
That's what the mess of scribbles
around the blob of black clay is
supposed to be. These two pieces
of toilet paper tube represent the
couple that murdered my parents.
A man and his wife who used to
live next door. They'd been up
for days on meth and they broke
in one night and carved up my
parents when I was ten. I hid
behind the couch. I still have
visions of that man's emotionless
face. It was just something he had
to do that night, like running
out for milk and smokes. (sobs,

collects herself) And this is my
ex-boyfriend who pimped me out for
crack before he got sent upstate.

                    MAGGIE
Poor. Such a poor effort. I'm
saddened, really. Very
disappointed.

                    BRUCE
The gas station is great, and I
can see the murder as displayed
by the tubes, but that's not
really a fear. You didn't follow
directions.

                    CHAZ
I think they did a swell job.
Another top-notch piece!

                    BRUCE
Alright, come up here and get
your slap on!

Gasman and Shelly hand over their project among
chants of SLAP, SLAP, SLAP! Gasman slaps the
project, knocks it to the ground, and stomps it
repeatedly. Shelly watches him. They return to
their seats.

                    MAGGIE
    Time for the last group.

Ronald Reagan stands and clears his throat,
holding the poster board, blank side to the
camera.

                    RONALD REAGAN
First, let me say the first two
groups did a great job. Tough
acts to follow. Especially Althea
and Haley.

Ronald Reagan looks at Dolph. Dolph pulls a loose thread from his shirt and wraps it around his finger.

                    RONALD REAGAN
          Dolph, want to take the reins?
          I need a coffee.

Dolph continues spinning thread around his finger till the tip is blue. He stands, takes the poster from Ronald Reagan. Ronald Reagan walks to the snack table.

                    DOLPH
          Guess our fears.

                    GASMAN
          Eight! The number.

                    SHELLY
          Dolph, honey! I know how you fear
          the pending government takeover.

                    RONALD REAGAN
          (Holding coffee by snack table)
          Close, Henry. Good try.

                    ALTHEA
          Ronald Reagan's biggest fear is
          the unknown as it pertains to
          letting down his family due to
          his inability to stop trying to
          control everything, which, in
          turn, leads to self-sabotage. So,
          I'd like to say, great job
          representing fear of the unknown.
          I didn't know you were such a
          talented artist.

                    HALEY
          (Nodding enthusiastically)
          I agree.

                    RONALD REAGAN
You guys got them both! Awesome
job!

                      BRUCE
Great work!

                     MAGGIE
Wonderful! Just great.

                      CHAZ
This might be the top-notch-est
project of all time!

While the others break into applause, Ronald
Reagan spits coffee all over the floor and makes
exaggerated GAGGING sound by the snack table.

                  RONALD REAGAN
    This coffee tastes like there's
    booze in it. What the fuck?

Judges glance at the snack table. Dolph sprints
toward the judges' table brandishing a pair of
safety scissors.

                     DOLPH
                 (Screaming)
    Bruce, you fuck, fuck you and die.

Ronald Reagan tackles Dolph. They wrestle.
Shelly dives on top of the pile and pulls Ronald
Reagan's hair. Dolph shakes free, waves scissors
at Bruce. Ronald Reagan grabs his leg. Shelly
steps on Ronald Reagan's wrist. Dolph turns,
ready to stab Ronald Reagan when he is overrun
by orderlies.
                                    CUT TO:

INT. SERENITY COVE - DAY

Exhausted, Ronald Reagan sits, smoking a
cigarette.

>   RONALD REAGAN
>   It was all instinct. We can't go
>   around stabbing people.

                                        FADE TO:

INT. SERENITY COVE — DAY

Bruce looks slightly disheveled

>   BRUCE
>   It makes me feel good that Ronald
>   Reagan would put himself in
>   harm's way to help me. The
>   lessons I'm teaching him about
>   selflessness appear to be taking
>   hold.

                                        FADE TO:

CONTEST RECAP MONTAGE:

(Thirty seconds of contest highlights with CHAZ
DORSEY CHORD PROGRESSION AND DRUM MIX playing, as
edited per pre-derived maximum viewer engagement
algorithm. FREEZE FRAME on each contestant as
their name is announced. Prize Graphics appear
in lower right-hand corner as necessary)

>   CONFIDENT MALE (V.O.)
>   The judges have voted and the
>   results are in. In third place:
>   Henry the Gasman! In second
>   place: Ronald Reagan! And your
>   winners: Althea and Haley! [beat]
>   Unfortunately, Dolph and Shelly
>   have been disqualified!

SPLIT SCREEN: still frames of Dolph and Shelly,
looking dejected and angry. TITLES: DISQUALIFIED!

DAY SEVEN - A LETTER FROM BOB[24]

RR,

What a goddamn cliché you've turned into. Meth? You deserve what you get. You're an adult.

A couple weeks ago, I got caught smoking pot after practice. Mom and Dad lost their shit and sent me to a shrink. Meanwhile you've been in jail all summer and they set you up in a resort. Perfect.

Every morning, Mom sets the motion sensors and goes to the club all day. I can't figure out the code. I set it off by accident once. Not good. She put a lock on the TV and my phone in the safe. I only go outside to take the trash down and to see my shrink on Wednesdays.

In the waiting room at the shrink's office, I met a girl who was all fucked up from speed and she told me, unprompted, how she once spent sixteen hours walking down 95 looking for bottles of piss.[25] She looks for meth-laced piss left by truckers who might have taken speed to help them drive all night, pissed in a bottle, and thrown it out their window.

That's the drug you've been all fucked up on. Sounds like a blast.

Then the girl quoted some shit you said on TV about recovery, and I about slit my wrists.

When Mom said you were on TV, I thought she was just drunk and confusing you with the guy from *Werewolf Hunter!*. But no. I can't even avoid seeing you on the fucking internet. You're all over the fucking targeted ads you talentless piece of shit. Enjoy your fifteen minutes, asshole.

The shrink told Mom and Dad I should go to your old boarding school in the fall. My goddamn senior year!

On top of all this, I got prescribed these green pills to help me concentrate. It's goddamn summer, why do I have to concentrate? The best part is Dad's company sells the pills. They're not even FDA approved yet. Nedvedol. He has cases in the basement. I'm getting middle-manned sketchy ADD meds from our father. What a scam.

Remember when Dad used to hit us tennis balls to help us practice catching flies? The way they stopped completely at the top for a second and almost disappeared before they crashed back to earth. Maybe if you try to remember those times it will help. Fuck if I know.

Also, I haven't forgotten about my CDs. You owe me like seven hundred bucks. Those were collector's items. Fuck you for selling my shit.

You better not be on TV drinking trucker piss.

– Bob

•

Fuck Bob.

He has no idea what it's like to do lunges for a living.

After this, I'll never have to work another pants-related job. As it turns out, the public loves me. I'm one of the most famous drug addicts in America and the show hasn't even aired yet. I've decided to finish my memoir. Celebrities and drug addicts write memoirs all the time. Most of them are functionally illiterate. When I get out of here, I just have to find Sophie and get the beginning. I could pay Bob back with the royalties. I better keep writing, and I better maintain my popularity.[26]

TITLES: DAY SIX

FADE IN:

INT. MAIN MEETING ROOM – NIGHT

VIEWER APPROVAL RATINGS: Althea 40.5%, RR 32.5%, Haley 10%, Gasman 6.5%, Shelly 5.5%, Dolph 5%.

Donuts and coffee pot sit on snack table next to bay window.

Window provides view of pool and courtyard. Tiki torches shaped like penguins burn bright orange. Above the tree line, stars are visible. Moon is full. Shadows float over ripples in pool.

Maggie and Bruce sit by fireplace full of blue flames.

The six addicts enter and sit across from Bruce and Maggie.

Ronald Reagan stands.

> RONALD REAGAN
> I'm Ronald Reagan M. and I have a tendency to abuse drugs and alcohol.

> GROUP (O.S.)
> Hi, Ronald Reagan!

> RONALD REAGAN
> Before we start the meeting, I want to tell everyone, especially Steve, that I was wrong to attack Steve. He was just doing his job and trying to capture my essence on film. Steve, if there's any way I can make things right, let me know and I'll do it.

Pan shot of group until camera stops on STEVE
holding his camera. CLOSE UP of Steve filming
the camera that is filming him. Steve shrugs
his shoulders, puts down camera. Ronald Reagan
approaches Steve. They embrace. Bruce smiles.
Ronald Reagan turns to Bruce. They embrace.
Ronald Reagan's eyes water. Raising a fist in
celebration, he returns to his seat.

>   RONALD REAGAN
>   I'm just going to listen tonight.
>   Thanks.

                                            CUT TO:

INT. SERENITY COVE - NIGHT

Ronald Reagan sits with unlit cigarette dangling
in mouth.

>   RONALD REAGAN
>   Normally I share. Tonight I
>   decided to just listen. Making
>   amends is exhausting.

Ronald Reagan lights the cigarette.

                                            CUT TO:

INT. MAIN MEETING ROOM - NIGHT

Gasman rubs his temple and raises his hand.

>   GASMAN
>   I'm Henry and I have a problem
>   with inhalants.

>   GROUP (O.S.)
>   Gasman!

>   DOLPH (O.S.)
>   Fuck you, Henry!

Dolph throws a pillow at Gasman, knocking off his glasses.

                    GASMAN
          I'm struggling really bad. I want
          to break into the storage closet,
          pour all the cleaning products
          into a bucket, and stick my head
          in it. After yoga yesterday, I
          opened the closet accidentally
          and I stared at the fireplace
          fuel for five minutes before I
          slammed the door and ran to
          Bruce. I don't want to feel the
          pain. (sobs) I want to thank my
          roommate Ronald Reagan for all
          his support.

Ronald Reagan rubs Althea's neck.

                    GASMAN
          And I want to thank Bruce for not
          being condescending like some
          people because my drug of choice
          is gasoline.

Dolph stands and points at Gasman.

                    DOLPH
          Fuck you, Huffers Anonymous. No
          cross talk!

Gasman cowers.

       SHELLY   HALEY
I was inhaling gas at   I bet you were.
ten, you pussy.

       DOLPH   GASMAN
(at Gasman) Daaaahh!   Bruce. Bruuuuce!

       SHELLY   HALEY
Oh yeah, princess? How   I told you that in
much cock have you   confidence.
sucked for dope?

SHELLY
Where was your kid
when you shot up with
that bass player?

HALEY
Leave my son out of
this.

ALTHEA
This is not helping
me move toward God-
centric thoughts or
actions.

DOLPH
How can I recover
when I'm in here with
people who have never
smoked crack?

RONALD REAGAN
It's goddamn Gasman's
turn. Let Hank talk.

ALTHEA
These poor birds are
trapped by their
earthly bonds.

GASMAN
Henry.

ALTHEA
Doesn't anyone care
about the birds?

Bruce stands.

BRUCE
Thank you, Ronald Reagan. Dolph,
a drug is a drug is a drug. We've
been over this. Now, everyone
calm down, it's Henry's turn to
share. Respect his need to share.

Gasman picks up his glasses.

GASMAN
Thanks. Ever since I got here,
I've been having this recurring
nightmare: I keep reliving my
last high when my wife killed my
pet rabbit Dennis Hopper. I'm in
the kitchen. The fumes course
through my brain, I drop the rag
and it smells like grapefruit
and Lysol. Then Susan breaks my

rabbit's neck and skins him right
in front of me. I try to get up
and save my rabbit, to stop her,
but I fall in a pool of tears and
my nose breaks and blood spills
on the floor and it's pouring out
of my face and I feel like I'm
drowning. I need to be here.
Thanks for listening. I hope I
don't get voted off.

                    GROUP
        Thanks, Gasman

                         DOLPH
        Homo!

PAN OF GROUP:

Ronald Reagan rubs Gasman's shoulders. Shelly
steals one of Dolph's cigarettes. Playfully,
Dolph smacks her in the face. Shelly punches
him in groin, they laugh. Shelly throws stuffed
rabbit at Gasman. Haley looks at her pack of
cigarettes, then at clock.

Bruce and Maggie take notes.

Althea walks to the window, stares at flamingos
sleeping in Outdoor Flamingo Cabin.

                                        CUT TO:

INT. SERENITY COVE - NIGHT

Bruce adjusts headset, winks.

                         BRUCE
        I'm so proud of Gasman and Ronald
        Reagan. So proud. They really
        want it. I've been in this
        business for twelve years. Drug
        addicts and alcoholics share

a common bond and our common
solution lives in the halls of
recovery. Helping other addicts
helps me stay clean, too. God
willing I will celebrate thirteen
years clean at midnight, tonight,
just before you...

Points at camera
                    BRUCE
     Vote out one of our addicts.

                                        CUT TO:

INT. MAIN MEETING ROOM - NIGHT

The group shifts into an uneasy silence.
Althea walks toward the women's room next to
the storage closet in the East Hallway. Ronald
Reagan pours coffee at the snack table.

                    MAGGIE
     Tonight is your last chance to
     make a lasting impression and
     improve your ratings before the
     Relapse Challenge.

She stops abruptly.

                    RONALD REAGAN
     Why is Althea outside?

EXT. ROSE-THORN RECOVERY CENTER - NIGHT

Althea slides the pool skimmer through the
handles on the front door of the Recovery Center
and reinforces the barricade with a lawn chair.

She walks toward the Flamingo Cabin, douses
Cabin and sleeping Flamingos in fuel oil.
Flamingos shiver, don't awaken. Althea throws
empty can in pool, produces matches, throws lit
matchbook on flamingos.

INT. MEETING ROOM – NIGHT

The group cringes at the sound of SCREAMING
FEMALE FLAMINGO and rushes to the window.

EXT. ROSE-THORN RECOVERY CENTER, POOL – NIGHT

The Flamingo Cabin is on fire. Flamingos SCREAM.
Althea runs toward pool, dislodges fish statue.

BURNING MALE FLAMINGO flies into pool, Screaming
Female Flamingo hops, tries to fly. Flailing, it
spins, almost jumps.

INT. ROSE-THORN RECOVERY CENTER, EAST HALLWAY –
NIGHT

Bruce sprints toward exit.

EXT. ROSE-THORN RECOVERY CENTER – NIGHT

Althea charges the window of the meeting room,
holding fish statue above her shoulders. Flamingo
Cabin burns behind her. Althea slams fish into
window, statue recoils off Plexiglas and hits her
face, bloodying her mouth.

                 ALTHEA (SUBTITLE)
        (garbled by mouthful of blood)
        Set the flamingos free! They
        belong on a higher plane, and I
        want out of here! Fascists!

INT. MEETING ROOM – NIGHT

Maggie waves at camera (Steve), points to window.

                 MAGGIE
        Steve, are you getting this?
        Steve!

Ronald Reagan stares out window, sips coffee.

INT. ROSE-THORN RECOVERY CENTER, EAST HALLWAY –
NIGHT

Bruce slams his shoulder into the double doors.

> BRUCE
> Maggie, call it in. Level Five!
> Emergency!

He slams into doors. Doors CREAK. Again, he
slams into the doors. The skimmer bends. The
chair falls.

EXT. ROSE-THORN RECOVERY CENTER – NIGHT

Althea slams statue into the window. The window
cracks, spider-webs.

> ALTHEA
> (To camera) Purge the birds'
> souls with fire! Where is God now,
> Maggie?

She continuously slams fish statue into the
window. Behind Althea, Screaming Female Flamingo
spirals into pool, floats alongside Burning Male
Flamingo.

INT. ROSE-THORN RECOVERY CENTER – NIGHT

Group stares out window at burning Flamingo
Cabin.

> MAGGIE
> Remain calm, everyone. She won't
> be able to break the glass. The
> fire department is on the way.
> Bruce will handle the flamingo
> situation. We will close the
> meeting with the serenity
> prayer...

EXT. ROSE-THORN RECOVERY CENTER, POOL — NIGHT

CLOSE UP: BURNT FLAMINGO CORPSES

Althea smashes statue into the window.

>ALTHEA
>I am the foremost Robert Johnson
>scholar in the Southeast!

Althea smashes statue into the window.

INT. MAIN MEETING ROOM — NIGHT

Dolph and Shelly run past TV showing *Werewolf Hunter!* Dolph inadvertently knocks over Gasman, stops, pushes him down again, SCREAMS. Haley dives under the snack table. Ronald Reagan helps Gasman up, points to their room. Gasman flees.

EXT. ROSE-THORN RECOVERY CENTER — NIGHT

Althea breaks a hole in the window and falls backward. She gets up, takes off her shirt, collects herself.

CLOSE UP: Althea's tattoos: A pair of shoelaces winds around her left arm from wrist to shoulder. Sheet music circles down her right arm, where notes are outlined but not colored from forearm to wrist.

She wraps shirt around forearm, pushes at cracked frame.

>ALTHEA
>You can't keep me here like a
>Goddamn animal, Maggie, it's not
>helping me get to the core of my
>problem!

EXT. ROSE-THORN RECOVERY CENTER, POOL - NIGHT

Bruce breaks through doors, jumps in pool, swims toward floating Burnt Flamingo Corpses. He holds the dead flamingos, crying.

EXT. ROSE-THORN RECOVERY CENTER - NIGHT

Althea covers her eyes, kicks in windowpane. She steps through the frame, lunges at Maggie.

INT. MAIN MEETING ROOM - NIGHT

Maggie runs toward Serenity Cove. Althea chases her, slams into door, falls.

INT. SERENITY COVE - NIGHT

Maggie locks herself in Cove, grabs a phone off the wall, pushes "!" button. BANGING on door increases in frequency and volume.

> MAGGIE
> We need the security team. Code Purple. (To camera) This happens on occasion. Nothing out of the ordinary. I spoke with Althea today in our one-on-one session and she was adamant she be released. However, we're still adjusting her medication. It's a delicate balance. I told her 'this too shall pass.' She needs acceptance.

> ALTHEA (O.S.)
> I'll kill you, bitch! Fascist!

> MAGGIE
> I told her to use the flamingos

as a model, to connect with the
birds on a philosophical level
and observe how they function
as a narcotic-free family unit.
She seemed to understand, but
kept talking about the Hampton
Aviary and her stepmother. [beat]
Security will be here in fifteen
seconds.

                    ALTHEA (O.S.)
You better pray to your bullshit
God I can't break down this door!

EXT. ROSE-THORN RECOVERY CENTER - NIGHT

Bruce places Burnt Flamingo Corpses in a trash
bag, picks up a shovel, and heads toward pine
trees near Detox unit.

DAY EIGHT - ALMOST SUNRISE

Last night, right before lights out, I was in the day room spacing out on the couch watching *Werewolf Hunter!* when Maggie walked in and asked me if I wanted to talk about what happened with Althea. "Do you need help processing anything?" she asked. I said I didn't, but Maggie sat down next to me anyway. How the fuck do you process the feelings that occur when your fake TV girlfriend who you're kind of falling for burns a pair of exotic birds in effigy? Insane, but also kind of hot in a fucked-up way that I'm not totally comfortable admitting. Hopefully Althea hasn't lost her shit. I'm thinking about how crazy Justin went at the end. All his paranoid nonsense about The Firm and Tom Canada. Could be Althea was just trying to boost her ratings. Hard to say.

I was thinking about all this when Maggie touched my thigh, gently grazed it, then played it off as incidental. She said, "Do you ever get lonely, Ronald Reagan? When the cameras are off, I get lonely."

I said, "Sure. Sometimes." Then I got up and left. This is all so surreal, one big trazadone dream come to life.

Six in the morning. I just lit a cigarette to hide the smell of Gasman's blister cream. Birds are booming outside my window and the early morning sky is bug zapper-blue, and when the little bubbles floating out of Gasman's greased face catch the light it looks majestic and sad.

Hearing the birds reminds me of the days before I met Jacky, when I had nothing altering my mood but coffee and cigarettes. That clean time doesn't feel real anymore. Those months might as well be someone else's time. I've been so fucked up and medicated one way or another since then, trying to draw from it would be pointless.

TITLES: CLEAN TIME, WEEK ONE RECAP

FADE IN:

INT. MAIN MEETING ROOM – DAY

The five remaining patients sit in circle of couches. A giant piece of plastic covers the window.

Clipboard in hand, Maggie stands by fireplace.

> MAGGIE
> Althea is in the hospital at the bottom of the hill in Detox. She's being treated for lacerations, smoke inhalation, and mania. Despite her inappropriate behavior, she still has a spot in Clean Time. Her honesty increased her Viewer Approval Ratings and that should be a lesson. What is not a lesson, however, is her cruelty to animals and abuse of center-issued matches. The other news is that Bruce has relapsed.

CUT TO:

INT. SERENITY COVE – DAY

Ronald Reagan wipes hand over his face, exhales.

> RONALD REAGAN
> I'm even more drawn to Althea after she stood up for herself and the birds. I know killing animals is wrong...I hate this music in here. Can someone change this shit? Sorry, that wasn't too serene. I was wrong to say that. I am making amends right now.

> There, I just did it. [beat]
> Bruce helped me a lot. His
> relapse makes me doubt the whole
> recovery process.

He lights a cigarette, looks away from the
camera.

CUT TO:

INT. MAIN MEETING ROOM – DAY

Maggie stands in foreground with Dolph and
Shelly. CHAZ DORSEY ORIGINAL SENTIMENTAL SOFT
ROCK BALLAD plays in background.

> MAGGIE
> Dolph [looks at Dolph]. Shelly
> [looks at Shelly]. The viewers
> were, unfortunately, not very
> kind to you. You two have the
> lowest ratings, and that means
> you'll have to fight to keep your
> spot here. But due to the…flamingo
> incident, we will postpone the
> Relapse Challenge until the end
> of week two.

Maggie walks from the meeting room, down the
hallway and out the front doors. She stops next
to the pool.

Cracked cement fish statue lies near burn mark
on patio. Maggie looks at the tarp covering the
pool, then the camera.

> MAGGIE
> Well, it has certainly been an
> exciting first week on Clean
> Time. Be sure to keep up with
> the day to day activities of
> your favorite addicts on our web

stream, keep voting, and tune
in next week. I'm Maggie Turner,
thanks for watching Clean Time.

ROLL CREDITS/DISCLAIMER:

FLAMINGOS WERE NOT INTENTIONALLY HARMED DURING
FILMING. DONATIONS HAVE BEEN MADE TO THE WWF
ON BEHALF OF THE RECOVERY CHANNEL AND JACKSON
ENTERTAINMENT, A SUBSIDIARY OF PHILSON & JACKSON
CORPORATION.

DAY EIGHT - LIGHTS OUT

After burying his flamingos, Bruce stole the Nedvedol reserves and left town. He drove to Trenton, sold the pills, and bought a bunch of dope. Rumor is the network hired a PI, who found Bruce the next day with the Governor of New Jersey at a motel in Chambersburg. The Governor was already in deep shit for some kind of sex-for-drugs scandal.[27] Now Bruce is in Detox down the hall from Althea, but the Nedvedol he stole is nowhere to be found. Now our pills are getting rationed out sparsely. I hid my afternoon dose under my tongue and stashed it inside my lamp. I'm going to try and see Althea.

DAY NINE - ONE-ON-ONE THERAPY

Since Bruce relapsed, I am the best looking guy in here who hasn't sucked dick for Benzodiazepine. My ratings have skyrocketed since my heartfelt speech in Serenity Cove aired on TV last night. According to Maggie, the show's audience has tripled.

With Bruce out of commission, Maggie is my therapist now. Earlier today I sat in one of the big plush chairs across from her. After filling out some worksheets, I talked about my past, my drug history, and my parents and stuff. I lied about most of it, but I made great eye contact.

Toward the end of our session, I looked past Maggie at the "Drugs of Our Times" poster and I remembered shooting morphine before my grandmother's funeral and falling asleep by the casket. Afterwards my dad told me the best decision he ever made was giving Bob his name. I tried to fight it, but started crying.

Maggie said, "It's, okay. I'm here for you. Right here."

She got up on my chair and sat facing me, on her knees, my nose right in her cleavage. She wrapped her arms around the back of my head and brought me in.

I kissed her neck. She smelled my hair.

Outside, Dolph screamed and Gasman banged on the door. "It's time for my appointment, please help me. It's Henry. Help, please."

I pulled away, lost my balance, and tumbled onto the floor. Maggie undid my belt as we tussled by the overturned chair. She started on my fly. "Fuck me, Ronald Reagan."

I buckled my belt. "You should let him in."

"Fuck Gasman." Maggie grabbed for my belt again.

The pounding on the door got louder. Dolph yelling at Gasman yelling at Maggie.

"He's throwing books at me!" Gasman stuck his fingers under the door. They wiggled like he was reaching for something. "Why won't you let me in!"

Maggie shoved me away and tied her hair back up. "Session's over," she said, and gave me a look that was supposed to be sexy.

I ripped the poster off the wall and left.

●

I've been running on very little sleep.

Last night I snuck out and visited Althea in Detox. Her bed looked like a gurney. The monitors and machines were right out of an HG Wells book. I told her about the basement full of Nedvedol in my parents' house forty-five minutes south of here.

I loosened her restraints. "Come with me," I said.

Althea's braces had punched through her lower lip sometime during the fire. A single black stitch closed the hole in her face. "I've only known you for like five minutes."

"It feels longer," I said.

"Sort of."

"Wasn't that what the flamingo thing was about. Escaping?"

"I need to get clean, but this place is a joke." Althea lit a cigarette and rubbed the red marks on her wrists. "If I'm sent home for reasons other than low VARs, my insurance will still cover my partial stay. I wanted to get kicked out. Plus I think Maggie's fucking with my meds."

I don't know if I buy Althea's excuse, but if she was lying, at least she realized the need to lie about why she burned those birds alive. "If you want out so bad, let's go," I said.

"Have you even read your contract?"

"Skimmed it."

"They will hunt you down. Even if you complete the program they can fuck with you after you're gone. There's not enough upside."

"We can outsmart them," I said. "I know people in Booth who can help us."

Althea remained noncommittal so I dropped it. We sat in silence until the first rays of sun cast light over the wires and the mess of tubes they'd hooked her up to, and I realized she had passed out.

DAY TEN - AFTER YOGA AND MORNING MEDITATION

I've devised a plan to get me and Althea out of here.

Maggie clearly wants me. So I'll tell Maggie we can fuck, on the condition she signs Wellness Certificates for me and Althea. If that won't work, we'll wait until everyone is distracted by the Relapse Challenge and make a break for it.

We're out of Nedvedol. I have enough to last three, maybe four more days, but there's tons of it in my parents' basement. We have to make a move. Worst case, I can probably arrange a sit down with Tom Canada and get him to forge us a couple certificates. As much as I don't want to deal with him, he's a businessman. He won't turn down the work.

DAY ELEVEN, ~4AM - BACK FROM VISITING ALTHEA

Sitting in my room listening to Gasman wheeze, watching the spit bubbles pop in his mouth while the sun creeps up behind the mountaintops. No way I'm getting any sleep tonight.

When I snuck in to see Althea earlier, I asked if she'd thought any more about leaving. I untied the leather restraint on her left wrist.

The silver machinery glistened even in the shadows. Althea untied the other strap and sat up in bed, shaking her hands as if to dry them. "Not without a certificate," she said. She leaned forward and undid the straps around her ankles.

"Look," I said. "I'm taking off. We're out of Nedvedol. I can take care of everything once we get to North Carolina. I swear."

"I don't need to ride off into the sunset with anyone."

I pushed the hair out of Althea's eyes. Between my fingers it felt thick and unwashed, strands of bright orange wire, full of a current I couldn't figure out. "Trust me, I have a plan," I said.

Althea brushed me off and lit a cigarette. "Have you thought this through? What's going to happen in North Carolina?"

I sat under the window in a stainless steel chair. Its legs screeched over the floor when I slid closer, close enough to take Althea's hand and rub the red marks on her wrists. She didn't stop me.

"What are you going to tell Jacky?" she said.

"What are you talking about?" I said, and pretended I heard something in the hallway. I got up and put my ear to the door, listening for orderlies doing their rounds. From down the hall I could hear Bruce screaming. I went back to the bed.

"Maggie told me about Jacky in therapy. Like I give a shit," Althea said, and pulled on the rubber band around her wrist. "I'm just making sure you're thinking straight, before you run off to find this woman who is probably fucking someone else right now."

"We're out of Nedvedol. I haven't heard from Jacky in weeks. I'm leaving. If you don't want to come with me, that's fine. Fake relationship or not, drive me to Booth, which is one county over from your place, in exchange for an essentially unlimited supply of pills you can't even get a prescription for yet and are stashed in my shady father's basement. Fair trade in my book."

Althea waved me away. "I need to think. I'm tired."

I snuck out the window and walked back across the lawn with a lot on my mind. Althea was right. I didn't know what I was doing, but I knew I wanted to run away with her, and I've always been pretty good on the fly. I hadn't heard from Jacky. These last few days, I realized I'd been thinking about her less and less. Sneaking toward the back entrance of the kitchen, before I went inside, I stood for a minute in the blind spot by the dumpsters. I lit a cigarette, and those questions about where Jacky was and why she hadn't written started to eat me up again.

DAY ELEVEN - SCHEDULED UNSTRUCTURED FREE TIME

Althea got out of Detox this morning. We were building sandcastles in the beach volleyball court while Maggie outlined the Relapse Challenge to Shelly and Dolph on a dry-erase board by the pool. In three days, they will fight it out in front of a live studio audience to see who gets to stay.

I motioned to Althea and she followed me toward the burned-out Flamingo Cabin, where we pretended to sort rocks. Keeping my back to the cameras, I smoothed a space in the ash near my rock pile and grabbed a stick. I wrote a message on the ground: "Your car?"

Wary of hidden microphones, I wiped out the message and, in a raised voice, started talking to Althea about recovery. "How do you feel about lighting the flamingos on fire?" I asked. "Now that you've had time to reflect on your role in the incident."

Althea wrote "mall" on the ground with her finger and breathed deep through her nose. "Well," she said, "I feel quite sad. I realize it was not the right action. No living thing deserves to die at the hands of another regardless of my own fear of aviaries."

"Run for it?" I wrote. I gave her a look and added a piece of flint to my pile.

Looking apologetic, she wrote, "NO. Cert. PhD."

Wiping out the message, she said, "I feel like sorting these rocks is a great metaphor for how we have to sort through our feelings. This flat, smooth one represents my need to take personal accountability for my actions."

I felt the cameras zoom in. "The mineral composition of these rocks parallels our makeup as complex and fallible human beings," I said. "We are all equal in God's eyes, yet unique in the particulars of our fears." Under my breath I whispered, "Don't worry, I have a plan."

Althea wrote, "?!"

Soot collected on my hands and forearms and our hips touched as we edged closer to the pines. I cleared a new spot in the ash and wrote, "I seduce Maggie."

Althea yelled, "Fuck you," and slapped my face.

Maggie lowered her pointer and the cameras turned toward us. Suddenly everyone was watching.

I gave Althea my best Jesus-be-fucking-quiet look. "I used to collect rocks and shells with my dad when we went on trips to the beach in Georgia," I said. "This was before I felt the urge to numb my feelings with chemicals." Then I whispered, "She'll sign our papers or I go to the press and say she took advantage of me in my fragile state."

"Bullshit," she said.

"Quiet."

She picked up a burned piece of the Flamingo Cabin, whacked me with it and said, real loud, "This charred rubble represents the way my heart burns when people tell me things that make me feel undesirable."

I grabbed her red curls and kissed her on the mouth. I knew the cameras would be all over it. Our Viewer Approval Ratings would be soaring.

Althea smiled and the sun reflecting off her braces made it look like she had a mouth full of glass. She hit me again.

"Quit it," I said.

She flipped her hair out of her eyes, grabbed me, and kissed me back.

"Maybe we can rebuild the cabin as a way to be of service," I offered. "The rebuilding will represent our need to restructure our feelings and discern our role in the performances we put on for others."

Ash covered my arms to the sleeves of my t-shirt. Althea threw a rock in the pool. The look in her eyes shifted from dark to light and back again. I swallowed hard and whisper-yelled, "I have contingency plans... Just in case."

"What?" She raised a piece of wood over her head. I put up my arms in defense and she hit me with a left to the gut. Doubled over, I grabbed her waist.

We rolled around in the dust by the edge of the woods. She pinned me and pushed up her sleeves, put her palms on my shoulders. For the first time I saw her arms up close, in the light. Cigarette burns, track marks, and white scars. I felt the texture rippling under her tattoos. Her thighs constricted around my ribs. She wiped dirt on my cheeks. Cast in sunlight, the imperfections in her face looked so beautiful. I felt ashamed I couldn't see it before.

"If you want that old lady's saggy tits be my fucking guest."

I looked over at Maggie standing by the white board and pointing at crudely drawn stick figures holding medieval weapons, arrows signifying attacking movements. Her tits are okay.

DAY TWELVE - "THERAPY"

I proposed my plan to Maggie in our session today. She agreed to sign me and Althea out and give us our certificates, but I was still wary. It was too easy, the way she just said, "Sure. You've made great progress and I'll be happy to be rid of Althea, of course." Then she dimmed the lights. "I think this will benefit us both in a very deep and meaningful way. Don't you?"

I asked her to pipe in the music from Serenity Cove. I said, "It helps me reach a stage of meditation that allows for complete honesty."

"I admire your honesty, Ronald Reagan. Right away I noticed that about you. Very honest." She walked behind me and turned a dial next to the poster of the two kittens and the music got louder. She put her mouth to my ear. "And I hope you're ready to fuck."

I said, "I am," and did the thing where I ruffle my hair. "But first you have to sign my certificate, and Althea's. Like you said, or no deal."

Instrumentals emanated from the walls in a weird electronic wave. Maggie peeked out the window behind her desk and tried to undo the top button on her blouse. Her tongue crested her lips while she focused on the button, fumbled with it. "Once we've explored each other naked and felt our collective weight sway in rhythm, together, we will be better able to express our feelings and create a more intimate state of emotionality." She tore open her shirt, the stubborn button fell to the floor.

I caught myself hoping she'd clear everything off her desk in one swipe, pin me down on top of it, and ride my cock while she smacked me in the face with a rolled up NA workbook. Instead, she lit some incense on top of the filing cabinet.

"That incense smells great," I said. It smelled like burning socks.

Maggie put her finger to my lips. A pair of shimmering pink panties, twisted in elastic, nipped at a birthmark on her stomach. She knelt in front of me. "Sex therapy is designed to break down the emotional barriers that prevent us from achieving true acceptance. True emotional freedom."

"I need to see the certificates first," I said.

"Let's not talk business." She rubbed her face against my crotch, looked up at me, and said, "This is an exercise in trust."

I pushed my chair back until it hit the wall behind me. "Do we have a deal?" I asked. "I need to know I can trust you."

"They're in the filing cabinet. You can trust me." Maggie slid off her panties and tossed them aside.

"Show me," I said.

"You're killing the mood."

I stood up on the chair. "Show me, or I'll run out of here right now."

"Fine." Maggie walked back to the filing cabinet, pulled out a stack of blank certificates and held them up for me. "See," she said, "right here. All I have to do is write your name and sign it." She placed two on her desk and put the rest of the stack back in the bottom drawer of the filing cabinet.

Everything looked legit. I slumped back down on my chair, relieved and ashamed.

"Now where were we." Maggie crawled toward me, and I was thinking about being in love with Jacky while also wanting to run away with Althea, and knowing I'd feel like shit after Maggie fucked me and that I'd go through with it anyway.

I didn't even get my pants all the way off before I came. My shoes were still on. Then we tried again, but I couldn't get it up. Maggie slapped me in the face.

"So, you'll sign us out?" I fixed my belt and fought the urge to pocket Maggie's underwear, draped over her desk lamp. "I did my part," I said.

"I've changed my mind," she said. "You need to make others earn your trust. You can't just give it away." She picked up the two certificates on her desk and put them in the drawer with the others. "Let this be a lesson."

I stared at the kittens playing with yarn. "Happiness is an Inside Job!" Heat from the lamp forced a thin strip of smoke and the smell of burning satin from Maggie's panties.

Maggie said, "It would be unprofessional to let you go. We can still fuck, though. I think we can do better than that little excursion. Can't we? I'd like to try."

I said, "Your pussy is disgusting." But it was actually nicer than most.

"Now you're just being cruel."

Maggie grabbed her underwear from the lamp and threw them at the trashcan under the window. They landed on the rim of the wastebasket where they hung like a dead rabbit.

DAY THIRTEEN - CONTINGENCY PLANS

Today was fucked. After lunch, I met Althea in the kitchen. She was sitting on a pallet of economy-sized decaf coffee cans in dry storage when I told her I didn't get the certificates. She didn't take it well.

"It's okay," I said, "I know a guy who can forge them for us in Booth."

"But we don't have certificates to forge." she said. "This is bullshit."

"The plan is not bullshit," I said. "The certificates are in Maggie's filing cabinet. I saw them. We can break in now while everyone's getting ready for the fight."

"What about Maggie's signature?"

"We'll worry about it later."

I knew there were too many moving parts now, it would take a miracle to pull this off. We needed to form a unified front. "We can break in through the ceiling tiles in my bathroom," I said. "It's right next to her office. My guy will take care of the signatures."

"Then what?"

"Run for it. Tomorrow. During the Relapse Challenge."

"You better be right about this."

We headed to the gym. Bleachers and wrestling mats were set up at center court. A steel cage hung above the makeshift ring, ready to descend when Shelly and Dolph stepped out under the lights in front of all the screaming fans.

Maggie was briefing the production crew: "To start the special, there will be a reflective montage played on a projector for the studio audience, while a local independent theater group in black latex suits performs an interpretive dance depicting what's happening on the screen behind them. While this performance takes place, I will narrate a synopsis of the first week of *Clean Time*."

Althea continued down the hall, and I was about to follow her when Maggie caught sight of me and called me over. She said I needed to pre-record some thoughts in Serenity Cove before the live feed tomorrow. They wanted footage to cue up before and after the Relapse Challenge. "Do a take as if Shelly won," she said, "then do one for Dolph. Try to seem sincere."

After my time in Serenity Cove, I spent an hour distracting cameraman Steve out in the courtyard. Then I spent another hour looking for Althea. At one point, I casually strolled by Maggie's office, but it was locked. Maggie was walking around and barking orders like nothing was wrong. We passed in the hall and she gave me a weird smile.

DAY THIRTEEN - ALMOST MIDNIGHT

It's almost midnight now.

Althea came by my room not long ago. "No certificates," she said.

"But I saw them."

"There was a folder but it was empty. Nothing in the filing cabinets."

"So that's it."

"It's in the contract. We are fucked without certificates."

"We're fucked anyway." I said.

Althea was more upset than I thought she'd be. I could smell her sweat. She hadn't showered, possibly since she got out of Detox. She said she went looking for me earlier but couldn't find me. When she went back to her room, someone had moved shit around and looked through her dissertation papers. Personal items were missing: pictures of her friend Leah, and one of Althea and her dad before he died. A keychain in the shape of an owl she stole off an ex-boyfriend. She needed to leave, she said, and I'd let her down with my bullshit plan.

"I'm sorry," I said.

"So am I," Althea said, and she went back to her room.

I'm resigned to fate. Stuck in rehab without Nedvedol, pretending to give a shit until I can't keep my TV face on anymore and my ratings fall and I have to fight Gasman.

ESCAPE

In the end, it was so obvious I wanted to kill myself for not realizing it sooner.

Althea and I were loitering by the gym doors, looking in. Maggie was screaming at the dancers. A team of trainers went to work on Shelly, stretching her out, massaging her calves. Dolph paced up and down the hall. His knuckles were taped, his arms swung wildly through the air as he walked past us.

I felt bad for Dolph. He had a thing for Shelly and everyone knew she was going to destroy him. In another life, me and Althea might have been the ones battling it out. If I had to fight Althea, I'd refuse. I would try to escape. I'm not sure she'd do the same.

Orderlies rolled in big plastic bins full of hockey and football pads, helmets without facemasks. Swords and nunchucks hung from a wheeled rack. The last orderly carried a gleaming silver tray displaying knives and handguns. All the cameramen were gathered in the gym. Everyone was in there, or so I thought. Sauntering down the hall with a girl on each arm and a big shit-eating grin on his face was the answer to all our problems. Chaz fucking Dorsey. "Sup guys," he said, nodding at me and Althea. "Ya'll ready to rumble?" He sniffled loudly and laughed to himself as he brushed by us. The moment he took his seat in the front row of the bleachers, I grabbed Althea's arm and dashed toward the kitchen, ripping Chaz's framed certificate off the wall as we fled.

All I had were the clothes on my back, this journal, the 12-Step workbook, my wallet containing the Griffey rookie card, and fifty bucks in my secret jeans pocket. I shoved the journal and workbook into Althea's big purse. She'd left most of her possessions in her room. We didn't have time to pack.

We crept past the dumpsters, ran across the yard, and stumbled into the woods in the middle of the darkest night in the history of North Jersey. Pine trees dwarfed us, blotting out the moonlight.

Holding Chaz's framed certificate, I followed Althea's silhouette through the inky blackness till she found the fence. The fence ran down the hill toward Detox. The space between the fence and the treeline narrowed. Rosebushes in various stages of decay scraped against us.

Althea stopped and looked back. I held up the frame to try to reassure her. "This certificate is as good as one with your name on it," I said.

"How do I know you're not lying?"

"You don't," I said. I wasn't lying, I just had no idea if Tom would do the forgeries, or if I'd even be able to find him.

We came to a break in the woods and a dirt road that led to the gate. Beyond the gate, the road headed south toward the highway and the mall and Althea's car. Peeking through the trees, we could see the Detox building across the dirt road, a fleet of Prii parked haphazardly in front. We used the woods as cover and ran alongside the road until reaching the gate.

"This is where we climb," I said. "You first." I knelt and made a step out of my hands to boost Althea up on the chain link.

"I got it," she said, and climbed up and over.

I slid the certificate under the gate, then climbed. I was halfway up when a siren went off and a floodlight on top of Detox cast the forest in electric white. The light started circling. The voice of God boomed from a loudspeaker: "The Rose-Thorn staff strongly recommends you reconsider your decision to flee the premises. You have violated your contract. Any liability on the part of Philson and Jackson Corporation and subsidiaries is effectively waived. We will find you."

Althea took off up the road. I climbed faster, swung myself over the top and landed on the certificate. When I picked it up, I sliced open my hand on the broken glass.

"Hurry," Althea said.

With my non-bloody hand, I slid the paper out of the frame, folded it poorly, and stuck it in my back pocket. Floodlights circled and the voice over the loud speaker repeated the message. I tried to suck on the cut running across my left hand and smeared blood on my face. I couldn't see Althea anywhere.

"Over here." Her voice came from the woods farther up the road.

I hurried to her. "I'm bleeding pretty bad."

Althea pulled an undershirt out of her purse, ripped it in half and wrapped it around my hand, pulling it tight. I screamed.

"Quiet," she said. "They're on our trail."[28]

A pair of headlights cut a crescent into the woods and onto the road. I spit out a mouthful of dirt and heard the gate open. We stayed down until the wheezing electric engine grew louder, then quieter, and the sound of the tires over the gravel dissipated down the road. We took a few deep breaths, stood, and ran toward the miserable light thickening over the highway in the distance.

•

The mall lot was packed with cars full of junkies shooting up and teenagers fucking, but the building was a shell of its former self. The biggest mall in New Jersey, boarded up and broken down. Althea was staring at the TGI Friday's. Part of the roof had caved in there. I told her how when I was a kid I used to come up to the mall before baseball season to buy new gear, and how great it felt to ride home with a new pair of cleats and a fresh Mets hat. She ignored me, trying to retrace her steps and find her car. "Macy's," Althea said. "I left her by the Macy's."

"This way," I said, and we made our way around the building. The Macy's sign was missing a C. The facade was scorched, like someone had tried to set it on fire. Althea's car was right where she said it'd be, so we hopped in and headed south.

We almost got turned around at the 78N/287W/87S clusterfuck

near the Route 80 interchange. But when we hit Hunderton County the sky cleared and Route 518 was empty. Nothing but farmland and moonlight and the smell of fresh cut grass. We'd get to my parents' house by midnight. North Carolina by sunrise. Althea told me her car predated GPS and the AC hadn't worked in three years, but she had *American Beauty* in the CD player.

"Stick to the back roads," I said. Ripped vinyl stuck to my scraped up back when I leaned forward in the seat.

"There's a roach in the ashtray."

I fished out the half-smoked joint and pressed the lighter on the dash.

"Floor's got a hole in it," I said.

"I kind of let things go toward the end."

"Rusted right through."

"Cover it with the mat."

The lighter popped.

"I can see the road."

My hand had bled through its dressing. I unwrapped it, stuck it out the sunroof, and let the bloody scrap of undershirt fly behind us.

PART THREE

SOUTH BOUND

A NOTE ON THE CONSTRUCTION OF THE NARRATIVE

As evidenced by the previous "escape" scene, it appears that there was a conscious effort on Ronald Reagan's part to construct a cohesive narrative from his journal. Primarily, he is trying to get the story down, but the reader will notice in certain scenes Ronald Reagan's desire to hone his craft and create work he can be proud of. Once out of rehab, his desire to record his journey south and his attempts to recover the early childhood memories documented in Sophia Trent's class reveal his motives to complete his story.

The forthcoming entries, and the second half of the work in general, were the most challenging, from an editorial standpoint. These journal entries were written in various tenses and with varying degrees of distance from the scenes they depict. It is helpful to think of them in three categories: (1) Entries Ronald Reagan wrote in the moment, full of power and energy, a mix of fear and exhilaration. These include lists and scraps of notes composed in the margins, diagrams we've rendered into prose due to budgetary limitations preventing us from including the actual drawings or illustrations. (2) Entries written with limited distance from various points along his journey that provide some self-reflection, but mostly confusion. (3) Ronald Reagan's voice recordings, which were transcribed after the fact and inserted into the narrative.

Bob and I worked to condense and restructure these entries for maximum thematic impact. The inclusion of the recordings and of the rough drafts of Ronald Reagan's journal entries ideally adds a sense of immediacy to the narrative. In a way, this aesthetic decision was forced upon us, as there were sections of the story, written in the moment or spoken into a recorder, that we felt compelled to include in order to tell the full story.

BOB

Gardenia Falls: The Finest in Suburban Living Since 1984. Between July 4 and September 11, the landscapers tint the streetlights in my parents' development red-white-and-blue. Colored light streaked across the hood of the car, through the windshield and over Althea's pale thighs. She drove and I navigated.

"Looks like you had it pretty rough growing up," Althea said.

"Awful, right?"

"Yuppie."

"Stop calling me that."

Houses scrolled past like a repeating background from a cartoon. I pulled the sticky note off my 12-Step workbook and read the note Bruce left me: *Prayer, meditation, helping others! Dentist 2PM!*

Time felt malleable since my arrest. Days never seemed to end, but the weeks flew past. Two weeks ago felt like another life.

"Is that a castle?" Althea said.

"That's what we called it, as kids."

"Because of the moat?"

"Yeah."

We wound all the way down to the end of Independence Way, where my parents' house sits at the end of a cul-de-sac. My old house looks exactly like the one next door and the one across the street except the first floor rooms are in different places. One time I blacked out, walked into the Murphy's place, peed in their broom closet, and tried to watch baseball on the fireplace. It was the middle of the afternoon.

When we approached my house, I saw a taxi idling at the end of the driveway. We parked in a dark spot between lampposts, and walked toward my driveway, where Bob was struggling with a duffle bag.

"Bobby."

"Ronald Reagan?" Bob said. I jogged to him.

"Let me help." I grabbed a bag from the curb and stuffed it in the trunk. Bob pulled it back out.

"You're fucking up my system." He rearranged his luggage like Tetris.

"Where you going?"

"Boarding school. Class starts the day after labor day. What the hell are you doing here?"

"Listen, I'm gonna pay you back for those CDs." We each grabbed the side of a chest and lowered it into the trunk.

"Sure you will."

"I swear. Hey, this is Althea."

Althea was across the street by the Murphy's mailbox, watching the notes on her arm change color in the lights. "Hi, Bob." She walked past us, lit a cigarette, and stared at our pool through the side fence.

"Where's Mom and Dad?" I moved around to the side of the taxi. Half of me turned blue, then red, then white again.

"Mom is passed out, Dad's on business," Bob said. "What the fuck happened to your eyebrow?"

"Bob, we need pills," I said. "Rehab prescribed us Nedvedol to help kick our respective drugs of choice, but then Bruce stole it all. Was that in the news? With the governor? There's some in the house, right?" I asked.

"It's September, and I haven't watched TV since goddamn July. Who's Bruce?"

"My ex-counselor Bruce. I got your letter, you said it was in the basement. We need to get back on the road, but we can't without the pills."

"Where are you going?" he asked.

"Georgia," I said, "I'm gonna get clean and start over." I patted myself but couldn't find my smokes. "All I want is peace and quiet right now. And a cigarette."

"You're out of your mind," Bob said.

"Got a Camel?"

Bob nodded at the cherry of Althea's cigarette bobbing toward our side gate. The motion sensor lights came on when she reached over and unlatched it. She puffed smoke and wandered around the patio, kicked an inflatable duck into the pool.

"How do you wind up with these women?"

"It's not like that," I said.

"Whatever." Bob handed me a cigarette.

I heard Althea splash into the swimming pool, out of view behind the house.

The cabbie leaned out the window. "It's your meter, buddy, but I got a six-pack and a Vincent Price movie marathon waiting for me at home."

Bob pulled at his shirt. Patches of sweat licked the faded Mets logo. He looked just like me, before I aged twenty years over the last two.

I told him, "Don't make the same mistakes I did."

"Don't come at me trying to sound all wise and shit," he said. "Did you mistakenly smoke crack? Did you accidentally pawn all my shit?"

I flexed my hand and rubbed my eyes. Fucking Bob always had to have the moral high ground. I tried not to yell, "Where are the fucking pills?"

Bob pushed on his luggage and closed the cab's trunk. "Basement storage room, near the water heater."

"I will get you your money," I said. "And I didn't drink piss on TV."

"Way to not drink piss," Bob said. He took a seat in the cab, and the cab drove off.

I walked down the driveway toward Althea, who was drying off with a beach towel she'd found.

"How's the water?"

"Cold."

The towel fell to her feet, and I realized I forgot to ask Bob for the alarm code. But even if we set it off, I felt confident Mom would stay knocked out on whatever super-valium my dad is selling these days.

We ducked under the half-open garage door, and I banged my hip on Mom's car. Forgotten hobbies rotted alongside Christmas decorations and tennis rackets. I stepped between a box of Pat Boone records and an old cat carrier, and I couldn't remember ever having any pets as a kid.

"I need this," I said, dusting off a big backpack with lots of compartments. I picked up a roll of duct tape and put it in the pack. Althea grabbed a coffee can full of detachable cleats.

"Can I have this can?" She held it up. "There's an owl on the label. I love owls."

"Sure."

Approaching the alarm code panel, I knocked over a box of half-finished sweaters from Mom's knitting phase. I had three tries to get the lights to turn from red to green or the cops would show up.

"Try one-two-three-four-five-six," Althea said.

I tried it, and the box said: *Please try again, you have two more attempts.*

Althea turned over the can and the spikes bounced and jittered across the cement.

"Quiet. I need to focus."

I punched in President Reagan's birthday.

No dice.

"There's only one more option," I said. I punched it in. The light blinked green and a metallic voice told me, *Please enter. Thank you for choosing Philson Alarm Systems.* Before things got bad between us, my folks loved talking about the day I was conceived, especially after a couple drinks.[29]

"What was it?" Althea asked.

"Tell you later," I said and opened the door. The tile floors had been replaced with marble since I'd left. There was music coming from upstairs.

Althea grabbed my arm. "This is the biggest kitchen I've ever seen not on television." Her hands were still wet and she smelled like chlorine.

I opened the freezer, grabbed a half empty bottle of vodka. "Take anything you want. They fucking owe me."

Althea went through the cabinets, opened and shut a few drawers. "These are all empty," she said. "Don't you use plates?"

"Should be cigs on the shelf below the phone."

Near the phone, Althea organized junk mail. She took the bottle when I offered it. Neither of us hesitated or judged the other for the drink. It was delicious.

"This tastes expensive." She put the bottle in her purse along with the remote to the kitchen TV and two candles.

"There's more liquor behind the bar. In there." I pointed across the kitchen table into the living room. "They'll blame Bob."

As I hustled to the bar I tripped on the landing at the base of the stairs and fell face-first onto the floor. I must have hit my head hard. I think I blacked out for a minute. There in my living room, I saw myself from above, the camera pulled back into an overhead shot of me splayed out like a cartoon character, face buried in the carpet, which strangely smelled like lavender. All I wanted was to tell Althea to go down to the basement, grab all the drugs she wanted, and leave. Then I would peel myself off the ground and curl up on the couch and watch baseball highlights until Mom woke up and maybe made some breakfast.

"You good?" Althea asked.

The sound of change clattering into a coffee can jolted me up to my hands and knees. "I'm good."

I stood and listened. Followed the music up the stairs to my mom's bedroom. An overflowing ashtray and a half-empty rocks glass sat on the nightstand. Mom grinded her teeth and snored while I took two twenties out of her purse. I left the credit cards. Then I turned off the radio and grabbed some clothes from Dad's dresser. Then I headed back downstairs, where Althea was going through my dad's office. I could see her from down the hall, through the open office door, reflected in Dad's big empty fish tank.

"Can I take this umbrella?" She held a glass of scotch in one hand, twirling the umbrella with the other. I said she could take it, and walked into the office, where I took a drink from her glass and sat down at the desk. The screen-saver on my dad's computer was a picture of him and Pat Boone with a bunch of politicians at some black-tie event. I clicked it away and spent a couple minutes searching online until I found Sophie's home address, which I wrote down and stuck in my wallet. It was easier than I thought. Things were looking up. I took another sip of scotch.

Althea dropped the umbrella and ran her hands over the fish tank full of bright blue rocks. She reached in and ripped out the toy mermaid and dropped it in her bag.

I grabbed a tape recorder and a box of blank tapes stacked next to the computer. I had no idea what my dad needed an old tape recorder for, but at the time it somehow seemed interesting or important, a relic. On top of the recorder I dropped five pens, a three-pack of legal pads, a box of pencils. I snagged a roll of stamps and some envelopes. In they went.

"We should get moving. Pills, remember?" Althea placed her empty glass on a coaster.

"Check it out," I said. "My dad thinks he's smart."

The drawer was heavy when I pulled it out and felt the full weight of it. Althea helped hold it steady, and I grabbed the key to the basement storage room that was taped to the back like it had been since I was in high school.

BACK TO BOOTH

I'm writing while Althea drives. The car rattles when we go over eighty miles per hour. We have $143 cash between us and a coffee can full of change. We grabbed six, 2,000-count bottles of 50mg Nedvedol.

Althea's hair is blowing all over the place in the wind from the open window. One of my mom's Marlboro 100s in the corner of her mouth. Her knee is cocked against the door. I'm happy for the company.

Althea and I left around midnight, but we're making great time. We've been heading due south for over six hours and are currently in a desolate patch of country that serves no purpose other than to hold this strip of interstate. Our soundtrack: a Talking Heads CD that only plays the middle third of the album without skipping.

We've got something like a plan. Once we get to Booth, we'll have Tom Canada forge Chaz's certificate in our names, and then get enough 12-Step meeting slips signed to meet the conditions of our various probations.[30]

I keep telling Althea we could just forge all the signatures on our meeting slips, but she wants to actually go to the meetings. Guess it couldn't hurt. While we handle the shit with Tom and get in our meetings, I should be able to track down Sophie and recover the beginning of my memoir.

Althea just told me to quit being anti-social and put down the notebook. She seems to be in good spirits.

TAPE EXCERPT

Looks like the tape is rolling. Hello?

That sound in the background was the CD skipping. I pulled it out and wiped it off with my shirt. *Remain in Light*.

I've driven this stretch of highway under the influence of any drug you could name, occasionally with a co-pilot, twice with a hitchhiker. Usually alone.

Like a subtle electric current, I felt it when we crossed the Mason-Dixon Line. We're somewhere in southeast Virginia. The green Prius up ahead has been following us in reverse and at high speeds since it pulled out in front of us near Newport News. We're almost out of gas.

Althea's car is a blue Taurus with a vanity plate that says, 4BLUES. I once had a theory about girls with vanity plates, but I forget what it was.[31]

"Okay, what's with the heightened language? And why are you

talking in a fake British accent?"

"This is how writers talk. How will people know I'm worldly? No one will take me seriously if I talk like I'm from New Jersey."

"Well you sound like a pretentious asshole."

"I appreciate your honesty."

"Honestly, that Prius is freaking me out."

"Everyone drives a Prius now. I'm not concerned."

THE WEREWOLF KILLER

Big noise barriers separate the highway from the hillside slopes dotted with houses and trailers and the occasional elaborate truck stop/porn stores called The Gryphon's Den, which are always across the street from a lonely church between a GasLand and a Waffle House.[32] Before long, we'll hit 40 West and should be in Booth by the break of day.

Is it fucked up that I haven't really thought about Justin since being locked up? Now his murder is all over the news, at least on the radio. Not just murdered, but killed by a serial psycho they're calling the Werewolf Killer. They say Justin was the first victim, and now two more have popped up in Durham and Raleigh, both heroin addicts. As we plummet down the coast these talking heads are blaming the addicts for getting themselves killed. Apparently the killer leaves a poem written in blood at each crime scene, just like the villain in *Werewolf Hunter! Season Eight.* I've had too much time to think about this, scribbling these words in bumpy silence. What if I'd stayed at Justin's party that night? Maybe I could have prevented his death. Maybe I'd have been killed. I change the station and there's talk of another body. I'm afraid of what might be waiting in Booth. Change the station again. AM radio conspiracy theorists blaming the whole thing on the "liberal media" and "inner city" drug dealers.

The sign up ahead reads FIRST IN FLIGHT: NORTH CAROLINA WELCOMES YOU!

Looking behind us as we cross into North Carolina, the WELCOME TO VIRGINIA! billboard greets the northbound traffic and, for a millisecond, I'm stuck in an empty line on a map.

KEEP RIGHT, PASS LEFT. IT'S THE LAW! Every sign I see is an exclamation.

We've been eating the pills, and that green Prius is still in front of us, and there's a serial killer loose in North Carolina.

TAPE EXCERPT

"I'm pulling over."

"We're making great time."

"We need to lose the Prius."

"Jesus, you're going to get us killed. Use your blinker."

"If you weren't so busy writing, maybe you could take a turn."

"I'm going to check out that memorial by the guardrail."

"I don't want to idle on the side of the road for too long. It's bad for the environment."

"It'll put more distance between us and the Prius. Anyway I have to piss."

"Fine."

RILEY SHERIDAN

The dead kid's name was Riley Sheridan, 16, hit by a truck over two years ago. Killed on December 26. Stapled to the peeling white paint on a cross that came up to my knees was an eight-by-ten photo, warped and faded by weather, of Riley in his baseball uniform, and that picture looked right into me and out the other side. The flowers were fresh cut.

I wanted so badly to feel sad, or even lucky that it wasn't my picture by the side of the road, or Bob's or someone I know, but there was nothing. Riley looked into my guts and found nothing. That poor kid who died the day after Christmas.

•

While we waited on the highway, I thought about last Christmas and the gift for Jacky that I worked so hard on.

The story starts before Christmas, in October, when Jacky and I went to this art exhibit at GSU. We got dressed up and drank wine out of plastic cups and ate cheese cubes and wandered around fucked up in this cool space with good music and weird people, and we came to this one exhibit that was a free-standing dresser with its drawers held together by only a vinyl strap, the kind of straps you see on eighteen wheelers that ratchet down tight and hold heavy shit to the bed. All the drawers were different colors and sizes. Coolest dresser you've ever seen.

"Imagine that in the sitting room," Jacky said and sipped from her plastic cup.

After the show, Jacky tried to buy it, but it wasn't for sale. She wasn't used to not getting what she wanted. It pissed her off. So I decided I'd build a set myself and give it to her for Christmas. While she argued with the curator, I noted what materials I'd need to make it. For the next few months, I collected drawers. I'd tell Jacky I was going to hang out at Dr. Blank's place, but instead I went to the wood shop at Prep. Mooch still worked at the school then, coaching JV football, and of course Cindy taught drama and dance. They both helped with the project. We sanded and cut and glued. My supervisor at the J$F warehouse, White Reggie, managed to get me the strap off of one of the delivery trucks that take blemished jeans to the outlet malls. With some help, I'd crafted a decent replica of the drawers at the exhibit. On the back, I carved RRM + JG with a heart around it. Cheesy, I know, but whatever.

Christmas Eve, Mooch helped me lug the drawers upstairs while Cindy took Jacky out to run some errands or something. When she got back, I unveiled the drawers for her.

"Oh," she said, "You made this?"

"Yeah, remember the exhibit at GSU? You tried to buy one. This is almost exactly like it."

Cindy and Mooch kind of shifted their weight and smiled. You could see the gears spinning while Jacky searched for the memory of that day. It took a while.

"That's so thoughtful," Jacky said. "I had a lot to drink that night."

"You don't like it."

"Of course I do."

The drawers are still in the sitting room, near the piano, full of random crap that people traded Jacky for meth.

"She trusted me," I said to Althea. "I miss that about her. Maybe it's how Bruce says addicts are naturally drawn to what's familiar."

Althea took a hand off the wheel and bit the rubber band around her wrist, pulled back with her teeth and let it snap. She looked at the gauges glowing white behind the wheel, then out her window, and finally at me. "I get it," she said, kissed me on the cheek, pulled back onto the highway and left Riley Sheridan behind.[33]

TAPE EXCERPT

When the sun finds the top of the tree line and first light hits my blind spot, I have to squint to see, and I feel like I'm watching the car from above. A child's toy on a plastic track surrounded by a setting that seems too perfect to be real.

"Been saving that one up?"

"Don't impede my creativity."

"That Prius is back in front of us."

"Let's burglarize one of those churches. It'll give me something to write about."

"You are insane. Stop talking in that accent."

"The trees look like witches."

"I hate all these Jesus billboards."

"Gas light."

"I know my car."

"There's a Gulf. Seventeen south."

OUT OF GAS

Wires and broken filament hung from the busted Gulf logo above rusty gas pumps and a boarded up mini-mart. Queen Anne's Lace pulled apart the black top. The place had been closed so long, the sign still said two dollars a gallon. We were about ninety miles from Booth, headed down Route 17 into town with a gas can and all our stuff, which was thankfully not much.

Althea finally asked the question that must have been on both of our minds for hours, "We're not really relapsing, right?"

I gave her the answer we both wanted to hear. "Of course not. We have a problem with narcotics. We are taking the medication prescribed to us, which we collected from my basement."

"Weed doesn't count."

"It's legal in many places."

"Liquor?"

"Non-narcotic."

I stepped over a dead cat where Route 17 turned into Lee Street. We approached a bar called The Wasps Nest, flanked by a row of sad houses with porches covered in rusted toys and plastic furniture, piles of unopened mail. I was feeling twitchy and wanted some pot to calm my nerves.

"Ask the bartender for weed," I said to Althea as we walked in. "It's better if a chick asks."

The place reminded me of Screwdrivers. It smelled faintly like fryer grease. An old jukebox in the corner played Bob Seger. Dressed in zebra patterned windbreakers and hats from another era, two old men sat under an old tube TV and stared at a dated Budweiser commercial like it held the meaning of life. I walked past the two men and slammed a ten on the other end of the bar.

"Two shots of whiskey."

"And we need to find a gas station." Althea held up the can.

The bartender looked like he could double as the bouncer. "Why doesn't your friend go find the gas, sweetheart, and I'll keep you company?"

"Don't talk to her like that."

"I was talking to you," the bartender said.

"She's my girlfriend."

"I'm not his girlfriend." Althea put the gas can on the bar between us.

The bartender held a dirty glass up to the light and polished it. He set it on the shelf behind him, still smudged.

We threw back our shots and I ordered two more. Suddenly Bob Seger started to make sense. When "Night Moves" makes me feel sentimental, I know I'm in a dangerous place.

Gathering quarters for the juke, I noticed the two Zubaz-wearing old guys were watching a replay of the Virginia Tech/Florida State Sugar Bowl from the late '90s, and for a second I couldn't remember what year it was or when college football season started or what time we had walked into the place. A greasy film covered the jukebox and there was sawdust everywhere. Three bucks bought me an entire Led Zeppelin album. A safe choice for this crowd. For the first time in a long time I felt almost grounded.

Back at the bar I ordered more shots and more beers. The two men cursed when Florida State scored.

"Who's winning?" I shouted over The Silver Bullet Band, but got no response.

Althea tapped her fingers on the bar top. The bartender set the drinks in front of us. "They've watched that same game every day for the last five years," he said. "It's all that comes in on the cable."

Three shots later, the front door opened and a young guy limped in wearing a white suit, tugging at a wavy piece of gauze wrapped around his right hand. Naturally, he sat next to Althea despite the large selection of open seats. He reeked of bad weed and burnt plastic. Spots of blood stained his dress shoes.

I nudged Althea and gave her my ask-that-guy-for-weed look. She just sat there ripping the edges off her bar napkin and piling the little squares by her shot glass.

"You know where we can find a gas station?" I asked the kid.

"There's a Gulf down the way, but it's closed." His words clicked together like scrabble letters. He couldn't have been any older than my brother, but the bartender gave him a pint of dark beer and a big glass of whiskey without question, then delivered Bud longnecks to the old men. "So that leaves the GasLand on the other side of town."

"We ran out of gas in front of the Gulf," Althea said.

The kid slugged whiskey, did a weird wince-snort thing and slapped himself in the forehead. "I'll give you a hand," he said, "but I got a pickup and a dog, so it'll be a tight fit."

We left just as my songs started playing.

•

We drove to the GasLand, got a gallon of gas, and headed back across town to where we broke down. I sat in the bed of the truck, gas can between my knees and whiskey burning in my throat. Sawdust covered my shoes. There was no dog, but a leash attached to a collar was looped around a tire iron and a car part that looked like a spider. The rear windshield on the back of the cab was covered in stickers. Classic rock logos and comic book characters. Calvin peeing on a Mexican caricature. *TRUMP!* centered on the little sliding window.

I banged on Calvin. "Slow the fuck down."

The kid put on Bob Seger and turned the volume up.

We hit a pothole and I puked over the side and smacked the window again. I wanted as much distance between me and the bar and that town as possible.

Back at Althea's car, outside the busted Gulf, I poured a gallon into the tank and traded the kid in the white suit a handful of pills for some weed. Before Althea and I went on our way, the kid handed us each a Gryphon's Den business card. Above his work and cell number the card read: *Geoff Sanderson, Talent Evaluator and Sanitation Technician.*

I traced the raised logo: a naked lady riding a gryphon over a rainbow shot from a cloud. Booth was listed as one of their North Carolina locations, but I didn't recognize the address.

"We offer safe, adult entertainment in an upscale environment," Geoff said. "And if either of y'all want to stop at any of our tri-county locations I'll arrange for some coupons."

•

When we got back to GasLand, Althea said she'd fill the tank. After some deliberation, I went into the bathroom with the intention of blowing a line of Nedvedol off the toilet paper dispenser while she pumped gas. GasLand bathrooms are prefect for this. Always single use with locking doors. I took a piss, then sat on the toilet and deliberated for a while before I decided I'd rather wait and do a line with Althea, and see how she felt about it. When I got back outside, the car was gone. I found my backpack and a letter wrapped around the strap with a rubber band. I'm sitting in the parking lot like an idiot, the letter at my side. It reads: "The Prius is relentless, but it can't follow us both. Left you some weed. Meet you at your old place. Don't worry, I'll find a way in. –AB"

I should have seen this coming.

TAPE EXCERPTS

There's a certain thrill to hitchhiking, but mostly it's a lot of disappointment...

•

Every thirty minutes, I take ninety seconds to inventory my pockets: weed, lighter, cigarettes, wallet. My wallet contains: $72, Ken Griffey Jr. rookie card, and rolling papers...

•

Every forty-five minutes I stop and re-organize my backpack: four pairs of underwear and socks borrowed from my brother's dresser, roll of duct tape, one pink *Clean Time* undershirt, one Mets t-shirt also borrowed from my dad's dresser, a coaster stolen from The Wasps Nest, coffee can five-eighths full of change, blank tapes, notebooks and writing implements, six 2,000-count bottles of Nedvedol...

•

Every hour I crunch a Nedvedol. Every two hours I take inventory, and allow myself one bonus pill. I left the gas station twelve hours ago…

•

It's getting dark. I estimate my position to be approximately seventy miles from Booth, proceeding at approximately three miles per hour, not-as-the-crow-flies…

•

I'm badly sunburnt from walking with my shirt off all afternoon, and I need water. Forward progress gained by walking is outweighed by the strain on my legs and back…

•

I will smoke half a joint at my next inventory point, this will occur slightly ahead of schedule as Routes 40 and 20 part in less than a mile. I'm going to stop at the giant rest area and wait for a ride…

•

My hand is starting to throb, which means a storm is moving toward my location. I'm stopping to duct tape a sock around the gash…

•

This morning the sky was streaked red, but I didn't think anything of it. I figured we'd be in Booth by now, that it would be a "we." Thus, I did not formulate a contingency plan based on this or a similar set of circumstances and must now rely on my guile and navigational abilities even more…

•

I've got money and a backpack full of drugs. Someone will give me a lift…

TRUCK STOP CONGREGATION

In the rest area parking lot, I passed a black boat of a convertible with a white cross hand-painted on the hood. There was a message written in a lopsided arc around the cross: "The Fear of God is the

First Thing We Know by Heart!" (but with a picture of a heart instead of the word).

The front entrance was blocked by a flock of churchy types. Adults and kids in matching white shirts, handing out pamphlets and singing hymns.

Crouching by my bag, I turned my *Clean Time* shirt inside out. It was too tight and it burned my skin when I put it back on.

The children held candles, waving them up at their shoulders, producing smoke the odor of burning hair. The adults chimed bells and triangles and tambourines.

I avoided the front entrance and headed toward the woods behind the building. In the jumpy shadows beyond the picnic tables, I took a couple puffs from a joint and headed for the men's room through the back way.

Sitting quietly in the bathroom stall farthest from the door with my pants around my ankles, I slid a frayed dollar from my wallet, folded it into an envelope around fifty milligrams of Nedvedol and twisted myself so I could use the back of the toilet as a surface. I crunched the pills with the butt of my lighter. Footsteps approached as I unfolded the bill and scraped the green powder into a pile. I wondered how the side effects of the pill would hit me when I snorted it.

"Howdy," a deep southern voice echoed under the divider. "How's the highway treating you?"

Who the fuck starts a conversation with someone in a rest stop shitter? I cracked my neck and stared at his shoes, scuffed black loafers with dimes tucked into them.

"Why are you talking to me?"

"Where you headed, friend? Are you lost?"

"Are you a cop?"

So many open shitters and Loafers took the one directly to my right. By my calculations, he had to pass ten stalls to sit and talk to me.

"No sir," he said, "I work for the Lord."

I pulled a line out of the pile and snorted it.

The voice said, "Have you heard the ringing bells of Christ playing the swan song of the wicked?"

"I have a cold. Stuffy nose."

"Is the Lord with you in your travels?"

"I hope." I snorted another line.

"I was lost once. Sin devoured my spirit. I lived in search of women and vice. Imprisoned by the bottle, crack cocaine, and the devil's music."

"I lost my girlfriend, and then my potential replacement girlfriend."

"Here, friend. Take this literature." He slid a pamphlet under the stall.

The picture on the pamphlet was of a white family holding hands in a circle around a teenaged black girl who looked like she just got pulled out of a dumpster. The caption read "God's Church of the Carolinas: Saving Lost Souls from Sin for Centuries." I kicked the pamphlet back toward Loafers and slid the rest of the green powder into one big line.

Is it a relapse if you're never really clean in the first place? As long as I'm not doing hard drugs, I thought, I'll be fine. But I've always been good at rationalizing, maybe I'm full of shit, deluding myself just like always. Then the pills kicked in and the drip down the back of my throat tasted chemically, the way cleaning products might, and I figured I'd be fine.

Loafers started in again, "I was wandering lost in the land of the wicked. Whores everywhere. I met my wife at a truck stop pornography palace and we spent half a decade probing the depths of God's wrath before we saw the light." His toilet flushed, and I heard him walk past my stall.

I snorted the last line, pushed up against my face with my thumb and forefinger to open my sinuses, and snorted again. Out of habit, I dipped my fingertips in the remaining green powder and wiped it on my teeth. The bathroom door swung shut and he left without washing his hands. I wondered: had I been talking to him in my writer voice the whole time?

With Loafers gone, I stood at the sink and let it run while I cleared my sinuses. Cupped my hands and slurped water. Hit the air blower, knelt beneath it and looked up, warm air on my face.

Back in the lobby, I recognized the loafers on the tall man in the sport coat and expensive shirt. I caught him pulling pamphlets out of a brown paper bag and placing them alongside the tourist info before walking outside into the bell-ringing hoard.

I was drawn to a claw game on the other side of the room, past the security desk, where the guard was watching a small TV. Behind the Plexiglas, I saw a stuffed owl in the back corner and thought it'd be a great gift for Althea, if I ever saw her again. If not, something to remind me of her. I realize how lame those thoughts would have seemed to any normal person, but I was honed in on that fucking owl. I stared into those beady plastic eyes and dropped a couple quarters into the slot.

Fifty cents lit up the machine and filled the lobby with a creepy, synthetic rendition of "What Do You Do with a Drunken Sailor?" Time ticked down on the machine and I hit the release button. The claw missed the owl by a solid six inches. I cursed. The security guard laughed.

Outside the parishioners played what sounded like a bell-only rendition of Ted Nugent's "Stranglehold," with lyrics about Jesus and smiting. Again I dropped the claw into the pit of plush toys and again the claw came away empty. I pushed another fifty cents into the machine and recalculated the angle of descent as I steadied the claw over the owl. "This thing ever win?" I asked the guard.

"Not really, man," he said. His eyes were dim and bored behind large glasses. He spit tobacco into a Styrofoam cup and fucked around with his phone.

The bells outside were crashing and tinkling like nothing I'd ever heard while the church people sang about sinning and penitence.

"What's with the sing-a-long?" I asked the guard.

"Dunno, man. It's bugging me out, though."

I checked the back door. Two parishioners were standing there talking to a trucker while a couple more of them walked over from the parking lot. All the exits were blocked. Lacking the necessary wherewithal to face the choir, I decided to stall and waved the guard over.

"Are you a real cop?"

"Fuck no."

I hit the release button and missed the owl again.

"Wanna burn one?" I asked.

The guard put a "Back in Ten" sign on the counter and a "Closed for Cleaning" sign in front of the men's room entrance. I rolled the rest of the weed from Geoff into a big joint and we smoked under the men's room window, taking our time until the sound outside dissipated and died.

He sprayed air freshener that smelled like lemons and burned my eyes. "I'm Matt," he said. We shook hands.

"Ronald Reagan."

"Bummer. Folks must be into him, huh?"

"More than they're into me."

"Lame. That's real lame." He seemed genuinely upset.

Back in the lobby by the claw game, Matt slapped me on the back. "Check it out," he said. "They don't even lock this thing." He knelt behind the claw and his hand appeared inside the glass, squirmed in the midst of the two-bit prizes and pulled out the owl. "Least I can do. I saw you gunning for this guy."[34]

It'd been a while since anyone did me a favor, and despite my hesitance to push it, I figured he might be up for one more, so I asked to use his phone.

I pulled Geoff's card out of my pocket. Geoff Sanderson of the Gryphon's Den. He picked up after a few rings. "Geoff," I said. "How many pills do you want for a ride to Booth?"

•

Just as the first bolts of lightning flashed in the distance, Geoff's rust-red pickup rattled to a stop between two handicapped spaces. When I pushed myself up from the curb, my hand throbbed. Rain began to hit the windshield just as I closed the door.

"Perfect timing," I said. "Let's get the hell out of here."

I didn't trust his grin. He adjusted the mirror and said, "I swear I've seen you somewhere."

"I was on TV, now I'm a writer," I said. Then I asked him if I could record the conversation for my memoir, but he told me to go fuck myself.

"Have any more weed?" I asked.

"If you got more pills."

The truck reversed, stuttered, and sped onto the highway, black clouds above us. Geoff asked, "You into glass?"

"Not anymore."

"Ever get that blue stuff that was around last spring?"

"You're asking a lot of questions for someone I've known for a few hours."

"I'm a connoisseur. Figured a man like yourself might have an appreciation for such a fine product."

"Are you fucking with me?"

"I haven't been able to get good speed since June. But I've got some to sell that's decent. Could trade you for more pills if you want."

"No. I'm trying to stay quit."

"Did you know Justin Haas?"

I swallowed hard, shifted in my seat, took a couple deep breaths. Something didn't add up, and I couldn't figure out what his angle was. "Seriously, what the fuck?"

"Easy, guy. Justin had a reputation, was steady with that Ghost for a while. Too bad about him is all."

"Don't fucking gaslight me."

"Just trying to make small talk," Geoff said. "We got some miles in front of us here. And you're selling pills I've never heard of to a stranger you just met and you look fucking stoned out of your head. Figured you heard of the dealer who got strung up on his front lawn."

Geoff had forced me to think about Justin and that night, and all the subsequent bullshit that led to the two of us in that truck... Even now, I'm so overwhelmed when I try to write about it I have to get up and take a break. Walk to the window and peek outside, and all I can see is Justin out there, gently swaying above all those cop cars.

I ignored Geoff, played dumb, though I wanted to say "Fuck Justin" and tell him all the shady shit I knew about him. But I couldn't shake the idea that Geoff knew exactly who I was and where I'd been. The storm picked up. Despite my posturing, I was terrified. I tried to change the subject and said, "What's with all the fucking Bob Seger?"

"Against the Wind" played on a radio that looked like it cost more than the truck. Geoff stabbed a finger at the blue display and it went quiet. Only the rain pounding and the arc and fall of the wipers broke the silence. The smell of burnt plastic and smoke pooled in the cigarette burns on the bench seat. One second I felt like I was sitting in Geoff's lap, the next I felt ten miles away. Thunder cracked and the truck hit a bump.

"About that weed," I said.

From my pack I produced the pills. Rain dripped red in the taillights in front of us. I counted out the twenty-five Nedvedol we agreed on for the ride and five more for the weed. While I was sorting the green triangle-shaped pills, I realized they should be called trifocals or maybe triceratopses, for their shape. Tri-something, definitely.

I asked, "How'd that happen?" and nodded at his hand on the gearshift. His middle three knuckles were swollen bad, bruised almost-black. The sleeve of his suit jacket was spotted red.

"Work," he said, and downshifted as the traffic around us slowed and the storm picked up. "How'd you do yours?"

"I fell."

I slid the cellophane off my pack of cigs and dropped in the pills. "Here's thirty." I ran my lighter across the slight edge of the plastic, sealing its contents. "Plus as many as we can eat on the way."

I shook the cellophane and gave him two more, which he crunched in his teeth. His jaw pulsed in time with the lone working wiper.

"Pot's in the toolbox behind the seat. Take more than your share and I'll push you out the door."

I took my share and no more.

Geoff stepped on the gas. "Ever want to just run your car into traffic?" His teeth looked rotten, covered in green residue.

"You have no idea."

I pictured blood pooling under my head on the side of the road. An empty funeral home with all my burnout friends sitting in shitty folding chairs smoking crack, listening to some recorded scripture. My family too embarrassed to attend. I thought about all the times I wanted to end it. The summer before college when I sold all my baseball equipment for a gram of shitty coke and a case of even shittier beer. It all seemed perfectly normal and extremely fucked up at the same time, and unless I stayed fucked up, it just ate away at me. But usually it was the more innocuous stuff that sent me spiraling into despair: mornings when Bob found me half in the pool and pulled me out so I didn't drown. Cleaning me up after I'd shit or pissed myself. He was just a kid and I'd basically ruined his summer break. Some mornings I'd wake up and beg him not to tell me what happened the night before, but he'd tell me what I did, and I'd sit there with him in the kitchen, trying to choke down my greasy breakfast, thinking I'd have to make any suicide look like an accident so I wouldn't put him through any more shit.

After what could have been anywhere between twenty minutes and ten hours Geoff said, "There's our exit!" and swerved around a tractor-trailer. I crunched another pill, hoping it wouldn't be the last thing I did in my life. The breaks screamed and we slid across the rumble strips along the exit ramp for Rural Route 404.

•

It was still pouring when we stopped in front of Screwdrivers. Geoff had business in Booth anyway, he said. Something about opening a new Gryphon's Den franchise on the other side of town.

"Keep in touch," he said. "If you need to move more of those pills."

"Thanks for the lift," I said, and stepped out into the rain.

I shouldered open the door to the bar. The jukebox played a Betz-era Allman Brothers song. Beneath the moose head, a group of college girls smiled and clinked glasses and the pool table cracked in the corner. Some new guy behind the bar wore neon pink sunglasses, laughing and pouring shots. One drink, I thought, to get my head straight. When the bartender pushed up his glasses and asked for my order, I couldn't hear my own voice ask for a High Life with a shot of whiskey. And when, as promised, the whiskey took off the edge and the beer cooled the burn, all I could think about were those two old men back in that ghost-town bar, rooting hard for Tech.

PART FOUR

MEETINGS, MURDERS, AND DESIGNER JEANS

AN INTERVIEW WITH MARGARET TURNER (CONTINUED)

Having addressed the commotion inside the Rose-Thorn facility, Maggie met us in the cafeteria to finish our discussion as planned. A life-sized portrait of Ronald Reagan Middleton looms behind the salad bar. A cafeteria attendant serves us pizza and Kool-Aid. We sit in Posture-iffic model chairs, like the ones from my undergrad days, that are set around a folding table bolted to the floor.

HS: Why did you follow Ronald Reagan and Althea when, according to his journal, it became clear Ronald Reagan just wanted to get on with his life?

MT: Quite frankly it's impossible for an addict to know what they really want, or what is best for them, while they are still suffering. The disease is in control. And he was under contract. Our plan was to put Ronald Reagan and Althea back in the spotlight, to highlight their personal struggles and gain insight into their thought processes.

HS: We, Bob and I, conclude they left because they ran out of Nedvedol, that Bruce stole the reserves, forcing them to choose between staying in rehab without the drug on which they'd become dependent, and taking their chances with what they might find in the Middleton's basement.

MT: First, let me say Bruce is clean and doing great work for us. Really great work. Just for today, as the saying goes.

As for their motivation, it's irrelevant. Legally we cannot keep anyone on the premises if they want to leave. Contractually, however, all our patients sign a waiver that gives Jackson Entertainment the right to televise their struggles with addiction for up to eighteen months after their stay in Rose-Thorn—to show America how the addicts are progressing after their treatment.

From a therapy standpoint, to *not* follow Ronald Reagan would have been horribly irresponsible. I believe in the Hippocratic oath. And eventually we completed our treatment plan, Ronald Reagan and I, so I ordered him cured of his drug addiction. But that was only after we worked through his issues. You can understand that, I'm sure. Of course you can.

HS: My understanding is tenuous at best. I see your desire to help Ronald Reagan with his addiction, to help him resolve his issues, but I don't feel your methods were entirely honest, and as Bob said earlier, Ronald Reagan wanted to find a way to dispense with the acting he had to do for the viewers and to live a normal life, which you must admit was hindered by your relentless pursuit of him.

MT: No, I don't think that's quite right. Not even close, really.

Bob Middleton Jr.: You can't possibly think you had his best interest in mind.

MT: I'd love to help you as well, Bob. I'm sure you have some issues about growing up in a family ravaged by addiction and alcoholism, and how Ronald Reagan's problems permeated through your existence. Would you like my help with that? How old are you?

BM: How do you sleep at night?

[Sensing the situation could grow ugly from here, I ask Bob to retrieve some of RR's notebooks from our car to try to corroborate Maggie's version of the story with RR's. I certainly agree with Bob, but with so much at stake, my acquiescence to Maggie's chain of events is purely motivated by my need to flesh out this narrative. When Bob leaves, I change the subject.]

HS: The Werewolf Killer. Were you frightened of him during your stakeout of Ronald Reagan?

MT: Quite the opposite, we viewed it as an opportunity. After his escape, we quickly developed a follow-up series around the search for Ronald Reagan. This was in production at the same time as Jackson Entertainment's documentary of the Werewolf Murders. When the route the two recovering addicts [RR and Althea] took down the coast merged with the pattern of recovered bodies, we were presented with the chance to combine our resources. Out of respect for the victims, we chose to delay airing the Werewolf Killer documentary. The viewing public will have to wait until this winter for that meaty piece of investigative journalism.

HS: In addition to profiting off Ronald Reagan, do you feel you're profiting off the deaths of dozens of drug addicts?

MT: Ronald Reagan became famous practically overnight, so we needed additional content, especially after he left the show. We expanded *Clean Time* almost immediately from a weekly show to a nightly live event, supplemented by a twenty-four-hour webcast, not for *profit*, but for the thousands of viewers who, like Ronald Reagan, were suffering and in need of help. That doesn't seem so different from your little book project. So I suppose I could ask you the same question.

HS: Fair point. Of course, I have nothing to hide, no ulterior motives. To be perfectly frank, the question of exploitation is something I've struggled with. But surely the publication of an academic work pales in comparison to the millions the network has made from not only Ronald Reagan's time in treatment, but the systematic slaughter of drug addicts by a madman.

MT: The killing spree in the South is one of this decade's great tragedies. Clearly, I do not condone murder. I am not a sociopath. However, as a television executive, it is impossible to overlook the impact of the killing spree on the ratings of *Werewolf Hunter!* and the buzz surrounding the movie franchise. Not only are werewolves hot, murder is hot. Put a reality television star of Ronald Reagan's caliber in the midst of the most prominent news story of our time, and you've got a ratings bonanza.

The opportunity to cover every angle in such a nuanced manner is a once in a lifetime opportunity. The plan was to put Ronald Reagan in a position to take credit for the arrest of the Werewolf Killer, or at the very least to get him in the same place with this monster. To capture his response to the actions of this horrific psychopath who had killed many of his fellow addicts and friends.

HS: That sounds incredibly dangerous and irresponsible.

MT: The desired outcome did not materialize. Still, our attempt to find Ronald Reagan created a huge following and led to the creation of our online magazine and our collaboration with several journalists and publications.[35] The reasons behind Ronald Reagan Middleton's sudden popularity are textured and multifaceted, but very real, I assure you. Viewer Approval Ratings don't lie. We still get letters begging us to follow up on Ronald Reagan and provide updates on his whereabouts.

Why am I telling you this? Because of Ronald Reagan's popularity, we were able to make arrangements with inpatient rehab centers and fractional living facilities up and down the coast, most of which had suffered the misfortune of losing their government funding, and, in case you aren't aware, *Clean Time* has become a multi-city show with a neutral site Relapse Challenge of Champions. Think of all the addicts we're helping now, just think. We are helping so much.

•

I was not there to argue, so I didn't push. The interview faded into banality. Despite certain outcomes, Maggie's admiration, perhaps even love, for Ronald Reagan shone through as genuine. For a moment, I pondered this. I told Maggie about my previous relationship with Ronald Reagan, what he was like before the fame, how he functioned in academia, his study habits. For that one semester, Ronald Reagan Middleton was my student, mine to mold. Now, in a way, I was a student of his.

THE RED HOUSE ON FREDERICK

The porch light was still on, and there was a pile of overdue bills stuffed in the mailbox, two months' worth of notices in pink envelopes. A faded blood stain streaked the front steps where I'd left Mooch. I guess it was probably better Jacky wasn't there that night, but standing in front of the house we shared, the sadness just about cut me in half. Then I got mad at myself for being such a fuck up, then mad at her because she wasn't there, because she hadn't even gotten in touch with me. I went back and forth between sad and angry and hopeful before I pushed it out of mind and focused on finding my keys. I patted myself down twice before realizing I'd left them in rehab.

I went around back, climbed up on the roof and crawled across it toward the balcony outside my bedroom. Flecks of red paint fell like confetti and stuck to my lips when I pushed open the doors and stumbled inside. I took off my shoes and grabbed the lamp on the nightstand, trying to find the on/off switch. Before I could get the light on, Althea flew out of the shadows and almost nailed me in the ribs with a baseball bat.

"Jesus Christ it's me."

"Oh shit, sorry. They're coming after us. I saw the Prius again."

"Hey, there are a million green Prii out there. No one at *Clean Time* knows where I live. My name's not on the mortgage or any of the bills."

I turned on the lamp. The room was cluttered with useless crap.

"Ronald Reagan, I can't go back to rehab."

"Why did you leave me?"

"I had a bad feeling."

"Please, don't leave me again."

She said, "I won't," but I didn't believe her.

Althea threw the bat aside, and it rolled in an arc across the floor and came to rest near the hole in the wall that led to the sitting room. She hugged me.

The mantle of the bricked-up fireplace was full of random stuff Jacky had traded for. Toward the end, she was pretty indiscriminant. Half a village worth of those ceramic houses my grandma always used to put out at Christmas, two iPhones with cracked screens, a pair of those expensive dolls kids were into last summer, and a lonely glass wizard. The dresser I made Jacky sat covered in a drop cloth back in the corner we started to paint one weekend before we got distracted and never finished.

Covered in dirt and bruises and sunburn, I stepped over an empty box and followed Althea through the hole in the wall. A record spun on the turntable Jacky got off a DJ from Raleigh—a fancy one, pushing a gritty blues song through the upstairs. Streetlights and stars cast light onto the piano. Althea sat at the bench and ran through a few bars, playing along with the record before deciding she didn't want to make too much noise. She was better than most half-assed musicians I knew.

"You need to get cleaned up," she said. She lit a cigarette with a match, and for a second her face held the flame like a lantern.

"This is for you." I pulled the owl out of my backpack. "I won it on one of those claw games."

Althea thanked me and set the stuffed owl next to the record player. She walked over to the bathroom and I followed her.

"Where'd you get the records?" she asked. "I've never seen a collection so sprawling, yet clearly self-contained and reflecting such taste."

"Didn't know we had them. I never looked in those boxes."

The shower curtain was full of holes and mildew so I pulled it off and shoved it under the sink. Althea drew a bath and I let her wash me.

"I don't normally do this type of thing, so don't think I'm the kind of woman who just gives men baths."

The tub wasn't quite big enough to fit us both. We sat in an awkward, angular embrace. She ran her hands through my knotted hair and over my shoulders. Fog filled the small room. On the back of the toilet, a small basket of soaps shaped like stars and baby elephants sat on the box mirror I used to blow lines off of with Jacky.

Althea crossed her wrists in front of my chest and I ran my hands over her scars. Water stung its way down my back. Mud and bubbles circled the drain.

"Sorry I left you."

"I'm drunk."

Blues played by the window while Althea cut my hair short. At my request, she died it bright yellow using bleach mixed with water. She fixed my eyebrows with tweezers and a little pencil. By the time she finished I felt almost whole. If they were actually after us, I figured I'd need a disguise. Even if they weren't, I didn't want anyone down here to recognize me.

Later, we smoked a joint by the piano. Althea flipped through the records and picked out one with a picture of a guy on a broken down porch. Something with "Blind" in the title.

"Let's go to bed," I said.

"I won't get in that bed with you." Althea said.

So I stepped into the bedroom, returned with blankets and sheets, and spread them out on the floor. I lay down with Althea and tried to align my breathing with hers until I fell asleep.

I didn't dream. It felt like I'd closed my eyes for just a second. When I opened them, Bruce was standing over us holding a Taser.

CAPTURED

Tied together with an extension cord, we rolled around in the back of the green Prius for half an hour.

To Bruce, Althea said, "You look like dog shit."

"The sedative should be kicking in soon," Bruce said. "Nap time."

"Fuck you," she said. "My wrists are burning."

Bruce itched his cheek. "Girl, you need an attitude of gratitude. At least no one lit you on fire."

"Is that a threat?"

"Principles before personalities, Althea. I'm trying to help you and Ronald Reagan complete your treatment." Bruce tapped his hands on the wheel to the tune of a Billy Joel song from the early '90s.

"Is assault a principle?" Althea tried to blow the hair out of her eyes.

Bruce said, "You need to retreat, rethink, and respond."

"Where are we going?" I asked.

"Not far! We've got plans for you two. You're going to be the focal point of our new special. Don't you want to help others? Helping others brings me closer to God. I'm helping you. Right now, that's what I'm doing. Helping others is how I've stayed clean for over thirteen years."

Althea shook her hair away from her mouth. "Bruce, you relapsed."

"My clean date is between me and God." He winked at us in the mirror and hummed along with the music. "It's just my experience, strength, and hope."

"Fuck your hope," Althea said.

"Couldn't they give you a bigger kidnapping vehicle?"

Bruce said, "I love this car, and so does Mother Earth."

He took a wide turn, and we slammed into the side panel.

"Everything you told me is bullshit," I said.

"Maggie will be here soon." He snorted and wiped his nose with a bare forearm. "I think you'll both really benefit from what we have planned!"

That was the last thing I remember hearing before I passed out.

•

I came out of a deep stupor to the sound of my own voice talking about how much I missed Bruce. Then I saw myself sitting in the Serenity Cove. My head was running through sand, trying to catch up with my body. I told myself to wake up, like when you're stuck in a nightmare and you know you're dreaming, but I was already awake. The blurriness dissipated, my head cleared a bit, and I realized I was watching a giant flat screen bolted to the wall. Me and Althea were tied up back to back at the foot of the bed. Bruce's laptop was hooked up to the TV, streaming the *Clean Time* website. Althea snored. Bruce thrashed through chemically enhanced dreams.

I wriggled free of the orange extension cord wrapped around our chests, but Althea wouldn't wake up and I couldn't leave without her. We were still in North Carolina, I figured, based on the license plates on the cars in the lot. The clock on the computer said 10:15PM. Bruce took us before dawn. We'd lost a whole day.

The room was freshly painted and furnished with industrial fixtures, fancy appliances, and weird furniture, but I could tell it used to be part of a fleabag motel. Our stuff was stacked neatly in the corner, my backpack with Althea's huge purse under a painting of the Atlantic City skyline. I popped a Nedvedol, chewed it into powder, and let it dissolve on my tongue until the taste got to be so gross I gagged and had to wash it down with a glass of foggy water from the bathroom. I peeled a piece of duct tape off the roll in my bag and covered the camera on Bruce's computer. I searched the room for additional cameras. Then I went through Bruce's shit.

What an amateur. It took me thirty seconds to find the econo-pack of needles and the sedative he shot us up with. It was almost like Bruce wanted me to steal it, practically begged me. Little glass bottles with holes in the top, tinted Philson's signature green. Justin used to score this shit from a nurse he knew. One weekend Mooch and I got pretty deep into it, so I was somewhat familiar with the effects. I assumed Bruce had a high tolerance, but I didn't want to kill him.

I pulled half the bottle into the needle and crept around to the side of the bed where he was sleeping in fits, legs twitching like a dreaming dog. As I slid down the elastic on his boxers and stuck the needle in his ass, I wondered what he was dreaming about. When Bruce woke up, would he forget for a moment that he'd relapsed and thrown away all that clean time? Would he think the relapse was a dream at first before it hit him? When it did hit him, would he want to get clean again? I couldn't imagine starting over after losing all that time. Most likely, he'd wake up and think about getting high. I depressed the plunger. His muscles flexed, then relaxed.

I tossed the rest of the sedative from Bruce's shaving kit into my backpack. He had a ton of Nedvedol in there, too, but I left most of it for him. I had more than enough, and didn't want him to wake up and get sick. I thought about stealing his car, but was certain the thing was being tracked and monitored.

I needed a plan. I figured I could glean something useful from *Clean Time* about their plans for us, and how to best proceed. I untangled Althea from the extension cord and put a pillow under her head. Then I sat in one of the futuristic-but-old-looking chairs and stared at the computer. I cut lines of Nedvedol on a table that looked like a cross section of a steel I-beam topped with glass. I blew a line and watched the streaming clips on the computer, curious how the public saw me. Had I made a total ass of myself? Maybe. Anyone who appealed to that many Americans couldn't be very cool.

I clicked around on the *Clean Time* website and found profiles about everyone, like baseball cards with up-to-the-minute stats, but nothing too interesting. Now that I was gone and stuck in this weird motel, I missed Gasman. I missed the idea of someone wanting to actually get their shit together with no reservations. It was also nice to be around someone who looked up to and respected me, even though the pretenses of that respect were essentially false. Gasman held steady in third place in the Viewer Approval Ratings, never threatening to take the lead but maintaining a solid cushion.

I was getting impatient, so I filled another glass of water and dumped it on Althea. No dice.

I clicked to watch some day-old web clips and saw Maggie heading to the train station. The caption: NEXT STOP NORTH CAROLINA! Apparently when Maggie left, her intern was put in charge, and there was a riot when the patients tried to overthrow the orderlies.

I clicked again. Shelly had dominated Dolph in the inaugural Relapse Challenge. It got bloody and I had to look away from the footage. After the doctors stitched him up in the infirmary, Dolph was sent off that night with $76 and a bus ticket to Greensboro.

At the bottom of the page, along with the VAR stream, there was a "Ronald Reagan Middleton Update" ticker scrolling across the screen. It said: "Status: Escaped." The trailer for *Werewolf Hunter! The Movie!!* played at the end of the Relapse Challenge clip. They're calling it, "The movie based on the show that spawned the real-life killing spree!"

Things started to make sense. Bruce was sent down here to find me and Althea. Maggie was on her way. It seemed like they'd rather have us on TV than arrested.

I stood over Althea and held her nose, but she wouldn't wake up. A noisy pop-up window appeared on the computer screen flashing the words "Breaking News." I put my face close to hers and felt her breath on my eyes. Steady, but she was out cold. I gently slapped her cheeks and they grew flush, but she wouldn't open her eyes. I gave her a kiss, just a quick one, but that didn't work either. This was no fairy tale. I was about to get the Narcan out of Bruce's bag when she mumbled something. Althea was finally waking up, slowly and unromantically, as I watched a helicopter hovering over a bombed-out radio shack. The reporter was saying Dolph's body was down there, somewhere by the dumpster. The feed cut to a picture of Dolph—one of those cheesy, mall portraits of him and his family before his wife left with the kids. "Flayed past the point of recognition," the reporter said. "A poem written in blood at the scene." But they didn't read it on air.

"What the fuck is going on?" Althea slurred, lolling her head in circles. "Dolph's dead."

"Christ, where are we?"

"I'm not sure exactly. We have to go. I shot Bruce full of sedative. He'll be out for a while."

Althea got up slowly, but then came around. She grabbed the keys from Bruce's pocket and flushed them down the toilet. Then we tied him up with the extension cord and left him drooling on the bed.

Outside, the parking lot was packed with cars. A neon sign bent into a buzzing arrow pointed at the First Lite Lounge on the other side of the parking lot. "Open 24 Hours."

I'd never been to or heard of the First Lite, and I knew almost every motel/bar in the state. I figured we were out in the new tech corridor where they were trying to attract businesses with tax breaks.

"Someone will have a phone we can use in there," Althea said. "We can get a cab."

"Perfect. I need a drink."

"Hold on," she said and walked back toward the dumpster. "His car."

Althea grabbed a piece of pipe sticking out of the dumpster, walked back to the car, and smashed the windshield. No one seemed to notice or care.

Then I took my turn. I hit it real good, a couple times, to the point where Bruce would have to stick his head out the window to drive.

Althea took back the pipe, smashed the driver's side window and reached in to pop the hood. She ripped a bunch of parts out of the engine and threw them down a storm drain.

We went to the bar, without the pipe of course.

The place was packed. Everyone was young and on drugs, dressed in designer jeans but trying to look poor. One of those fake dive bars where everything is goddamn expensive. All the tables were full of kids yammering about money and *Werewolf Hunter!* and *Clean Time.* The TV in the corner played local news on mute and it looked like the anchor was singing along with the country music playing on the jukebox. A couple swayed in time in the middle of the bar, joined at the hips and hands. We walked past a booth where a group of kids shared a bucket of Busch pounders and looked at us a little too long before chugging beer until it spilled down their chins.

Althea broke off to go to the bathroom. There were two stools by the poker machine at the edge of the bar. A flyer for God's Church of the Carolinas was taped to the side of the machine. I took a stool and ordered drinks.

The bartender wore a Guilford Prep shirt and I swear I saw the Pirate on her chest wink at me when she poured the shot.

"Are we in Booth?" I asked.

"Twenty miles east."

"Where'd you get the shirt."

"They make me wear it for work. It's supposed to be ironic."

A pained look settled on the bartender's face when she dried her hands, like she was trying to scrape the scent of the place out from under her fingernails and couldn't. She turned to another customer below the muted TV in the corner. The sink squealed. A song about whiskey and women faded into one about patriotism and Chevy trucks. I emptied my glass and tilted it toward the bartender when she walked back my way.

Althea sat down beside me. "Vodka," she said. She drank it down in one gulp. "And we need a cab."

Our ride showed up fifteen minutes and two drinks later and we were on our way to Booth again.

CINDY

It took six dollars in quarters and forty-five minutes at the payphone by the 7-Eleven to locate Cindy. She'd been staying out by the airport, running with a burnout college kid named Kevin who used to know her sister. The light rail ran out to the airport, and things in Booth seemed quiet, so we jumped on and rode out to yet another motel. The Layover.

I knocked on the door to room 107 and stood in front of the peephole so Cindy would see it was me. Her room was cramped and covered in musty, bald carpet that was supposed to be pink or red. At the foot of the bed, the weather station came in blurred on a credit card-operated TV. The water was running in the bathroom.

It was the first time I'd ever seen Cindy with her hair down, hanging past her waist almost to the end of her shorts.

"Oh," she said. "There's two of you."

"I'm Althea."

Althea and Cindy smiled at each other in the cramped entrance. Or they could have been cringing. It was all kind of awkward. I stepped between them and tried to give Cindy a hug, but she backed up into a handshake.

"Have you heard from Jacky?" Cindy asked. She looked better than I remembered. A pack of Camels stuck out of her hip pocket.

"No." I tried to sound nonchalant, the way I would if she were asking about Mooch or somebody. "I figured she would have gotten in touch with you."

Cindy banged the side of the TV and the image corrected. The weatherman smiled and pointed at a series of sun logos in the Carolinas. All the suns wore sunglasses.

"So what's your story?" Cindy asked Althea. "I don't know whether to trust what I saw on TV."

"I'm a scholar."

"Cool," Cindy said. "I'm working on a play. It will be adapted for the stage, but really it's more of a mixed-media documentary. Still in the research phase."

I brushed off a chair and sat down. "What happened to your faculty housing?"

"Prep is still doing renovations," Cindy said. "I'm staying here in the meantime. Nothing like teaching high school with a shitty motel as your office."

Althea crawled over the bed and grabbed the clock radio off the nightstand. She rolled it over in her hands. Intent focus settled on her face while she played with the dials: static, commercials, news, more static. She settled on a spot between a blues show and a Christian rock station.

"Guess it's good you didn't try to come with us," I said.

"I had to deal with the fallout," Cindy said. "While you got famous."

"Fallout? I was in jail."

"You were in jail for two weeks."

"Six weeks," I said. I lit a cigarette.

Cindy took off her glasses and rubbed her eyes. "I don't know how long I'm going to stay here." She set her glasses on top of the TV. "This play is based off Kevin and Nancy's business dealings with Justin and my theory about her death." Cindy appeared to be searching for a word or a phrase, motioned her hands like she was trying to wave one up from the floor. Then she sat on the carpet and lit a cigarette.

From the bathroom, Kevin announced himself: "Fuck Justin."

"What's with him?" I ran my hand down the strap of my backpack, then up again and back down while I shifted my weight from foot to foot.

"Antabuse." Ash from Cindy's cigarette fell to the carpet.

Althea kept fucking with the clock radio.

I picked up the remote, but it didn't change the channel.

"TV won't play anything else without a credit card," Cindy said. "I spent more than I should have watching you two."

In the bathroom Kevin gagged and vomited. The toilet flushed. He left the water running and stepped into the room. Acne scars cratered his cheeks and forehead. Big pink sunglasses pushed back his hair. I recognized him as the bartender from Screwdrivers. The coincidence was unsettling, but not terribly shocking. These social circles get smaller and smaller the longer you stay in them.

"Do you have any chapstick?" Kevin asked.

"Will you just quit taking that shit?" Cindy said.

"I'm trying to get sober." He took a swig from a big can of generic beer and dropped it in the wastebasket at his feet.

Cindy looked at him, then at the air conditioner. Blue fluid dripped onto the carpet.

"I have lip gloss." Althea held it out while her other hand fiddled with the radio in her lap.

Kevin grabbed the tube and examined it. He applied the pinkish gloss and smacked his lips. "Well, I have to get back to the house now. This Tier Two shit. I'm only allowed out past ten for work." Kevin made it sound like this was the worst news any of us had ever heard.[36]

I crushed a couple pills on the table.

Like an afterthought, Cindy kissed Kevin quietly on the cheek without getting up. Before the door closed behind him, I swear I caught a glimpse of a green Prius pulling into the lot.

"He'll be on Tier Three soon. More freedom," Cindy said. "I don't miss him at all when he's gone. But he's really helping inform my work. Justin fucked him and my sister over real bad." Cindy bent forward like she wanted to get up, but reconsidered. She ran her fingers through her hair. "Kevin's helped a lot with research. You can't have too many primary sources."[37]

"I'd love to read your work." Althea poked at the radio with a bobby pin.

"It's not done yet," Cindy said.

I stepped over Cindy and looked through the peephole. No Prius. I put my back against the door and exhaled. "You really haven't heard from Jacky?"

Cindy extended her arm and I helped her up. "Maybe she ran. I'm sure she's fine. Probably just waiting for things to blow over."

I thought about the killer out there murdering addicts, wondered if Jacky would be safer in a halfway house or on the run. Any halfway house she might be in, it would have to be nearby, but I didn't know what I'd even do if I saw her again.

Althea stood on the mattress, slowly waving the radio over her head, searching for reception. The weather channel showed the temperature in Atlanta, Baton Rouge, and Birmingham.

I pressed my palm against the wallpaper, dark red and bubbling, and picked at a hole. "Jesus. This room. Aren't you guys claustrophobic?"

From the bed, Althea said, "When you find your friend, tell her that Ronald Reagan fucked his counselor."

"That was a tactical move," I said.

"From what I saw on TV, it looks like you're fucking him, too."

I tore off a piece of wallpaper, rolled it up, and blew a line with it. "Let's get a drink. We need to figure this out. I'm suffocating in here." I handed the rolled-up wallpaper to Cindy. "Everything got so fucked that night. We shouldn't have taken the bus."

"No one blames you," Cindy said. "Not for that, and really, it is good to see you. Who you're fucking is none of my business."

"Got it," Althea said, and the radio sounded perfect. The college radio station played an old country blues song.

She left the radio strung by the cord over the curtain rod. On her way to take her turn at the desk, Althea ran a finger down the back of my arm. I shivered and stared past the radio at the dark highway streaked with blurry headlights.

"All right, let's get out of here," Cindy said, pulling open the window.

"What's wrong with the door?"

"I'm billing the school for a room at the Hyatt. I can't be seen."

We found a cheap place that wasn't full of college kids one town over, with a decent jukebox and a dartboard, and we ordered round after round. We kept eating pills, too. Mostly, there was a lot of reminiscing about old times, that deep painful nostalgia that's so hard to let sit. At first, I had to maintain a pretty high level of inebriation to stand it. Althea looked uncomfortable, fidgety, but as the evening wore on, she opened up and talked about her childhood in North Carolina and her time at UNCG, avoiding any talk of her family and birds. Eventually she and Cindy bonded over teaching and art and, for a moment, I felt at ease. We all did. The fleeting sense that it would all work out. Foolishly thinking we had formed a bond that would last when we sobered up. I outlined my plan to go to Georgia, talked about my memoir, and how Tom Canada would help forge our certificates. We bought a case of cheap beer after last call and kept the party going in the motel room. We may have figured it all out that night, but by the morning it was all forgotten.

•

I woke at 11AM hung-over and terrified by the sound of the air conditioner. It sounded like an engine that wouldn't turn over and it spit blue fluid into a puddle on the carpet between the desk and the TV. Cindy was gone. Althea and I were naked. Empty Brewtown Ice cans glistened like a silver moat around the bed. I covered Althea with a sheet and grabbed my pants off the TV.

"Have you ever heard of Brewtown Ice?" I examined a can and tossed it in the direction of the garbage can. "Regular Brewtown for that matter?"

I tried to shake Althea awake and found a note from Cindy and two NCDOT cards on the nightstand. The note said she was off doing research, that she took ten pills as room tax, not to let Kevin in if she wasn't there, and to clean up the mess.

I shook Althea's shoulder again. She told me to fuck off and covered her head with a pillow.

"It could take some time to get a forged certificate, at least a few days. We can track down my memoir and get my travel itinerary set up." I squatted and picked up an armload of cans and dumped them by the trashcan.

"Get fucked." Althea sat up and threw the clock radio at me. I caught it and set it down on top of the TV.

AMERICA

We stood at the light rail stop, achy and anxious, sweating out booze and waiting for the Nedvedol to kick in. The morning was mild, but

I didn't trust it, like the air was just waiting for the right moment to burn us alive.

We took two seats near the middle of the car, and it seemed like everyone on the train was staring at us, eyes darting back and forth from their phones. The rail system was put in a long time ago, badly in need of renovation, but in the wake of the recent murders they'd installed security cameras in every car and at most of the stops.

Barely concealed whispers increased as the seats around us filled. I swear a man was filming us with his phone for our entire twenty-minute trip. When we passed the guy on our way off the train, he snapped a picture of us and smiled. "You two are my favorite," he said.

Althea and I got off a couple blocks from the post office with some time to kill before Screwdrivers opened, so we decided to hit the thrift store. The mystery of last night hung between us as we headed into town. I waited for her to say something like "that was a mistake" or "let's just let that be a one-time thing and not make a big deal of it." But nothing like that happened. We stayed quiet and sweaty, walking close, almost holding hands as we passed the pawnshop and turned toward the GSU campus.

Althea lit a cigarette as we neared the Poseidon fountain. "Pretty random that we met in a New Jersey rehab after living so close to each other for five years."

"What if it wasn't random?" I asked.

"Don't you dare start with that rehab, God-Puts-People-In-My-Life bullshit, Ronald Reagan. You're too smart for that."

I dipped my hand in the fountain as we passed it. Across the street a woman held her phone out in front of her, recording us as we walked. I grabbed the cigarette out of Althea's mouth and dragged on it. "Hey, act normal," I said, "but I think that lady is recording us."

Althea pretended to stretch and snuck a quick look over her shoulder. "I don't recognize her."

The lady followed us from the other side of the street, recording the whole way until we ducked in to the thrift store.

Inside, I picked out a pair of aviator sunglasses and a three-dollar corduroy blazer with patches on the elbows. "I can't have Tom Canada thinking I'm some kind of amateur," I said and slid on the blazer. The sleeves were a little long, but it fit pretty well.

Althea laughed. "It's ninety degrees out. You look ridiculous."

"Writers wear coats like this. All the good ones."

While Althea tried on ten different dresses, I went back outside to smoke. Two cop cars and an ambulance flew past, sirens wailing, and disappeared around a corner a few blocks down. I waited for Althea by a telephone pole covered in rusty staples and "missing" posters. We had it so easy in rehab, now that I was thinking about it. Put on a show for the public. Fill out some worksheets and pretend to care. It was hollow, sure, but no more dishonest than scheming to score meth, trying not to get busted driving back and forth from the city with Jacky. Even then I was always putting on a show for someone.

Althea left the store wearing a new old dress, and we cut through the brush behind the thrift store. When we emerged onto Wicker Avenue the same woman was there with her phone, recording us from the far side of the street, and now there was a news reporter with a cameraman walking behind her.

The temperature rose quickly as we headed away from the fountain. Althea stepped over a broken chunk of sidewalk, pulled her hair back and tied it with one of the rubber bands from her wrist. More "missing" posters wrapped around lampposts and covered storefront windows.

The community bulletin board at the edge of campus was covered with warnings: "Inside before sundown!" and "Werewolf Killer still at large!!" At the center of it all hung a generic police sketch that resembled every white guy I'd ever met. The text beneath it read, "Artist's Rendering of the Werewolf Killer. Do not approach him, contact the proper authorities and return to your home or proceed to one of the designated safe areas." A map of the town with the fire station and the police station, all marked with stars, was stapled next to the picture. A cluster of candles and flowers commemorating the dead surrounded the three-sided base and pooled out onto the sidewalk. If my memory of the night before was accurate, I could have sworn the news at the bar had reported even more bodies found.

We turned down Main. An unmarked cop car sat in the alley and, beyond it, I could see a news truck and another camera crew getting set up.

"Maybe we shouldn't be seen together like this," Althea said, reaching for a cigarette before realizing she still had one burning.

"Screwdrivers is close. We can get the forgeries started. How else am I going to disappear to Georgia? You can come with if you want."

"To Georgia? No."

"I'm sure you can finish your dissertation there. It's quiet. We'll stay in my old family vacation home. Completely deserted."

"Yuppie."

We turned down College and saw a cluster of reporters circling a crime scene in the library parking lot. TV cameras filmed cops yelling and trying to control the crowd. The lady with the phone saw me and headed toward us, and a few more reporters followed suit. I recognized Steve from *Clean Time*, but didn't see Bruce anywhere. Still, he'd be close.

Pulling up the collar of my blazer, I kept walking past the yellow police tape and tried to look writerly.

"Ronald Reagan Middleton," Steve shouted. "If you really want to make amends, give us an exclusive. Let me take you to Maggie. We'll all sit down and talk."

"My name is Riley Sheridan." I spoke in my writer voice. I figured the best way to play this was to create the persona of someone who hates the cameras and just wants to be left alone.

"Ronald Reagan, how did you escape Rose-Thorn?" asked a pale reporter with a scar on his forehead.

"I don't even know what that is." I started walking faster, pissed that my disguise was ineffective.

The lady with the phone questioned Althea: "How does it feel to be Ronald Reagan's girlfriend?" Her clothes were wrinkled and she looked old when she smiled.

"I'm not his girlfriend," Althea said. "And that's a bullshit question."

More microphones were shoved in my face, and a crowd hovered close around us, chirping like birds, shouting "Ronald Reagan" over and over, as if they didn't already have my attention.

"Who is Ronald Reagan Middleton? People love Ronald Reagan because of what he represents in their minds." My response, I hoped, sounded thoughtful but annoyed. Like why are these reporters insisting I talk about Ronald Reagan? I kept trying to convince them I was someone else, but no one bought it.[38]

The scar-faced reporter looked confused, so I elaborated, "Ronald Reagan is America."

"Ronald Reagan, how do you feel about the Werewolf Killer?" Steve asked.

"*Is America?*" Althea said, baffled, and pulled at her rubber band.

"Silver bullets," said Scarface, "what are your thoughts?"

"The moon won't be full for three weeks," Althea said.

"Yes, America." I rolled down my sleeves.

"Don't you think you should be worried," Steve said, "given his propensity to kill drug addicts? The latest body was found right back there by the library."

"The killer could be a woman," I said. "And I'm not a drug addict."

Althea's face grew darker and more twisted as the questions kept coming. "Do you realize what y'all are doing to our culture?" she asked.

Steve smiled. "We're providing a service. Ratings don't lie."

"You can't do this," Althea said. "Not to me. I didn't sign up for this."

"You signed a contract." Steve shoved a microphone in Althea's face, hurrying to keep up.

Althea swung at Steve and I held her back. Give the impression of a peacemaker, I thought. Stay consistent with the image you're cultivating.

"We're leaving," I said. "No more questions. We have rights. America." I hurried Althea down the alley connecting Mason and East, and we left the cameras behind us for the time being.

MEETING WITH THE FORGER

Screwdrivers was the same dingy college bar full of Vancouver Canucks memorabilia it had always been. It felt like home.

"This better work," Althea said.

"It will. See, we know that guy." I pointed at Kevin, who was holding a clipboard behind the bar, checking the liquor levels.

Without turning around he said, "We don't serve lunch anymore."

Althea said, "I want my lip gloss back."

"We need to see Tom Canada right now," I said. "And I need a whiskey and she needs a vodka. Neat."

Kevin poured our drinks. "Did the cameras follow you? Tom won't like that."

Althea pushed a loose strand of hair behind her ear. "*Neat* means no ice. I'm not paying for this."

I'd already gulped down my whiskey. I hadn't noticed any ice.

Kevin came around the bar and frisked us, then Tom Canada buzzed us in through the Employees Only door next to the kitchen. We walked down a long hallway covered with fake wood wallpaper until we came to another door with a security camera blinking above it and a buzzer by the knob. Althea hit the buzzer and we stood there in a drawn-out silence, breathing stale air, not talking about what might happen if Tom wouldn't help us. Althea hit the buzzer again and we waited until he finally let us inside.

Tom's office was set up in the middle of a room the size of a high school gymnasium. Tom sat at his desk. Next to him, hanging from wires attached to the rafters, was a ten-foot-tall print of that famous picture of Mooch and the Guildford Prep Pirate. The print glowed in the light of a vintage neon Löwenbräu sign humming on the wall.

"You have ten minutes," Tom said. "If you want to waste it standing there, that's fine with me."

"We appreciate your time, Mr. Canada," Althea said and started toward his desk, but I was stuck staring at the picture of Mooch and that one-eyed pirate.

TVs lined the wall to my left, playing high school football highlights and security footage. Chicken wire covered a row of windows near the ceiling and the light falling through them landed in a honeycomb pattern on the floor. I felt dizzy and anxious in all the open space, out of proportion, shrunk like Alice, unable to comprehend how the room could be so wide open. Maybe the hallway had led to some kind of basement. Maybe I was trapped underground. Thoughts of traveling into Hades surfaced and subsided.

"Come on," Althea said and waved me over.

I moved one foot and then the other, like I was walking through mud, but I made it to Tom's desk and the looming photo of Mooch and the mascot. The picture was a replica of the front page of the *Picayune* from ten years ago, the same picture that dickhead CO had in his office in jail, the same picture that hung on every barbershop wall for three counties and above every urinal in every shitty sports bar across the state. Up close the photo looked glossy, slightly pixelated. Something about the way the blue and yellow neon light hit the Pirate gave it the illusion of three-dimensionality.

Tom Canada said, "Nine minutes left."

"Mr. Canada," I said, "great to see you."

Althea passed him Chaz Dorsey's certificate. "We each need one of these," she said.

I swear Tom Canada's desk was the size of a sailboat. The certificate's reflection swam in his glasses. He wore one of those translucent green visors, like a card dealer or an accountant, and his hair shot from its center like a patch of weeds.

I said, "I also need a fake ID." Changing my identity was inevitable at this point. I wanted to start over completely and I'd never be able to do that without at least a driver's license. Better to ask right off the bat. With so much Nedvedol to trade, I thought I'd probably get a decent deal. "A Georgia ID."

"Before we do business," he straightened a ceramic dragon on his desk pad, "I want to get on the same page." He took off his glasses and pointed them at me. "I'm only doing this because you're a friend of Jacky's, and the expiration of Justin Haas benefitted me greatly."

"I had nothing to do with that," I said. "Neither did she."

"We'll never know what might have happened if you hadn't seen Justin that night." Tom's skin looked gray.

Althea snapped her rubber band.

"I stood up for Jacky."

I slammed my hands on the desk and the dragon shook and Tom straightened it.

"We aren't friends Ronald Reagan," Tom said. He put on his glasses, relaxed in his chair. "If you ever think you need to get in touch with me, you don't. You talk to Kevin out front. If he's not there, go to Drew."

"Fuck Mooch and fuck Kevin."

"Can you forge it or not?" Althea pointed at the creased certificate on his desk. "With my name there."

Tom said, "I can do two of these and fax them to the proper authorities for three-hundred each." He shuffled through a stack of glossy paper and held up a sheet next to the certificate. "A fake Georgia license can be had for five-hundred dollars, but won't be ready for a week. Maybe two. I need to get the proper templates and holograms."

Stomach acid rose in my throat. I swallowed it. "How do I know the forgeries will even work?"

"I'll finish Althea's now, but you're on the hook for it, Ronald Reagan. I'll even cut you a break. One thousand even for everything."

"Okay, Tom, I don't have the money, per se," I said. "But I have over ten thousand Nedvedol. Kids love them, they adapt to the individual. The pills do." I shook one of the 2,000-count bottles in front of me. "Something about synapses. They're as good as money, if not better." I set the bottle on his desk next to the small ceramic dragon.

Tom said, "Get that off my desk."

I grabbed the bottle. "You can get at least fifteen bucks a pill on the street. I swear. They're like molly, speed, and oxycodone all in one." Saying it out loud like that made me feel shitty about snorting them for a second, but I assured myself again that everything was okay because I was not using meth, coke, crack or heroin.

Tom put his visor on his desk and opened the cigarette case beneath his desk lamp. Staring at me the whole time, he pushed on the dragon's tail and fire shot from its mouth. He held a long cigarette to the flame.

Althea's leg jittered and sent echoes through the room. "So you'll forge mine, right?" She got up, put her hands on the desk and leaned toward Tom. "If he's not good for it, I am."

Tom held up a finger, closed the cigarette case. "I don't want your pills. I don't want any drugs tying me to you. I'm hesitant to do business with you at all." A vent in the ceiling pulled the smoke away from his face and he looked like he'd just as soon smash that lighter over my head and leave me bleeding in the alley as help me. "But you are a friend of Jacky's. So I'll let you sell those pills without a hassle from any of my associates. And I'll help you with the documents."

With the cigarette pinched between his teeth, he held the certificate before him and walked past the TVs and the picture of Mooch and the Pirate to a smaller side-desk with a light box in it. He wore Guilford Prep gym shorts and an unbuttoned short-sleeve dress shirt that he took off and hung on his chair. I assumed he would digitally copy the certificate, but he worked by hand.

Althea sat on the floor and dumped out her purse and the bag of clothes from the thrift store. "Your friend Mooch looks so happy." She started sorting her things into color-coded piles, pausing to apply more lip gloss.

The Pirate's head was angled so his good eye looked straight ahead. Mooch's shoulder pads obscured the eye patch. I swear the Pirate's gaze followed me while I paced between Althea and Tom Canada's desk. I stopped pacing, stood in front of the picture, and reached toward the Pirate's hat to make sure it wasn't three-dimensional.

"Keep your hands off that picture, or I'll have them cut off and buried in West Virginia."

I backed away.

Without looking up from her piles on the floor, Althea asked, "What's so special about it?"

And while we watched him forge Althea's certificate, Tom told us the story behind the picture.

It was common knowledge that, among his various illegal business dealings, Tom Canada ran the high school football racket in the tri-county area. Ten years ago, he made $750,000 when Guilford Prep converted a meaningless, last-second 2-point conversion to cover a 14.5-point spread and win their fourth straight title. The promising young athlete who scored the conversion was Mooch (Tom called him Drew). "At the time, it was my biggest profit on a single game," Tom said. "So I decided to get a copy of the print blown up, life-size, to commemorate the occasion."

"I don't give a shit about high school sports," I said and lit a cigarette.

"What *do* you give a shit about," Althea said.

After almost an hour, Tom stood up. "For you, my dear." He handed Althea the certificate, an exact copy with her name and Maggie's signature on it.

"Oh my," she said. "It's perfect.

"Now, to whom should I fax it?" Tom asked.

Fuck, I thought. After convincing Althea to come all this way with me, I didn't know the fax number to the magistrate's office, what department or anything.

"Here's the number." Althea gave Tom a piece of paper with the fax written on it. Tom faxed it to the office.

Althea gave me a weird look and lit a cigarette. The return fax came a couple minutes later. My plan actually worked.

"Althea Blake," Tom said, "you have completed the first step in your state-mandated rehabilitation."

On his way back from the fax machine, Tom stopped in front of me and stared at my pants. "What?" I asked, and I checked myself out, thinking I must have a stain somewhere. "Seriously, what are you looking at?"

Tom took off his glasses. "How does a person in your situation acquire a pair of six hundred-dollar jeans?"

My jeans had come courtesy of the Employee Free Jeans Incentive, and though the J$F bridge was one I'd burned to dust a long time ago, I told Tom I had a connection, and my payment plan was officially decided.

Tom said five pairs would cover our certificates. Another five would pay for a fake ID and give me some more traveling money. Soon, I'd literally be a new man, on my way to Georgia.

Until then, the plan was to unload a bunch of Nedvedol, get the last of my signatures, and connect with Sophie. I couldn't wait to show her how good I was doing.

Tom dropped his Guildford Prep shorts and flung them at me with his foot. He pointed in the vicinity of my crotch and said, "We'll start with that pair."

.

Althea and I left Screwdrivers and walked to a nearby GasLand. We got coffee and sat by the air machine, watching the clouds grow fat with sunlight.

"You're welcome," Althea said.

"For what?" I clicked the air compressor a couple times and stared at my Styrofoam cup.

"The fax number," she said. "Did you even read the contract? Do you have any idea what is going on right now?"

"What are you talking about?"

"You don't have a clue how selfish you are. I put myself at risk, riding down here, and you didn't even have the fax number to the magistrate."

"Why didn't you ask me if I had the number? I figured I'd just get it off the internet or whatever. Besides, you had the number."

"The number isn't the point."

"Then what is the point?"

"The point is I wanted you to want to know what the number was before we left."

"But you had the number?" I raised my voice and I didn't want to. I couldn't help but feel flustered. "Why are we even arguing?"

"I covered my ass. You didn't even think to read the fine print. You're used to showing up and shit just working out for you."

"Yeah, shit's really working out for me. I have to steal a bunch of pants to trade a lunatic drug dealer for a forged rehab certificate while avoiding the police and the media and a serial killer. Living the motherfucking dream."

"You don't have anything to worry about. Even without a certificate, they won't arrest you. You're the star. In their eyes, I'm just Ronald Reagan's girlfriend."

"What the fuck? That was *your* idea."

Althea snapped the rubber band around her wrist. "They can still film us, you know. It's in the contract." She rummaged through her bag, pulled out a pack of cigs and lit one.

I dropped a Nedvedol in my cup and waited. "We still need to get our slips signed."

"No shit," Althea said.

My meeting sheet was identical to Althea's. A perforated page torn from the back of our Rose-Thorn workbooks with twenty-four lines, each with blanks needing a meeting name/time, date, and chairperson signature.

"My first time around," Althea said, "I went to a lot of meetings at the Alano Club on Confederate. North of town." She ran her fingernail under the rim of her cup, took off the lid and stirred her coffee with her finger. "They have meetings every hour there. We could get eight signatures a day and be done in a week."

"Alright," I said. "Listen, I don't want to be fighting right now. I have a lot on my mind. Are we cool?"

"We're cool," Althea said, but I had my doubts. "And thanks. The forgery worked. I'll give you credit for that."

Commuters stopped for gas, cars full of people on the way to work or someplace important, fulfilling real world obligations that seemed terrifying. I picked my cup off the pavement and swirled it, watched the pill melt into green pixels and disappear.

THE ALANO CLUB

After walking through the woods to avoid the media, we came out on Confederate Street near the Alano Club, right by the last light rail stop on the north side of town. The clubhouse lounge was filled with smoke and folding tables with matchbooks under the legs to keep them level. A couple people ordered food from a counter. A group of God's Church of the Carolinas followers handed out literature and proselytized by the Pepsi machine. They had a stack of pamphlets with the same big cross and fear-of-God slogan I remembered seeing on that loafer-wearing preacher's car at the rest stop.

Althea walked over and stood under the TV on the far side of the lounge, twisting her hair into braids. People gave us looks and nods, whispered to each other. They walked past Althea into the meeting room and she said a few hellos and smiled, dropped her hair to shake an occasional hand.

The kid at the check-in desk was upset: "You think you can waltz in without signing the sheet because you're some kind of celebrity?" It was Geoff, sitting with his dress shoes, polished to a bright shine, up on the desk.

"What?"

"Sign in. It helps the Club get funding if we can prove people are showing up."

"I'm not signing anything. You didn't make her sign it." I pointed at Althea.

He addressed the whole room when he spoke. "Look at Mr. Clean Time," he said. "Can't get twenty-four hours together."

Everyone stopped and looked.

I picked up the pen, spun it in my hand, and dropped it. "I'm just another addict trying to get a day clean."

After a brutal few seconds, conversation in the lounge resumed and the rest of the meeting-goers filed into the meeting.

"That was shitty, Geoff. I thought we were friends."

"Aren't we?"

"Why are you even here?"

"Recruiting."

I signed in as "Riley Sheridan" and hurried into the noon meeting.

Althea and I collapsed in our seats. Torn pieces of pink and red streamers stuck in the corners where the ceiling met the walls. It felt like we'd entered the shittiest high school auditorium of all time, but we stayed there all day, meeting to meeting, alternating between the upstairs and downstairs rooms, occasionally napping, steadily accruing signatures despite being legally drunk. Apparently, it's okay to be drunk at meetings, as long as you don't start a fight or talk the whole time.

I spent the 8PM meeting drinking disgusting coffee, watching the streamers flutter in the wind generated by the giant oscillating fan in the corner. After the closing prayer, I was dazed and dying for a cigarette when a kid in a white shirt shoved a 12-Step book in my face and demanded I take his phone number and call him every day if I wanted to "bask in the sunlight of the spirit."

"No. I don't want your number."

The kid persisted. "Take this literature."

"I don't think so."

He flashed a smug smile. "You'll never make it."

"I think that's been established."

Outside the club, orange construction cones cordoned off the smoking area. It took me a minute to register that the sun had set. I watched people wander around the cones, hugging each other and talking about various stages of recovery and potential triggers and things that might take them out. I sat on the picnic table by the side entrance and lit a cigarette, carved a Mets logo into the soft wood with my pen. There were a couple reporters that I recognized from earlier hanging around talking to each other, but nowhere near the numbers from this afternoon.

Althea sat down on the bench at my feet, let her head rest against my knee, and I thought about touching her hair, but held back. Smoke rose and dissipated above her while the lot grew busy with the back and forth between meetings.

"I think this might actually work," Althea said. She snapped her rubber band and stared out at the abandoned A&P across the busy street. The banner over boarded up windows read "Gryphon's Den, Coming Soon!!!"

"I told you it would," I said. I still couldn't figure out what she'd been so pissed about.

"I'm going back in," Althea said.

"I'll see you back at Cindy's. I've got other business to tend to."

As I crossed the parking lot to get back to the woods, I almost got hit by a car pulling into the Alano. That big black convertible with a white cross painted on the side.

WHITE REGGIE

It was a warm night and quiet. Not much traffic as I walked through the woods along the highway headed toward the J$F warehouse. But first I stopped at Cindy's room and emptied out my pack of everything but about 500 Nedvedols. If my spatial cognition held true, I could fit five pairs of pants in the backpack. I'd have to carry the rest. Tom Canada wanted me back with the pants tomorrow.

My jeans connection was White Reggie, the second-shift supervisor at the warehouse. I figured he could be bribed with pills. Reggie was a coward, and he loved pills. If he wouldn't negotiate, I'd just take the jeans by force.

A truck sped past on the interstate, and I stepped over the guardrail. Walking in the ditch by the side of the road, I thought about how much I hated Reggie.

Back before I got arrested, White Reggie came out to Screwdrivers one night to meet Cindy to discuss plans for some protest she was organizing for Columbus Day. Cindy knew him through mutual creative friends. I'd warned her that he was an ass, but Cindy said she was only interested in his connections and influence. Anything to spread word about the protest.

When Reggie showed up, aside from discussing social media strategy and promoting the cause to his minor-celebrity connections and how he could leverage his reading series for political activism, he spent all his time trying to impress Jacky. I'm not super possessive, at least not outwardly, but I swear, I was sitting right there while this fedora-wearing asshole flirted with my live-in girlfriend. He told us how great his fucking poetry chapbook was, and how he tried to capture the female and the African American experiences in his work, and how he could relate because he was a feminist and one-sixty-fourth Native American.

On top of all that, Reggie let it slip that he had inherited a couple million bucks from his dead uncle, but demanded his dad get him a blue collar job so he could better understand the working poor and more accurately depict their plight. Which might not seem so bad, but this asshole hardly worked. He spent most of his shifts sitting on a pile of boxes watching everyone on the line while he took notes and drafted bad poems. Sometimes he read them out loud to me, and I wanted to die. During that time, I wished every day my parents hadn't cut me off, and this guy took the job for street cred with some asshole poets.

The more I thought about Reggie, the more he pissed me off. By the time I climbed the fence outside the warehouse by the dock, I was half-wishing he'd try to start something. But he was actually happy to see me.

Reggie hopped off the dock and gave me a big bro hug. "Ronald Reagan motherfucking Middleton," he said. "How was it on the inside?"

"Not bad. Just a quick bid."

White Reggie lit a cigarette and offered me one. He said, "Saw you on TV, brother. I know C-Doors…" he paused for effect, maybe noting the puzzled look on my face. "Chaz Dorsey. I booked him for my next event this month, little spoken word thing the two of us have been playing around with. Nothing major. Anyway, when I told him you and me were like fam, he said how cool you were on the show. Top notch."

Of course that asshole name-dropped Chaz Dorsey. "Chaz is solid," I said. "Good guy."

The break horn sounded and a dice game started up at the foot of the dock. A few of the guys gave me pats on the back and handshakes, and a couple weird glances went my way, as in "why are you talking to that dick head?"

"What brings you back to the warehouse?" Reggie said.

"Actually, I have a business proposition," I said. Then, for effect, I asked, "Is it safe to talk here?"

"Step into my office."

His office was a broken-down tractor-trailer cab by the edge of the lot. On the way back we passed my station wagon that'd been there since July, sitting on four flat tires with a new crack in the windshield. I ran my fingers over the letters I'd keyed into the side, thought about the miles I'd put on that thing, and then hurried to catch up with Reggie.

Once we were up in the truck, he sparked a joint. "I've been wanting to ask you. Who's Bobby Junior?"

I ignored his question and laid out the plan. I'd give him 500 Nedvedol (which, for the sake of this transaction, I priced at $7.50 per pill, but could be resold by him for $15 or more) and he'd give me ten pairs of pants, which he seemed confused about. I told him I had a guy who was willing to pay me top dollar for them, but needed the pants up front.

Reggie hogged the joint, but the pot was good. He told me he got it from his man in San Diego who owned a dispensary and was going to set him up with a grow room or some bullshit. I tried to tune him out. The weed helped. At least when the joint was finished, there would be a natural end to this meeting.

"What if I can't sell these?" he asked.

"I could get rid of them right now, twenty-five a pop, but I want to give you a chance to get in on the ground floor. Plus, I need the pants. You're my man." A little too direct, maybe, but I was getting impatient.

"I appreciate it, brother. Me and my boys love pills. Plus these rich girls will do anything for a couple Oxys."

The joint burnt my fingers so I gave it back to Reggie, who put it out in the ashtray.

"Alright, brother," he said, "wait here."

I stood outside the truck while Reggie walked to the dock and came back with the pants.

"Listen, cuz," he said. "I can only do five pairs for two-fifty. If I flip these easy like you say, I'll do five more for another two-fifty."

I should have seen this coming. Motherfucker just wanted to hang out again. Even if he couldn't sell any of the pills, he'd want to look like he did. I knew he didn't need the money, but I wasn't sure if he knew that I knew. Mostly I didn't want to have to listen to this asshole talk anymore.

"I can only fit five pairs in my bag anyway, man," I said. "If you want,

I'll front you the other two-fifty now and you can owe me the pants."

"Nah," he said. "It's cool. How do I get ahold of you if I need to re-up?"

I said, "I'll be back around."

"My man," he said, and gave me a business card. I put it in my wallet next to Geoff's. "We should grab a drink."

"I'm trying to quit," I said.

CYCLOPS

It took me three hours to sneak across town with all the press. I showed up at Screwdrivers around last call, thirsty and out of breath. Althea was at the bar bullshitting with Kevin. The stuffed owl I'd given her poked out of her purse. Kevin brought me a shot and a beer on the house and I drank fast but my nerves wouldn't settle.

"Got some pants," I announced, and dropped my backpack at the foot of the barstool next to Althea. She said she needed pills, so I rattled a handful out of one of the bottles in my bag and dropped them into Althea's cigarette pack.

She finished her drink and gathered her stuff to leave. "I'm going to Alano," she said.

"Can you wait real quick?" I asked, "I have to see Tom."

"Sorry," she said. "Don't want to be late."

"Maybe I'll be there later." I said.

Althea left.

Kevin shrugged, poured me another shot, and provided a sympathetic ear while I lamented my state of affairs and the need to get my memoir from Sophie. Kevin's phone chimed, and he typed a quick response. "Mr. Canada will see you now," he said, and nodded at the door to his office.

The Löwenbräu sign glowed yellow and blue next to the picture of the Prep Pirate. Tom emerged from behind the picture and sat at his desk. He wore only his green visor and the stonewashed J$Fs I'd traded him the day before. I pulled the jeans out of my backpack, folded and stacked them on the desk next to the ceramic dragon.

"We are not off to a great start, Ronald Reagan. Ten pairs means ten pairs."

"My guy could only do five right now, but I'm meeting him in a couple days." I sat on the floor and smashed a Nedvedol on the tile with the butt of my lighter.

"The price has gone up." Tom spun the ceramic dragon on his desk and lit a cigarette. "Ten more pairs."

I railed a line of Nedvedol off the floor. "The fuck. We had a deal."

Tom took off his visor and scratched his forehead. He said, "If you want your certificate, I need ten more pairs."

"How do I know you won't just tell me you need twenty pairs next time?" I tried to stare him down, project strength, but Tom grabbed the jeans and walked into the shadows behind the picture. He changed the music to some kind of ambient noise that sounded like cicadas looped over late-70s synthesizer. It reminded me of Serenity Cove.

Left alone with the picture of Mooch and the mascot, I tried to compose myself while the Pirate stared at me, his one open eye like a fucking Cyclops looking into my soul. My right eyelid started fluttering, and I nearly vomited. Now the Pirate was laughing.

MEMOIR RECON MISSION

A candlelight vigil for the victims of the Werewolf Killer had formed near the bulletin board on the edge of State's campus, sprawling all the way down around the corner and across the street from Sophie's house. For several blocks in both directions, students and townies fanned out, engaged in deep discussion about whether or not the dead addicts had it coming. Everyone wore black clothes accented by silver wristbands and little silver ribbons pinned to their shirts. I'd never seen so many candles. They reminded me of the lights in the valley behind Cindy's sister's house.

I dropped a handful of change into a coffee can that was supposed to go to the victims' families and a stoned-looking girl in tight jeans pinned a ribbon on my lapel. I took care to make sure no one had followed me from Screwdrivers, but it was hard to tell with practically the whole town surrounding the vigil.

When I turned the corner, the crowd continued to stretch all the way down in front of Sophie's house, not just the folks mourning the dead, but a whole mess of reporters. I tried to blend in with the crowd and press on. As I got closer I saw a tent with a *Clean Time* logo on it set up across the street. More tents: Lifetime, AMC, MTV, were all represented. Corporate logos everywhere. I knew I'd never get through everyone, so I tried to double back and come around from the other direction, but a reporter cut me off at the pass. "Another addict turned up dead," she said. "Are you frightened?"

"This fear is a media creation," I said.

Another reporter was close behind and asked, "How do you feel about the upcoming *Clean Time* spinoffs?"

A man in a suit shoved a mic in my face. "Are you more afraid of werewolves or junkies?"

"Junkies."

"How do you feel about the final line from the Killer's last message. 'Purge the vermin from the South.'"

"I know a good place to start."

I pushed my way through the pack, but I couldn't gain ground. The path leading to Sophie's front porch was blocked and the lights were out inside. It seemed like nobody was home. When I tried to turn around, I was swarmed.

How's the memoir coming? Will you emcee the nation-wide Relapse Challenge Battle Royale? Do you have any advice for other addicts? What advice would you give Gasman if you could speak to him now? Is the killer coming for you? Where were you the night of the thirteenth?

When a smashed-up green Prius parted the crowd and sped up to the curb, I turned and fought my way through the reporters and took off across campus. I ran until the yelling faded behind me. I ducked into a utility shed by the track. Figured I'd wait it out until I was sure they'd given up looking for the night.

I picked up a discus and traced its edge.[39] Over and over, I replayed the series of events that led to me hiding out in a shed full of sports equipment, then I tried hard to think of anything but those events with little success. When I cracked the door and peeked outside, no one was around. Just the vigil glowing on the edge of campus.

I got all the way back to the motel before I realized I'd stolen the discus. Approaching the back window of Cindy's room, I wondered how many Nedvedol I could eat without having a heart attack. I opened the window on the first try and felt a sense of accomplishment greater than I'd known in some time.

Cindy, Kevin and Althea were somewhere else. I collapsed on the bed for what I intended to be a short nap before the midnight meeting at the Alano Club, but passed out for almost twenty hours.

The sound of Cindy and Kevin screaming woke me. I'd never heard Cindy yell. Kevin must have done something terrible. I faked sleep until the two of them left: Kevin out the front door, Cindy out the back window.

The bathroom smelled like puke, and I gagged as soon as I stepped inside. I showered until the hot water ran out. In anticipation of another hot night, I cut the sleeves off my blazer. I stuffed a mostly full bottle of Nedvedol in my backpack and took off for the 33/77 bypass, toward the highway. Back to the warehouse and White Reggie.

PANTS RE-UP

The night's silence held a weight I couldn't place, like it was keeping a secret. My face itched where my eyebrow had started to grow back and I jumped every time a car passed. Days were starting to bleed together and I hadn't even been back for a whole week. Maggie was lurking, Althea thought I was an incompetent dipshit, and I hadn't seen Jacky in over a month. I had no clue how to get ahold of Sophie without getting mobbed by people. On top of everything, White Reggie was the closest thing I had to an ally. Maybe I should have just given up on finding Sophie, but I didn't want to be wrong about the importance I'd placed on those pages. I needed them. If the increasing amount of bullshit I'd been through since the cops pulled me off that bus led to anything meaningful, it would be the composition of those pages in jail. Sophie's class was the spark. Completing the manuscript was the light at the end of the tunnel full of fucked up prescription drugs and 12-Step cults and asshole hipster poets. I'd prove to myself and my fucked up family that I could see this thing through. Stay the course, I decided, and I crossed the highway toward the warehouse.

Reggie jumped off the loading dock when he saw me, arms spread wide. Big hug and a pat on the back from him. Fewer nods from the other guys on the dock this time. No one came over to say hi.

"Ronald Reagan, bro, glad you swung by."

"Those Triple-beam Balances move for you?"

"The Tri-planes?"

"You selling any? How's the product?" I asked.

"Bro, they're moving fast," he slapped me on the back. "You know, brother, we should really kick it some time. I'm brewing my own IPA. It's bomb. We should imbibe. Just rap about stuff. Really, I much prefer doing business with friends. Feels less corporate, you know?"

"Yeah, hey, listen, I need more jeans. Ten more pairs."

"Ten pairs?" He took off his fedora, wiped his forehead and looked back toward the dock where his crew was unloading a shipment.

"I'm in deep with some bad people." I'd started talking business too soon. I pulled a joint from the pocket of my blazer to try to seem less needy. "I scored some good shit. My treat. And I was thinking I could probably give you better numbers on the Trifocals, especially for ten pairs."

"Step into my office," he said.

We started back for the truck.

"I don't think you know how tough a spot I'm in," I said.

"Ten pairs is tough. Variance reports. On top of our quarterly employee mark outs, we ship the blems to the outlet malls every week. All accounted for. Five I can make disappear. Ten more might raise flags with corporate."

Motherfucker was full of excuses. I thought about how Tom Canada would dispose of my body while Reggie talked down about the pot I had, in that kind of way people do when they don't even realize they're being condescending. "Pretty good for east-coast stuff." Then he asked if I'd given any thought to coming to the poetry reading he was hosting. I was non-committal.

"Next week, every fourth Friday. You should come out," he said. "September is usually solid, all the college girls are back and we give away boxed wine and cheese. Didn't you say on *Clean Time* you were working on some stuff? Memoir? We do mostly poetry and more progressive multi-media non-narrative pieces, but there's an open mic before the headliners. Might be a good forum for your nonfiction…"

I hit the joint hard. The last goddamn place in the world I wanted to be was at a poetry reading, but I remembered one time Sophie said it was important to participate in the literary community and it gave me an idea.

"…Or I could put you on the bill. It would be an honor to share the stage with you."

"You ever have anyone from the GSU MFA program at your reading series?" I asked. "I'm trying to get in touch with a student there. Sophie Trent. Know her?"

"Don't know her. Honestly bro, I try to avoid MFA students. Bunch of suburban kids trying to sound edgy. Too academic. Is she hot?"

"She was my teacher in jail. She's a great writer."

"Well, if you vouch for her, I'll check her out."

"If you can book her and have the rest of the jeans, I'll read at your event. Just don't publicize me. Say 'with special guest' or something," I said. "And if any of the *Clean Time* people come around, you can't let them in. The press has been up my ass lately."

"Deal. You're in for a treat, brother. This will be the event of the year. And I'll make sure you're comfortable. No unwanted guests."

•

I left White Reggie with 500 Nedvedol and promised another 500 pills upon delivery of the jeans. Ten pairs of pants more or less secured. I looked over my shoulder the whole walk back. Every blinking light was a camera, every figure in the shadows a reporter, a cop, or a killer. The relief I felt immediately after setting the deal up with Reggie fell further and further out of reach with every step along the highway and was replaced with a growing sense of dread. By the time I made it to the hotel, I was exhausted but still jumpy. As I climbed back in through the window, I half expected Bruce and Maggie to break the door down and throw me in the back of a Prius. Instead, I saw Althea lying on the bed, throwing the stuffed owl between the blades of the ceiling fan and catching it on its way down.

"Kevin should really quit drinking," I said. "The bathroom reeks."

"You missed a good meeting," Althea said.

"Why the concern about my meeting attendance?"

"I'm not concerned, but you look like shit. If you fuck up too much, it'll draw attention to both of us. I don't want an investigation into the veracity of my Wellness Certificate."

"The late meeting is depressing. Fuck that place."

"I get a lot out of it. This woman there tonight reminded me of my friend Leah. She was so honest."

"What did she say that was so fucking honest, the lady who looked like your friend?"

"Nothing that I can repeat."

"So you're miss confidentiality all of a sudden. You two make some kind of deep connection, or was it just false intimacy?"

Althea threw the owl at me, but I ducked and it landed in the puddle under the air conditioner.

"You're not even clean," I said. "Neither of us are."

"At least I'm trying," she said.

"Trying? You're watching *Werewolf Hunter!* reruns."

"People who judge don't matter and people who matter don't judge."

"Why are you watching TV anyway? They can trace your credit card."

"Kevin used earlier. It's fine. What's your problem?"

"Nothing."

Althea rolled over and faced the wall, and I flipped the TV to The Recovery Channel. On TV, Sophie returned home to the crowd on her front lawn and freaked out. She refused to answer questions about me or show them my work despite repeated requests for information. Eventually the police showed up and the reporters moved across the street, and after a while they dispersed. Then I saw Maggie walking around in my old house on Frederick Street, speculating about what kind of home life I must have had.[40] It creeped me out, watching her go through my things, but at least she wasn't outside waiting for me.

These images blew in and out of my dreams, as I lost consciousness and passed out on the floor. When I woke up, Althea was gone.

MEETINGS

In a fit of ambition, I decided to go to the Alano Club and hit the 9PM, 10:30, and midnight meetings all in a row. I left the motel just after dark and took the long way to better avoid the press.

At the Alano Club you don't hear stories about lawyers fucking their secretaries or professors losing out on tenure. You hear about stick-ups and murders. Overdoses that don't make the news because they happen in the wrong part of town. The guy stabbed in the parking lot for fucking his sponsee's girlfriend. Or the gun nut who holed up in his house in the sticks with a cache of assault rifles when he relapsed after ten years clean, firing at anyone who set foot on his property.

From the crest of the hill, I could see the Alano Club parking lot and the Preacher's followers picketing in front of the Gryphon's

Den across the highway. A cluster of white shirts swaying to hymns I couldn't hear. I thought about the rift within the Alano Club meetings. The less-crazy people versus the Preacher's followers. Some questioned whether the Preacher had any clean time at all, said he showed up out of nowhere claiming he had thirty years. Others swore they'd been seeing him for decades at meetings all up and down the east coast, that he personally started the midnight meeting, ages ago, and had exemplary recovery until his wife relapsed and he found her dead of an overdose and went crazy. He blamed the program for her death, and after that he grew more dogmatic and more corrupt.[41] Maybe I just wanted my signatures and didn't really have a dog in this fight, but I knew a con man when I saw one.

I came up through the woods and slid down the bank toward the light rail stop, then doubled back around the club and snuck inside through the kitchen entrance. I'd made friends with the woman who worked the counter, and she let me in without a hassle. Outside the cameras waited, but they respected the meeting.

The Preacher wasn't at the nine o'clock meeting. While I listened to everyone share, I felt something resembling peace. The unity in the room was overwhelming, everyone there trying to get better, at least for an hour. But the feeling didn't last. Toward the end of the meeting, word got out that another body was found on the other side of town. All the reporters outside left to cover the murder, and the parking lot was empty when I went out to smoke. I hated myself for feeling relieved.

During the 10:30 meeting, I scoped out potential escape routes while the Preacher's followers espoused nonsense. Althea sat on the other side of the room and avoided eye contact.

Three industrial coffee pots were lined up on a card table against the far wall, near the entryway. The Preacher sat just in front of them at a table covered with candles. Whenever anyone got up for coffee, he stared them down until they returned to their seat.

I poked at the candle on my table and listened while a kid with "depraved" and "inconsiderate" scrawled on his white t-shirt said his disease was running laps around the building, and he needed to remind himself how fired up his disease was or it would eat him for breakfast. "At the end of the day," he said, "I really consider how Jesus will help me change my conditioned responses." Everyone applauded.

For the first time since rehab, I raised my hand to speak in a meeting. When the chairperson called on me, the Preacher stood up and told me to shut up and listen. "Take the cotton out of your ears and put it in your mouth," he said.

"Cotton?" I said. "Go fuck yourself."

"No cross talk. Not even for celebrities," someone said. People laughed.

The Preacher stood, picked up a candle and pointed it at me. Wax dripped down his knuckles and onto the floor. He said, "You don't have anything worth sharing until you have a year clean, or have finished your fifth step."

The chairperson, Dick, stroked his moustache and said, "Ed, sit the fuck down and let the kid talk, you fucking bully."

The Preacher sat down.

"So, I'm a writer," I said and poured candle wax on the table. "An artist. So how can I conform to this regimented line of bullshit? I read all the literature when I was in inpatient, and there's no mention of Jesus, or half the shit you assholes talk about. I've been clean from amphetamines and other street narcotics for about two months and meetings just make it worse."

The Preacher stood and said, "First of all, I'm Ed and Christ has cured my addiction to drugs, alcohol, processed sugar, and pornography."

"Ed," Dick said, "please, leave Jesus out of it and keep your comments to drugs and alcohol. Oh, and sit the fuck down."

Ed ignored him. He said, "Keeping addicts from finding Christ is as bad as dealing heroin."

I said, "Fuck off, asshole."

The Preacher walked over to my table, he stood over me. "You're going to die. You will never recover. You lack the honesty, open-mindedness, and willingness. HOW!" The Preacher turned and addressed the room. Chants of "HOW, HOW, HOW" rose from his followers.

I would've left, but Dick had my signature sheet.

The Preacher's voice grew louder as he spoke. "The problem with the fellowship is the way y'all," he said, waving a hand across the room, "have strayed from the Christian principles on which the Twelve Steps were founded. Principles that have been cast aside by the weak-minded. Salvation will not come by the hands of man, and the righteous shall rejoice when he seeth the vengeance: he shall wash his feet in the blood of the wicked."[42]

He walked right up to Dick as he spoke. Through the small window on the side door, I noticed the blinking light of a cell phone camera and turned away.

The Preacher raised his arms as he spoke, "We need to do God's work if we wish to see the glory of a sin-free existence. Jesus will conquer my addiction in whatever form it takes. Whether it's liquor, crack-cocaine, pornography or cake. I pass."

Dick said, "Sit the fuck down, Ed."

Shadows cut into the dirty walls. Candlelight flashed around the coffee pots. The Preacher went back to his seat and closed his eyes. An awful smile crossed his face as he put his palms together in prayer. All but a handful of people sitting near Dick looked at the Preacher wide-eyed and clapped. Clapping quickly grew into shouting and chanting and wild applause. As if this man would answer all their prayers.

I stood and addressed the room. "Can't you see through this guy's bullshit?" The cheering drowned me out. At least Althea wasn't clapping. She got up and left out the side door.

Dick rang the bell several times before he could quiet the room. The meeting ended early. Everyone circled up for the Serenity Prayer, which I skipped.

Geoff had just shoved a reporter out of the lobby. "No cameras inside the club!" he yelled. "Can't you motherfuckers read the sign?"

Geoff spotted me and pulled me into the empty game room. "You got any more of those green pills?" he asked.

I told him I did, and we negotiated a Nedvedol deal that would finance my trip south. 2,000 pills at $3 a piece.

"I can only give you five hundred bucks up front," Geoff said.

I slid the cue ball down to the end of the pool table and watched it roll. I had no leverage and we both knew it. Without Tom willing to take anything in bulk, Geoff seemed like my best bet. I talked him into a thousand bucks up front, which would buy me a car in good enough shape to drive all the way to Georgia. The rest of the money, I'd get before I left.

"I don't feel good about this. I need the money by next Friday."

Geoff loosened his tie. "Already have buyers lined up. Next Friday. Five grand."

I placed a sealed 2,000-count bottle on the shitty green felt and took a stack of twenties from Geoff.

I counted it twice and we shook.

Back in the lobby Geoff was immediately occupied by a pair of young women hanging out by the check-in table. He handed them both his business card and started chatting them up. I went out for a smoke.

"No questions," I said to the lone reporter standing in the middle of the parking lot. He was rubbing his arms where Geoff had grabbed him. "No comment, no nothing."

Dick was at a picnic table near the entrance. He lit a cigarette and I sat next to him on the table, resting my feet on the bench. I was hoping to see Althea out there smoking, but she was long gone.

The reporter had started recording us on his phone but didn't ask any questions, and I figured this was a great time to show the public that I was interested in recovery, and therefore, when published, my memoir would be filled with the heartfelt agony of really trying hard to get clean. Struggling with it, failing occasionally.

"Hey," I said to Dick, "you've got time right?"

"Twenty years."

"Without Jesus?"

"Without Jesus."

We talked about the program for a while. Dick seemed all right. Honest at least, and willing to admit there was more out there than just the 12 Steps. Plenty of methods worked for other people, he just wasn't one of those people. Still, I remained skeptical of the whole thing.

"Why don't you get upset at that fucker? I mean really upset and fuck him up? You could take him." I tried to make a point of not looking at the reporter and his phone, of really engaging with Dick.

"People like him come and go." Dick looked like he'd been an offensive lineman in his day. He tossed his cigarette aside and lit another. He offered me one from his pack. I shook him off and lit my own.

Across the street the Preacher's followers were still picketing in front of the Gryphon's Den in anticipation of the grand opening. Bells chimed while the children joined together in a rendition of another generic Bible song that sounded vaguely like bad '80s rock. I thought they were too young to be up so late.

"Can I have my slip?"

Dick pulled the slip out of his pocket, signed it, and gave it to me. Then Dick looked at the reporter and said, "Those kids can't sing worth a shit."

·

After smoking another cigarette and eating three more Nedvedol, I went back inside with some time to kill before the midnight meeting and got my slip forged by the girl working in the kitchen. Soon I'd have enough legit signatures to justify missing a couple meetings. A 3-to-2, real-to-forged ratio seemed reasonable. I crossed the lobby into the game room to play some pinball. The silver ball bounced beneath the Plexiglas of the *Werewolf Hunter! Pinball Experience!*, and I thought about getting clean.

Most great writers have substance abuse issues, I thought, and I want to be a great writer. Getting clean might hinder me.

I banged the flippers and shot the ball into the werewolves' hideout in the abandoned warehouse, setting off a series of red lights and mechanical howls. "You've got him cornered, go for the silver bullet!" the machine said.

I thought: if clean means hanging out with these assholes I'll take my chemical maintenance program. No meth. That's my only rule. As long as I don't do meth, I'm fine.

Playing three balls at a time now, I had a shot at the high score, but the right flipper stuck and my balls fell into the Wolf's Den.

"Goddamn Lycan!" I banged on the machine. A drastic series of blinking lights and zapping sounds told me to try again. From behind the snack bar, the cook yelled last call for coffee and the kitchen went dark. A large van made an illegal turn into the parking lot. The headlights hit the windows and the glare made the woman behind the counter look like a demon. I dropped my stack of quarters and one went rolling under the Pop-a-Shot machine on the other side of the game room.

I crawled after my quarter. From my spot under the Pop-a-Shot game, I heard the Preacher in the lounge. "The meeting starts in five minutes. We have lives to save!"

Listening to him order those poor fucks around, the hatred in his voice, I was tempted to spend the rest of the night there on the floor in the relative safety of my alcove until I saw the bottom of a faded blue dress swishing toward me.

"Jacky?" I said to a pair of knees.

Jacky ducked down to my level. "Ronald Reagan?"

We sat on the dirty floor and kissed each other like it might be the last time.

"Your hair." She touched it, frowning as she rubbed her fingers together.

"Your eyes," I said. Her irises were outlined in sleepless red. So wide and wet you could fall in and drown. She smiled, and I realized I'd undersold how much I missed her.

My signature list crinkled in my back pocket. Jacky scooted backward out from under the Pop-a-Shot game and stood. I crawled toward her. Jacky pulled me up and the bottles of pills rattled around in my backpack.

"I wrote letters," I said.

"Your lawyer gave them to me. I still have them. I wasn't allowed to write, but I watched you on the internet." Jacky told me she had stayed at her aunt's place while she waited for a room to open up at some fancy rehab in Florida where she spent a month before she was released to a halfway house in Greensboro.

"I'll be out soon," she said. "You're not doing so good, are you?"

"What do you mean?"

A truck rumbled past. The windows shook, and Jacky looked out toward the highway. "Did you fuck your counselor?" Her hair was a wild wavy mess. A thick piece of faded blue ribbon wrapped around her forehead caught the light from the Pac-Man game and shimmered like a river.

"I've done things I'm not proud of." I stared at that ribbon. "But I did not fuck my counselor."

She backed away, skeptical.

"Meet me somewhere to talk," I said, "away from all these people."

"I don't know," she said.

I followed her out of the game room and through the lounge. Above us, the TV showed coverage of the murders. Pictures of dead addicts from *Clean Time* hung there, suspended over the entrance to the meeting room.

"Please," I said.

Haley laughed on the screen.

"Alright," Jacky said. "I'll meet you at the diner, later tonight. I can sneak out and get there by two." She shouldered open the door. "You coming in?"

"I've had enough for tonight," I said. "See you around two."

THE INFINITY DINER

In a booth by the window Jacky and I talked until almost four in the morning, reliving the last eighteen months and all that had happened since we'd been separated. Bittersweet is an overused term, but I can't think of a better one. Going into it, I prepared myself for the worst. For her to say, "I'm sorry, but I've changed," or something like that. Maybe it would have been easier if there was no spark. If Jacky had just said she needed to stay out of relationships and get clean, take some time to work on herself, or whatever, I could've dealt with that. But that's not how it went. We were like high school kids, sitting in that diner crushing pot after pot of coffee, playing songs on the little jukebox stuck in the wall above the condiments.

"I don't know how you could stand being on TV," she said. "All that attention."

"I guess you get used to it."

"They're going to start a spinoff show at my halfway house at the end of next month," she said. "On Halloween. Thank God I'll be out before then."

Last Halloween, me and Jacky got high, tried to fuck, and spent hours nervously talking about where we could go out for music and dancing. Eventually we just stayed in and fed meth to a line of costumed freaks that rotated in and out of the living room, and handed out candy to trick-or-treaters.

"I'm leaving soon," I said. "For Georgia, like we planned. I just have to meet White Reggie and get some pants."

"Pants?" she waved to the waiter to bring us our check. The couple sitting across the aisle were recording us with their phones. "You sure you're clean? You're not making sense."

"Come with me. I'm leaving in less than a week."

"I don't know."

"I'll never stay clean here."

"I better get back to the house," Jacky said, and got up to leave. "Let me think about it."

"I'll take it."

Jacky laughed. "You better because that's all I have to give right now."

AMENDS

For five straight nights, Jacky snuck out of the halfway house and I met her in Greensboro. With nowhere else to go, we walked around the public golf course in the dark, away from the cops and the cameras. We left tracks in the dew on the greens and lay next to each other on the cusp of a sand trap, watching the stars. She wouldn't commit to leaving. I didn't want to push the issue. Her company was enough. But as Reggie's reading drew near, and the prospect of leaving together or apart loomed, I got anxious.

The night before the reading, we were walking down the fifth fairway when I brought it up again.

"Are you going to stay in Georgia permanently?" she asked.

"I need to reset," I said, and looked around for a place to sit. I had no intentions of returning, but if Jacky was hesitant to leave Booth for good, I didn't want to be so absolute in how I explained my plans. "I'll need at least a month away from here." If I could convince her to come initially, I figured she'd decide to stay down there with me.

"Won't they just follow you?"

"Maybe," I said. "But no one knows where it is. No one followed me here, right? If we left right now, we'd be in the clear."

We sat in the rough by a water hazard. I tossed a stick at the pond and sent the reflection of the moon spooling out toward the banks.

"I don't know, Ronald Reagan. I'll be out of the house soon. All my connections are in Booth."

I lay back on the grass, propping my head up with my backpack. "We can start over."

"Stop by the house on your way out of town," she said. "I'll either come with you or say goodbye." Jacky rested her head on my chest, put her arm around my waist.

I wondered what could possibly happen in a day to make her change her mind. My heart sped up. An intense urge to do something, to take some kind of action, welled up in my gut. I wasn't sure if I was about to scream at Jacky to make up her fucking mind or start begging when she got on top of me and kissed my neck. Jacky reached back for my belt and hiked up her dress, and I was certain this was either her way of assuring me things would be okay, or her way of saying goodbye, but I couldn't figure out which.

•

When I wasn't with Jacky, I was making arrangements to get the hell out of Booth.

Cindy set me up with a car for nine hundred bucks. She said she'd have it waiting for me at her sister's place by the Park 'N Ride. "I'll leave the keys under the grill in the back yard," she said. "If I can't make it to the reading, make sure you say goodbye before you go." I promised her I would.

Althea made herself scarce around the hotel room, and I didn't know how I felt about it. Kevin and Cindy were on the outs, and Althea didn't waste any time making her move. My heart was set on Jacky, but I still felt like an asshole for being theoretically passed over for a guy on Antabuse who had just moved out of a halfway house and back into a college dorm.

When I had time, I went to meetings and racked up ten signatures. I even put together a couple days without pot or alcohol. Geoff had threatened so many reporters that the media pretty much stayed off Alano property altogether. Meetings wiped me out, so I also watched a lot of *Clean Time* on the motel TV using a prepaid credit card Cindy hooked me up with. Gasman was still holding on in the ratings. It surreal, how I watched Maggie roam Booth in search of me, bouncing between my house and Sophie's. Only blind luck and serendipity kept me from getting caught and brought back to rehab or taken into custody.[43]

The morning of the reading, I woke up early and went over to Mooch's place to apologize for the fight we got into before I was arrested. He'd been living in one of Tom Canada's buildings out near the Greyhound station, running errands for Tom when he wasn't coaching JV football at Prep. I hadn't seen him since the night I was arrested, and I wanted to make things right with him before I left town. The 12 Steps were probably bullshit, but making amends made sense to me. Mooch and I had a history, and it wasn't all bad.

When I opened Mooch's door, I knocked over a Gatorade bottle full of piss. "Careful," he said.

"My bad."

Cigarette butts in old takeout containers, burnt spoons and candles by the bed. It smelled like body odor and rot. Mooch sat under the window, his cigarette ash growing long before it fell to the floor like snow.

There was nowhere to sit, so I stood by his bed, fumbling with my words, unsure how to segue into the amends, terrified he wouldn't accept my apology.

"Listen, I want to make things right. I fucked up that night. None of that should have happened." I said. "For your face, I'm sorry." A framed copy of the picture of Mooch and the Prep Pirate hung on his wall. "How can I make it right?"

Mooch stood, scratched his cheek. "Know what they're going to do, Ronald Reagan?"

"No, who's *they*?"

"Halftime of the Columbus Day Weekend game. For the tenth anniversary of our championship team, I have to be a part of the ceremony. Then I have to deal with Justin's mother. The team is retiring his jersey and she's giving a speech at halftime. You know what it's like to be bred to play sports, and then you can't anymore and you just don't know what to do?" Mooch lit another cigarette. "But at least I've got a roof over my head. Some people don't and I'm not doing that bad, but I thought you might get it."

"I get it," I said, and it worried me how much I had in common with Mooch, a junkie surrounded by home enema kits and bottles of his own piss. It made sense, the whole scene, wanting to just check out, and I told him so, kind of rambled it to him because I didn't like to think or talk about myself with such honesty. When I realized Mooch was passed out, and I had no idea how much he heard of my response, I decided it didn't matter.

THE GARDEN

After I left Mooch's place, with a few hours to spare, I lost the cameras and made it to Screwdrivers to prepare for the reading. I was careful not to get too drunk as I revised a story I'd written in my jail journal about the last time me and Jacky went into the city to get meth. Before everything went to shit. I wanted to look good for Sophie, so I read it out loud until I almost had it memorized. Though I thought the idea was stupid at first, this reading would be a good opportunity to show the public I wasn't just some asshole who did a bunch of drugs and wound up on TV. My memoir would hold much more credibility if people thought of me as an actual writer.

If everything went well, I'd put on a solid performance, get the pants from Reggie and the beginning of my memoir from Sophie. Then I'd settle up with Tom, collect the rest of my money from Geoff, and finally get the fuck out of Booth—hopefully with Jacky. I felt good. It was almost as if I'd planned it this way.

•

The reading was held in a giant garden hidden behind an old textile factory that had been repurposed into lofts. To get to the garden you had to walk through the Communal Art Space on the first floor. I grabbed a can of Pabst from a clawfoot bathtub full of ice and made my way back, looking for White Reggie and Sophie or any friendly face. Fake lanterns were strung up on clotheslines along the fence around the garden. There was a lonely chair and a mic in front of a camera set up on the stage. Guys with aggressive beards and side-ponytails sipped from cans of cheap beer and hit on women covered in tattoos. Silver ribbons and wristbands were worn in unironic solidarity with the victims' families. A pack of crustpunks threw a hatchet at a bullseye painted on an old oak tree. There was so much space. I wanted to lay down in the grass with my beer and listen to the punk music playing over the PA. I was about to do just that when Reggie found me. After excessive hugging and pleasantries and introductions to a bunch of other poets, he took me inside to get the pants.

I stopped by the tub again and grabbed a couple more beers. "Sophie coming?" I asked.

"Sorry, bro. She flaked last-minute. But she told me to tell you she'd meet you with your papers at this address." Reggie handed me a folded-up map of GSU campus with one of the dorms circled in purple ink, and a short note: *Staying here for the week. Media. Room 324. Stop by before you leave town.*

"Shit," I said. "What's the plan for the reading?"

"We probably won't start till nine. Let the place fill up a little."

"Right. Cool. Guess I'm early."

"No worries, brother. Once you've done a few hundred of these things you get the feel of it."

"Right," I said. "How'd you get this setup?"

"I got in before the developers. It's technically a private club. That Maggie chick was waiting outside earlier, but I told her she wasn't welcome. She left without too much hassle, actually."

"What about the rest of the press?"

"No press. We just live stream it, and let the internet do its work. Gives it a more DIY, grassroots feel."

I thanked Reggie and followed him upstairs.

"My studio." He opened the door to one of the lofts. There was a writing desk near the window overlooking the garden. On the opposite wall was a big mural of Bukowski's face painted on exposed brick, and a small stereo speaker playing the same obscure punk I'd heard outside. On the couches in the center of the room, Chaz Dorsey was engaged in deep conversation with four topless women covered in Day-Glo paint. They were circled around a fancy coke plate on the coffee table, sharing a plastic bottle of whiskey.

"Have a seat," Reggie said. "I'll grab the pants."

Chaz stood. "Ronald Reagan," he said. "So great to see you again. Odd to meet in this arena, but great!"

I stared at the coke and the women and there was so much coke. Mid-level-pop-star coke. I knew it'd be good.

"Hey Chaz," I said and shook his hand. "I'm just here for some business with Reggie. Sorry to interrupt." I still had his certificate in my backpack.

"Please, my brother, sit. Help yourself to the finest uncut we have here. Right off the boat."

I pretended to think about it, but I was fucked as soon as he offered. Me and Chaz made eye contact and understood that neither of us would say a word to anyone about what was going down right then. Two of the women made room and I sat between them and did a line. My face went numb and it felt fantastic. How could I have ever dreamed of giving this shit up?

"Not to be rude, but what's up with the paint?" I asked the blonde to my right.

"We're part of Chaz and Reggie's performance. Living Poetry. We each have a stanza written on our bodies."

They all looked about college age. The woman on my left handed me the bottle. "It's going on my CV. Plus we're getting paid. It's hard to find paying gigs as an artist," she said.

Reggie came out of the back with the pants. "I think it's really pushing the boundaries of genre and form. The female figure should be celebrated. Poetry should live and breathe as a form of self-expression for the underserved and underprivileged. Fuck the patriarchy!"

I nodded. Poetry never made sense to me.

Reggie and I settled up for the pants, and we bullshitted and blew lines until it was about time to get back to the guests. Reggie said I could stash my backpack and the jeans upstairs. I slid a pair on over my shorts for the reading and dropped a few pills into a cigarette cellophane so I'd have something to munch on. On the way out, I made sure Reggie double-checked the lock on the door. After we were all downstairs, I ran back up and checked it again.

The crowd in the garden was standing-room only by the time we got down there. Reggie emceed the event. We had a moment of silence for the recent victims of the Werewolf Killer, during which I chain smoked and drank Pabst and felt like a million bucks. This was going to be great. My debut performance in the Central North Carolina indie reading scene.

Reggie made a long rambling announcement about the upcoming protest to be held during the Columbus Day parade and how important it was that we all stood in unity. He pointed out Cindy in the crowd, acknowledged her efforts in organizing the protest, and plugged some of her other projects. I walked over and sat with Cindy on a bench made out of halved logs, next to two women who talked shit about Reggie in half-whispers, smoking cigs as fast as I did. They were the first two readers on the bill and were both good. While they read, the crowd grew.

A third guy read a story about fucking and liquor that didn't make any sense. Then it was my turn. I got on stage, steadied myself, and read my story.[44] It went okay. Lots of cheers as I stepped off the stage, but I wondered whether they actually thought I was good, or if they just applauded because I'd been on TV. Did any of these hipster assholes even watch TV? Probably ironically. Or if they did, they wouldn't cop to it. What if they thought I was only asked to read because I was on TV and that I wasn't that good, but were cheering because they thought *I* was being ironic and non-sincere? I crunched a Nedvedol to calm down and tried to enjoy the rest of the reading.

Chaz and Reggie took the stage. Chaz played a single drum, keeping the beat while Reggie read his poem and the women from upstairs stripped down and stood in a line. They stepped forward when their respective stanzas were read.

"Lonny's, Curbside, 1AM"[45]

I was coming off my shift
Four tens at the garden
Sweat drenched, t-shirt stretched,
Reeking of stale Pall Mall Reds
Badly
in need of a drink.

Old Lonny's place
Down by the train yard
Pulsed "Coors" in blue neon
– Hopeful as a vacancy sign,
humming like the promise of cool water
in a far off mirage
or the legs of a girl just a little too far gone.

On the curb out front
I nearly tripped over a girl
Legs outstretched, mini skirt riding up.
Her dog on the ground.
Scrappy.
He had mange all around his ears.
The girl was scrappy too,
Looked like she'd seen some things
Looked like she could show me a few more.

Why do the pretty ones always slouch?
"Bad day, honey?"
She rolled her eyes up and lifted her chin
her red rimmed mouth, a perfect gaping 'O'
"Cigarette?" I held the pack out.
"I don't smoke. It's bad for you."
I dropped a cigarette on the ground
just in case.

Almost everyone cheered. Cindy and the other two writers lit cigarettes and looked disinterested.

After that, Chaz played a set that included a bunch of cover songs, and actually didn't sound that bad. Halfway through Chaz's performance, Cindy wanted to leave. I figured I'd walk her part of the way home before splitting off to see Sophie.

"Just have to grab my stuff," I told her. I found Reggie and we walked upstairs to get my backpack and pants. He offered me another line and a joint for the walk, both of which I accepted. He was ecstatic about the reading.

"You should stay and chill for a bit, brother," he said.

"I gotta run," I said. "Next time."

"Next time, brother. You're always welcome at The Garden."

Me and Cindy smoked the joint on the way to Sophie's and talked about art, and I started thinking I could stick around for a while if my life would be full of nights like this. Past the vigil, we cut through campus, turned a corner, and were greeted by a horde of media and the Booth police department. Yellow tape roped off another crime scene. I couldn't see the body. We stood still, like idiots, pot smoke swirling into the air.

One of the cops turned around suddenly, nose pointed skyward like a hunting dog, before looking down and settling on me and Cindy. He tapped his buddy cop on the shoulder and now they were both staring at us.

"Run," Cindy said.

I tried to make a break for it, but I was tackled, pepper sprayed, and thrown in the back of a squad car.

BACK IN JAIL

I called the Layover repeatedly until I got ahold of Althea. I asked her to find Geoff and get the money he owed me to pay for my bail. She refused. She sounded fucked up, talking fast about Kevin's ankle bracelet coming off and how Cindy needed her help with the musical score for her play. I hung up on Althea mid-sentence and called my attorney.

I waited almost forty hours in the holding cell before they moved me back to the interrogation room, where Pete was sitting in front of his open briefcase, flipping through a manila folder. The guards chained me to the chair across from him.[46]

"You believe she wouldn't bail me out?"

"We've got bigger problems." Pete took a long drink from a bottle of water and set it down beside his briefcase.

"What's the strategy? I'm not ratting anyone out."

Pete slid a sheet of paper out of the folder. "Your counselor," he scanned the sheet, "Margaret Turner."

"Maggie."

"Right. Maggie spoke with the judge."

I closed my eyes and tapped my feet. "What did she say?"

"Maggie assured her that jail was not the best option." Pete rubbed his five o'clock shadow and returned to the document. His shirt was wrinkled and he smelled heavily of mouthwash and cigar smoke.

"What's in the folder?" I asked. "You look almost as bad as I do."

"Rough trip down. You won't have to rat anyone out. It's your file. They have you for possession of a controlled substance, which is one of many violations of your probation. But we were able to cut a deal. Maggie said the Nedvedol in your backpack was prescribed to you. She offered to sign your Wellness Certificate, which will negate your probation."

I looked up, then back at my feet. The interrogation room was freezing but my face was drenched in sweat. Drops of it fell on the table. "Can I have some water?"

Pete poured water down my throat. I gulped and let it drip over my cheeks.

"You're lucky the judge is a fan of yours," he said.

I licked my lips. "Thank God for that."

"You have to sign this form and pay a small fine." He slid the sheet across the table.

"What's the catch?"

"Read it. Sign it."

The form made no sense. I recognized the Philson & Jackson logo on the letterhead, but the words looked jumbled and random. "Give me the gist." My eyebrow itched something terrible, like a worm trying to crawl out of my face.

"You will be released into Maggie's care until she is satisfied you have met the conditions necessary for her to sign your certificate." Pete rubbed his temple. "Sign the form or you're going upstate for two years. To a prison without cute MFA students teaching you poetry."

Pete put a pen in my mouth, held the paper to his briefcase and the briefcase near my face. I used my teeth to scribble a signature.

"Maggie is waiting for you outside." Pete closed his briefcase and left.

QUEEN MARGARET

Maggie took me back to the First Lite Motel on the other side of Greensboro. The honeymoon suite was covered in stained faux-velvet. It felt like the inside of a casket.

A large mirror hung over the bed across from an equally large flat screen TV. The cameras were already set up: one above the mirror, one above the TV, and one on the ceiling over the bed.

"Would you like to play a game?" Maggie asked.

"No." I stood by the bed and tried not to touch anything.

"Once we get started, I'm sure you'll love it. It's a great game."

At the foot of the bed was a room service platter, stainless steel, with a white napkin draped over it. Neatly arranged on the napkin was a rig like a junkie's—spoon, lighter, syringe—also a small ceramic dish full of blue pills, a TV antenna, and a rubber mask that I think was supposed to be the Queen of England. An old Chaz Dorsey album played from a wireless speaker sitting on the desk.

"Can you take the cuffs off now?" I asked.

She picked up the antenna and whacked me on the leg. "You will address me as Queen Margaret."

"God. Fuck. Why?" I thought about running for it, then of my certificate and prison.

"Maggie, I'm not into this. You broke the skin."

She hit me again. "On the bed."

"Yes, Queen Margaret."

"I think some time in the hot tub would be wonderful. Wouldn't it, Ronald Reagan?" She pulled open a curtain that led to the bathroom. A Jacuzzi shaped like two doves bubbled and died when she tried to turn it on. "Well, this won't do."

Maggie changed out of her pantsuit and into a purple leather bustier that pushed up her tits and left her nipples exposed. She approached me in a forced kind of strut that made me feel sorry for her.

Maggie uncuffed me, only to re-cuff me to the bed. I stared up at a sculpture that looked like a bunch of gears but turned out to be the light fixture.

"This is going to be lovely. Don't you think?"

"No."

I was terrified and a little excited, like the first time I went to score coke. Maggie whacked me in the leg again, and the excitement left.

"Queen Margaret, it will be lovely!" Rivulets of blood from my calves stained the faded pink sheets.

She pulled off my shorts, tied my feet to the bed frame, and licked the back of my knee. "You have such nice legs, Mr. Middleton."

She knelt next to the bed and held out a handful of Nedvedol. "Here you go," Maggie said. "I have a whole bottle, along with the rest of your things. All in here with us. Safe." She nodded toward the corner of the room and my bag sitting on a paisley ottoman. "You want your Nedvedol, right?"

"Queen Margaret, yes I do." I ate the pills from her hand, slobbering on her as I licked them up. I hadn't taken any since my arrest and my thoughts felt scattered and slow.

"Do you know what Sildenafil Citrate is, Ronald Reagan? I bet you don't." Maggie walked over to the platter and smashed the blue pills in the ceramic bowl. "Viagra, Ronald Reagan. Blood pressure medication. Now it's sold for its side effects."

"Why are you doing this?"

"We never finished your therapy, and I want to make sure these sessions are more fulfilling. More effective. That's why I brought our blue friend here."

She dosed blue powder into the spoon and started cooking the Viagra. "And please, right now, it's Queen Margaret." She put on the queen mask.

"My wrists are bleeding."

Maggie walked toward me. Less than gently, she shot half the Viagra into my arm. "And some for the Queen." She pumped her fist a few times and emptied the rest of the needle's contents into the top of her left hand. Maggie returned the syringe to the tray and switched on the cameras. "My wearing this mask will help you identify the source of your reluctance to submit to authority figures. The antenna represents a mode of connecting with the viewing public. Quite an antique, isn't it?" Her breath felt warm on my legs as she crawled across the sheets. I stared into the dark eye sockets of the mask.

•

I can't be sure how long Maggie fucked me. It's all a blur, but I know she stopped once in the middle to shower and shoot me up again. The whole time she narrated how the sex would allow me to practice acceptance and better understand powerlessness. The entire thing was streamed live on The Recovery Channel's website, which had been playing on the flat screen at the foot of the bed the whole time. If I looked up at it, I got that weird TV-in-TV effect with the mirror behind the bed reflecting the TV that showed Maggie fucking me in front of the mirror. For a minute I believed the idiot on the screen was someone else, or me in a parallel universe, but the physical sensations were too intense to ignore and, with the slight TV delay, it started to seem as if I felt everything twice.[47]

•

When it was all over, Maggie and I walked out into the lobby and she signed my certificate as promised.

"Would you like me to frame it for you?"

"Just fax it," I said.

"I'm happy to. And congratulations on completing this big step in your recovery." She walked over to the concierge, who took the certificate and faxed it to the county office. Maggie touched my arm. "I'd also like to thank you," she said. "Our ratings have never been higher. Your escape has helped so many people learn about the dangers of addiction. You're a star. A hero, really."

The concierge brought the confirmation slip back and I studied it closely to make sure the certificate had been faxed to the appropriate authorities.

Maggie thanked the guy behind the counter and offered me a ride. "Where do you want to go, Ronald Reagan? I'll take you anywhere you want."

"I need a meeting," I said. One more signature and my debt to the state of North Carolina and Guilford County would be paid in full. Forging the last signature felt cheap, and fuck, right then, I figured a meeting might do me some good.

"See, it worked, didn't it? You're much more in touch with your disease now."

"Forget it, take me to Screwdrivers," I said.

"I know of a meeting this afternoon," Maggie said. "It's not in the book, but someone there will sign your slip."

"Fine." I was sick of the Alano Club anyway. I didn't want to see anyone I knew.

I leaned my head against the window of Maggie's Prius as she drove through Booth. Maggie occasionally tried to start up conversation, but I just stared at the passing scenery. I thought about last December and all that optimism, when my life was finally looking up. We drove past the J$F factory by the 33/77 bypass, past Prep's campus, the Poseidon statue by Guilford State, and kept driving until we hit Rural Route 404. We crossed the bridge, passed Justin's old house, and kept going for another ten minutes, twisting and turning along the hilly backroads until we came to a giant church that was half McMansion, half Astrodome. A building I'd never seen before. A cross covered in LED lights lit up the massive yard. I half expected Jesus Christ himself to beam down from heaven and sit on top of that fucking thing as we drove up the winding driveway to the church-mansion, where a group of the Preacher's followers were outside smoking.

As the car idled, Maggie fixed my hair and helped pencil in my eyebrow. She straightened my collar, gave me a kiss goodbye, and I hopped out with my stuff. I wore only my sleeveless blazer and torn gym shorts.

I went inside, and of course the meeting was run by the Preacher. His followers sat around in a circle while their children waited in the next room singing hymns. Everyone had on a white t-shirt with character defects listed on the front. "Lazy," "Masturbates too much," "Self-centered," "Gluttonous," "Judgmental."

A hand grabbed my shoulder from behind. I turned and this kid was staring at me, trying to look concerned, wearing a shirt that said "Slothful."

"Listen," the kid said, "you gotta get your mind in the right place. You'll never make it."

"Get your hands off me and sign this." I handed him my signature sheet. The kid retreated and I yelled after him, "I'm not the slothful one!"

I turned back toward the circle and came face to face with the Preacher, who smacked me. "You will die and rot in hell and there's nothing anyone can do to save you if you don't submit to Christ and the Twelve Steps."

I wanted to fight, fight any and all of them, but I was outnumbered twenty-to-one. They had the home-field advantage. I settled down into the circle.

Slothful looked flush, leaning and panting in the doorway. He wiped his face with his shirt, a cigarette burn in the cup of the U, and sat down next to me. "I'm sorry for putting myself in a situation that caused you such anger," he said.

"Go fuck yourself," I said.

The Preacher scowled and led the group in a prayer I'd never heard before. He looked feverish standing in the middle of the circle. The meeting began and the Preacher listed off the rules. His face coiled and puffed when he spoke, "If you want the Lord in your life you have to remove the man-made obstacles that bind you to your former lifestyle. You will wear your hat correctly, remove all piercings, and change your vocabulary." He pointed at me. "Your dyed hair, makeup, your lack of sleeves and appropriate pants. Your celebrity does not give you the power to walk above your fellows."

"How many times do I have to say it, the makeup is functional, not cosmetic. And who are you to judge me?" I stood and got in his face, close enough to smell his minty breath through his perfect teeth. "Most people relapse," I said, "I'm working on it. And it's not my fault I'm famous."

The Preacher continued: "My followers don't use the terminology of the sick. Relapse is not in our vocabulary."

"Does this meeting even count? Why does it say Homosexual Tendencies on his shirt?" I pointed at the bald man across from me.

"Members of God's Church of the Carolinas are required to point out the flaws in each other which they cannot see themselves and these flaws are reinforced with black marker on white fabric."

"I'm done here. Fuck this, fuck you. Profanity: got that one? Profane. Whatever. Suck my fucking dick, motherfucker."

As I walked out into the foyer, I felt a yank on my collar. Then the group pounced. The Preacher said, "You didn't ask permission to pass through that threshold." They held me down and beat me till I stopped struggling. Magic marker ripped through my chest hair. I lay on the floor covering my balls with one hand and my face with the other. I thought about screaming, but realized there was no one within earshot who could help me. At least they signed my slip.

·

It was well past dark by the time I made it back to the Layover. Cindy's room was empty. The bathroom didn't smell like vomit for once. I thought about how I could get even with the Preacher, but I was too tired to come up with a good plan. My brain was fried.

Looking back on it, I probably should have just left town then. I had my signatures and my certificate. Legally I was in the clear, but I couldn't do it. I told myself I had accomplished something important, finished rehab, and was on my way to getting clean. If I could do this, I should keep with my plan, see it all the way to the end.

I drank a couple beers and watched The Weather Channel and flirted with sleep. I went in and out of this dream where I was in Georgia with Jacky. The two of us in that little house. I sat in the living room and wrote while she played Justin's piano, and it was beautiful. She was a virtuoso. We lived our lives, smoking pot but keeping off the hard stuff. We walked along the quiet Georgia beach in the morning before heading off to our honest jobs—I was a minor league third base coach, and Jacky taught piano lessons. Our lives were boring, we agreed, but we were adjusting. Together, we could make it work. I'd never been more certain of anything.

NEGOTIATING

The next day, I banged through the doors at Screwdrivers with the last of the jeans I owed Tom and the last of the signatures I owed the state. The afternoon crowd was unsettling, sagging lonely pockets of faded flannel shirts and middle-aged women dressed like teenagers, everyone clouded in cigarette smoke.

I nodded hello when I saw Althea sitting at the far end of the bar, trimming the filters off her cigarettes with the knife Kevin used to cut limes. She nodded back. That was our dynamic now, no cameras or games. I was about to buy a drink when I noticed the stuffed owl next to Kevin's tip jar. A sign had been stapled to its wing that said, in Althea's handwriting, "Tip if you give a hoot!"

"I gave you that owl," I said.

Althea said, "Who gives a grown woman a stuffed animal?" and it hurt more than it should've.

Kevin was staring at a drink recipe card. He looked up briefly when he heard me order a whiskey and a High Life, and he tucked the drink card into his pants. "Comin' right up," he said. "On the house, buddy."

When Kevin brought my drinks, Althea pulled Kevin across the bar and kissed him recklessly. I downed my shot, left them locked at the face, and took the jeans and my free beer into Tom's office.

Tom was sitting with his feet up, engrossed in high school football highlights playing on one of the TV screens. He straightened up when I approached with the jeans. On his desk, I placed ten pairs of J$F Acid Washed Skinny Dungarees of various color. I set my beer down and lit a joint with his dragon lighter. The flame singed my hair.

"I don't need my certificate anymore. Taken care of. Those jeans are a good faith offering. For my ID and the use of your fax machine. I need to get the fuck out of here."

Tom nodded at the fax machine, granting me access. I walked over and faxed the last of my signatures to the state.

"My hologram guy is still backed up," he said. "But it'll be here before Columbus Day."

"This is bullshit. Why don't I keep these jeans until you get me my ID." I waved the joint for emphasis before I passed it to Tom.

Tom said, "Why don't I call the cops and give them an anonymous tip about your deal with Geoff? I could have them waiting at the Gryphon's Den, or I could have them pick you up right outside the Layover when you go back there. Better yet, I could call some friends of mine and have them pick you up."[48]

"Alright, alright, I get it," I said and finished my beer in one gulp.

Tom handed me the joint and tended to an incoming fax. Smoke hung in the air between us. The machine made that screeching bumblebee sound, and I swear it was coming from the Pirate. I swear that goddamn Cyclops winked at me. I covered my ears, closed my eyes. There was no way that picture was directing messages into my brain via the fax machine, I thought. No way, no way, no way. I took the last of the roach and hit it so hard I accidentally swallowed it.

The fax machine stopped and Tom pulled the fax from the bay and held it up. "Here you go, Ronald Reagan. You're officially off probation," Tom said, and handed me the return fax from the magistrate. "What are you going to do to celebrate?"

Something chimed in Tom's pocket and he pulled out his phone. He looked at the screen, then grabbed a remote from his desk and a TV I didn't know was there clicked on behind me.

A reporter was on screen, some national network, nearly blocked out by the words "Breaking News Alert."

"Henry 'Gasman' Reed, best known as Ronald Reagan Middleton's roommate on the hit show, *Clean Time*, was found sliced open and hammered to a railroad tie in Booth, North Carolina this morning. He was said to be searching for his counselor, Bruce, and Ronald Reagan Middleton, whom he considered friends and pillars of his recovery community. The following footage is graphic in nature."

I dropped my backpack.

Tom got another joint going.

The reporter seemed genuinely sad. She said Gasman took a Greyhound all the way from Jersey. When he got off in Booth he headed toward the Alano Club, which must have been the last place he saw me, on TV or the internet or whatever. The news cut to a clip from his last Serenity Cove confessional—"Bruce and Ronald Reagan are the only people who understand me," he said, scratching at his hair plugs—before cutting to footage of the murder.

If I had to pinpoint where everything started to really go wrong for me, it was when I watched Gasman die on TV. If I hadn't left rehab, he would still be alive. I thought about the bubbles floating out of his face in our room in Rose-Thorn, and how jealous I was that he actually wanted to get clean. Henry didn't deserve this. He was a genuine human being, and I'd never felt more like a fraud standing in that fucking office with a Cyclops, thinking about my fake ID and bullshit memoir. Suddenly none of that seemed to matter.

The camera picked up Henry walking past the abandoned houses by the 33/77 bypass, across the construction site a couple miles from the Alano Club. He was a scrawny figure carrying a duffle bag through whorls of muted light.

"This is fucked up," I said. "No way they show him getting killed on TV." I didn't look away. Maybe they got it wrong. Maybe he escaped.

Tom said, "I'm sorry," and passed the joint.

I held back tears and kept watching. "Who the fuck is filming this?"

The shadow of the killer appeared behind Henry and followed him at a distance. The camera zoomed in. Henry tripped on a bag of cement. The picture jittered as the cameraman brought Henry into focus, the lights from Route 77 edging close enough to reflect off the ointment glazed around the spot where his lips should have been. The air in my lungs went stale. I felt my head drift behind me and up, watching myself watching Henry and knowing how it would end, but still hoping I was wrong.

Now there was another camera and a reporter in the shot. Henry screamed, startled by the sudden light of the news crew, but unaware of the killer at his heels. He began to run toward the camera. Maybe he thought it was Steve. He held his side like it hurt but he kept moving until he stood before them, his face glowing in the camera's bright light. That's when the black figure swooped in from outside the frame, wearing a wolf mask and holding a knife the size of a Cadillac, and Henry's neck was slit and he was gone. Swallowed up and dragged into the ally between abandoned houses.

"His body was found behind the Gryphon's Den," the reporter said. "Similar to the latest victim on the hit show *Werewolf Hunter!*, in which the serial killer murders the lead detective's high school friend and nails him to a cross behind the fictitious strip club featured in the show."

Mercifully, Tom turned off the TV.

"They just filmed him," I said, "They could have done something."

The Cyclops glowed beneath the Löwenbräu sign. It flinched at me, smiled wide, and I picked up my bag and hurried back into the bar full of living breathing people.

THE SHOW

Out toward the edge of town, buildings sagged around vacant lots and trashcan fires and walking past it felt like I was about to be chewed up by a giant mouth full of rotten teeth. Down the road was the Gryphon's Den, where Geoff was supposed to be waiting.

Above the front entrance to the Gryphon's Den was a big neon sign bent into the outline of a naked lady riding a winged lion under a rainbow. I walked around back and sat on a milk crate and picked at the hole in my shorts. Almost five grand Geoff owed me. I considered this figure and a number of other things while I threw rocks into the gully and listened to cars whip by on the overpass.

Geoff showed up two hours late with "Hollywood Nights" blaring from his pickup. Since I started dealing with Geoff, I heard so much goddamn Bob Seger it made me suicidal. If I could, I would punch Bob Seger right in the balls.

The crate cracked when I stood. "Took you long enough," I said, and waited for Geoff to open the back entrance. The air inside was thick with the smell of fresh paint and pot smoke. In the center of the room, a crooked wire rack held two Penthouse back-issues and a bottle of lube. There was a bar set up in the corner, the kind you'd see in a frat house basement. My sneakers squeaked over red linoleum as I followed Geoff to the register, where he handed me a paper bag full of small bills and a stack of play money.

"What the fuck is this, Geoff? You owe me like five grand."

"Best I can do right now is eight hundred and seventy-five bucks and some coupons."

"What am I supposed to do with these coupons?"

"They're as good as money," he said. "Tonight's the soft opening." He gave me a flyer and a VIP pass.

The cheap lighting made the walls glow red and gave Geoff's white suit a pinkish hue. I started to sweat. "I'll have cameras all over this place if you don't get me my money." I said.

Geoff walked over to the bar and filled two plastic cups full of whiskey. "Listen," he said. "Relax. The boss will be here soon. I can pay you then. Why don't you head back and watch the show while you wait?"

I took a plastic cup from Geoff and downed the whiskey. "Fuck it," I said. "What's another hour."

"There you go. Have a beer. Use some of those coupons." He handed me a Busch pounder. "Second door on the right," he said. "Enjoy the show."

There was no reason for the coupons to go to waste, I figured, and walked down the hallway. The door opened into a dark room the size of a closet. I took a seat in a leather chair, opened my beer and set it on the ground. To my right: a control panel with an illuminated bill slot and a stack of flyers listing the services available.

Coupons in one hand and my dick in the other, my life had devolved into a series of cramped rooms and two-way mirrors. I chose the Gryphon's Deluxxx option.

I tried to put all the coupons in the slot at once, but it only accepted one and spit out the rest. Rows of lights blinked to life above me. The front wall parted, slowly disappearing into the ceiling and floor. Behind the wall were two girls, one dressed as a mermaid, the other, as best as I could tell, had on a sexy-pilgrim outfit. They felt each other up for a while, then the pilgrim grabbed the pole out in the middle of the floor and spun around on it, and the mermaid walked into the closet-sized room with me. "You look like you could use some company," she said.

"I've had a rough week."

The mermaid put her hands on the back of the chair and pulled herself close. "I'll suck your cock for two hundred bucks. Four hundred to fuck," she said, before sticking her tongue in my ear.

The pilgrim looked at us upside down from between her legs, nodding her head to a twangy song about prison. It occurred to me that fucking both of these strippers at the same time might be a good chapter in my memoir. I picked up my beer and drank.

"I'm waiting for someone," I said.

The mermaid smiled and shrugged. I recognized her from the midnight meeting but couldn't remember her name. Under the colored lights she looked shot-out and vacant. She said, "We'll be here all night if you change your mind, sweetheart."

Then the lights started blinking and I thought about laying out under the night sky with Jacky, waiting for our eyes to adjust to the dark, dew soaking through my shirt. A sultry robot voice spoke through the speaker near the bill slot, asking for another coupon. The mermaid walked back toward her co-worker and the wall started to close. I fumbled with the stack of coupons and they scattered over the floor. When I finally slid one into the slot, the wall parted again. Mermaid and Pilgrim were really going at it, and I was so focused on the two of them, it took me a minute to recognize the third woman.

Jacky walked through the curtain on the far side of the room and out onto the stage. She wore a slinky blue dress with white lace and her hair was done up all fancy. She smiled at the two girls as she moved toward my booth. She was carrying something. From a distance, in the low light, it looked like a brick of coke in a paper bag, but when she got closer the proportions were wrong.

"What're you doing?"

"Working," she said.

"Jacky, what the fuck?"

Jacky looked high, but sounded sober. "Move over," she said, and squeezed in next to me.

"Let's leave together."

"I can't." She reached out and pushed the hair out of my face. She said, "Here's your money," and handed me the taped up brown paper bag. I stuffed it in my backpack without counting it, or even checking the contents. The lights started blinking again and the wall started to close.

"Please, Jacky. Come with me. You don't have to do this to yourself."

"Do what?"

"I don't know, hand jobs, lap dances, whatever Geoff has you doing." I took a long drink.

"You think I'm fucking truckers for pocket change?" she asked. "I own this place. Geoff works for me."

"You're high as fuck right now."

"*You're high as fuck right now.* I'm managing fine," she said, and I knew she was right. For now she was at least. And I hated myself for it, but I wished that she was in a bad spot, wished I could swoop in and save her, but I knew that would never happen. Jacky would never need me like that.

The wall closed all the way and we were sitting in the dark. With shaky hands I put another coupon in the slot. The wall parted and we had enough light to look each other in the eyes.

"We had a plan," I said.

"All the money we made," she said. "I invested it." Behind her, Mermaid and Pilgrim were spinning around in circles.

"In a truck stop strip joint?"

"Across from a recovery house, on a major throughway. It's the perfect location."

"What's with the get up?"

"Soft opening is tonight. I've got to schmooze. Sorry, honey." She'd never called me honey before. "Don't worry," she said, "I'll give you your cut. Ten percent, for the risk you assumed and the leg work. It might not seem like much, but you'll have passive income for years."

If we had just made it to Georgia that day, everything would've been fine. We'd be down there now, together. "Passive income? Fuck this. We had plans."

"You had plans."

I drank as fast as I could, crushed the empty can and let it drop under the chair.

Jacky said, "My girl up north is cooking Ghost again. I'm back in business."

"Why don't I stay and work for you?"

"That didn't work last time. I can't take that chance again," Jacky said.

"Jacky, I love you."

"I love you, too, but things are different. You're famous, and I can't have that kind of attention around me. It's bad for business," she said.

"Fame doesn't last," I said. "I love you."

"I could always meet you down there in a few months, after you get settled in. Come down for a week or something."

I didn't buy it, but I wanted to. Pilgrim and Mermaid were doing pirouettes on the dance floor. I held Jacky's hand. "Please, Jacky, leave with me. We'll get clean," I said.

"I can't," she said.

"What changed since last summer?"

"Nothing," she said, "I never planned to stay."

All of those sharp memories of us stabbed into me all at once, cut me open, the last year and a half spilling out in front of me. Jacky leaned in and kissed me, and I tried to hold on to the feeling so I could remember it later.

From a speaker near the bill slot, the sultry robot voice asked for money. "I have to go," Jacky said. She stepped out of the booth and walked back across the shimmering floor.

I sat there and watched the wall close around Jacky, kept watching until the lights in the booth went dark.

THE GIFT OF DESPERATION

It hadn't really hit me yet. Outside under the buzzing neon of the Gyrphon's Den, I didn't want to look back.[49] Whatever existed between me and Jacky was not only gone, but might not have even been there in the first place.

I stood just beyond a large group of the Preacher's followers. They held signs and sang violent hymns. Judging by the crowd forming at the Alano Club, a meeting was about to start. I lit a cigarette and waited for a break in traffic. For a second I considered blindly running across, thinking maybe I'd get lucky and a truck would hit me, but decided against it when I saw Althea break off from a circle of smokers and wander over to the light rail stop. I crossed at the light, and sat down next to her on a bench under the shelter.

Althea lit a joint.

"Nice night," I said, and it was. Unseasonably cool, the first bite of autumn on the leaves, one of those evenings you get in the late summer that make you glad you slept all day.

Althea said, "I miss my dog."

"Me too," I said, even though I never had a dog.

We watched the stars and the clouds shift while our hands steadied and our thoughts slowed.

"You think about getting clean ever?" she asked.

"All the time," I said.

"I mean really getting clean."

I picked at my nails. "Sure," I said.

"Kevin left."

"Fuck that guy anyway."

Althea passed the joint, and when our fingers touched I felt her shaking, the tiniest connection fighting to hold a current.

"This is it for me," she said.

"Really?" I thought about how many times Jacky and I had said that to each other. I inhaled deep and let Jacky float in my head for a minute.

Althea rubbed her arm. "We were so young. My friend, Leah, her and me shot up in my car and she turned blue. It's amazing how quickly you turn blue when you stop breathing." Althea slid the rubber band off her wrist and shot it onto the tracks. "I drove to the good part of the city and dropped her off, I thought, outside the ER, but it was an office building. It didn't hit me until later."

"Jesus," I said.

I was witnessing an actual epiphany and I resented Althea for it. I handed her the joint.

"Did she die?"

"It was a long time ago," Althea said.

For a while we sat in silence, twitching at the sound of the Preacher's followers singing across the street.

"I'm gonna go to the clinic," she said. "Get on a Nedvedol taper. I can work at the Humane Society until I go back to school. I'll take care of animals."

"Admitting you're powerless is the first step," I said, but what did I know.

We sat there waiting for the train, and I was sure before it got there she'd say "just one more night" and I'd say "yes." For us to go to some abandoned house, under the guise of summoning the spirit of her friend or something, and then Althea would end up killing herself somehow—overdose, or maybe fall down the stairs and break her neck, or just walk out into traffic like she was following some vision. Because that's how it would go, that's how it always goes when you say it's the last time. But none of that happened.

The approaching train doused us in light. We stood as it slowed to a stop, and Althea got on her tiptoes and kissed me on the cheek. She said goodbye and her braces sparkled as she stepped onto the car. The doors closed as she looked around for a place to sit.

As the train disappeared around the bend, all I could think about was that Geoff had meth, good meth from Jacky's connection, and I had a ton of money. Traffic whizzed by. The protesters in front of the strip club were calling to me with their song. It took every ounce of strength I had to walk back to the Alano Club.

I snuck into the meeting late and stood in the nook by the literature rack, waiting for a break in the discussion to take a seat. Candlelight filled the room. There were only a handful of normal people in there, badly outnumbered by the God's Church of the Carolinas folks. One of the Preacher's followers was condemning a new guy for drinking, screaming at this poor kid who just wanted to get his life together but couldn't admit he was an alcoholic. I was about to walk to the back of the room and sit when I recognized the Slothful kid from the megachurch. I thought about how badly they'd fucked me up out in the sticks. A few feet ahead to my right, the Preacher sat with his head bowed in prayer, guarding the oversized metal coffee urn that loomed behind him. I considered my options. My chest buzzed. I breathed deep, waited, and stayed in his blind spot. Carefully, I walked over to the urn and removed the top. For a passing moment I grew wistful for a time that hadn't yet happened, and might not ever. I picked up the silver urn and doused the Preacher with hot coffee. Then I smashed the pot over his head a few times, until it was dented, and tossed it out into the middle of the meeting room. I ran through the lounge and out the door, dodging traffic across the street. When I got to the Gryphon's Den, Geoff was out front checking IDs, a savior in his white suit.

•

I heard that the first draft of *On The Road* was written in one drug-fueled haze. In a similar manner, I have tried to recount everything that's happened in these notebooks, composed in various states of intoxication, in an unreasonable amount of time. But I'm tired. I can't work on this anymore.

In the moonlight I can barely make out Apollo among the hedges. I still have that discus tucked in my backpack. I've considered throwing it out the window at the beaten pantheon as a nod to the games the shrubs might play if they were to suddenly come alive, but something like that might be bad luck, like when Apollo's lover Hyacinth tried to impress him by catching the discus and was killed for it.

What would Odysseus have done, I wonder, if upon his return to Ithaca, Penelope had decided to buy a franchised strip club and become a pimp and a drug dealer?

Fuck it. Who cares? You know how the story goes.

After I fucked up the Preacher, I went to the Gryphon's Den, shoved a bunch of money at Geoff for some Ghost and here we are.

Thanks for watching.

PART FIVE

ODYSSEUS AND THE CYCLOPS

BRAVELY INTO THE CYCLOPS' LAIR

Though the previous scene appears to be the end of Ronald Reagan's story, there are more journal entries and an enormity of tape recordings that clearly follow this last entry, chronologically speaking. Unfortunately, most of these journal entries are incoherent, much of the tape garbled and distorted. To be frank, they sound like the rantings of a lunatic. This decline in the lucidity of his writing occurred when Ronald Reagan's methamphetamine use took a drastic turn for the worse. As his drug use escalated, his mental state deteriorated at an alarming rate. No longer concerned with composing a cohesive narrative, we're only given fragments to piece together the rest of the story. Below is one brief entry, relatively coherent, composed in what may have been a respite between meth purchases:

```
Deep down I think I knew we'd never be
together again after Justin died and
we got pulled off that bus, but I still
had hope. Without that hope, I didn't
know what to fucking do with myself.
I've never felt that kind of pain.
Heartbreak that physically hurt me,
heartbreak I couldn't just drink and
fuck away. I wanted it to stop hurting.
So I paid those two strippers to stay
with me for a long weekend at that fancy
hotel where Maggie fucked me and Bruce
held me captive, and we stayed there
for days getting high and partying with
```

strangers. We didn't see daylight. I
think we had fun but I don't remember
much. I'm going to get my ID soon. Geoff
said he'd meet me later with more Ghost.

Ronald Reagan was no doubt dejected from his loss of both Jacky and Althea. With his Georgia ID not yet ready, he had nowhere to go. Just as Odysseus was trapped in Polyphemus' cave, Ronald Reagan, as his condition deteriorated and his nerves grew increasingly frayed, became convinced that he was trapped in Booth.

I do not draw this parallel arbitrarily. It is clear from journal scraps and tape excerpts that Ronald Reagan, as he gave in to his addiction, descended into the world of myth he'd been creating with Dr. Blank, back in the "good old days" of undergrad when working on his play. Evidence of Ronald Reagan's less than sound mental state and renewed obsession with *The Odyssey* is made clear in the following partial list, which was found written on the back of a torn envelope and paper-clipped to one of his notebooks:

Revised Odyssey Parallels
- Sophie/my memoir = Penelope
- Reporters swooping around her = Suitors
- Bruce and/or Maggie = Head Suitor
  (If the head suitor falls, the rest will flee.)
- ? = Ithaca/home

In addition to this, the later journals are scrawled with drawings of massive floating eyes and several barely legible references to being "under the eye of the Cyclops" and "destroying the Cyclops." We know from previous, relatively sober entries that "Cyclops" equates to Guildford Prep's mascot, The Prep Pirate.

While the obvious, looming threat was undoubtedly the Werewolf Killer (a monster perhaps comparable to a minotaur), who was in the process of murdering the entire original cast of *Clean Time*, for Ronald Reagan, the biggest threat was the Pirate. The Prep Pirate came to embody the town's love of/addiction to high school athletics and the role that dependence played in trapping and eating its fans/addicts, so to speak. Booth is where Justin was killed, Jacky and Mooch succumbed to addiction, and Cindy lost her sister. Althea, it seems, is the only one of Ronald Reagan's friends—or shipmates, to continue the metaphor—who escapes. Ronald Reagan projects the blame for all of these deaths (both literal and figurative) onto the Pirate. It is not much of a stretch to believe that Ronald Reagan, in his altered state, would even see the Werewolf Killer as operating under the influence of the Pirate. So it is no wonder that his attempt to destroy the Cyclops (in the form of the Pirate in the form of Booth) came to fruition at the Guilford Prep Columbus Day Game.

One might assume from the final entry in Part Four that Ronald Reagan had given up on the goal of rescuing his memoir and escaping to Georgia. That his attack on the Cyclops (depicted below) was the result of blind, meth-addled rage. However, one must reckon with the near constant rolling of the tape recorder. Ronald Reagan, perhaps influenced by gonzo journalism, seems to have wanted to keep some record of what was happening during his bender. One must also explain why, if Ronald Reagan had given up, he bothered to visit Tom Canada to retrieve his Georgia ID. We are lucky to have clear (albeit crazed and grammatically confusing) audio from this encounter, in which Ronald Reagan appears to be narrating his own story out loud:

```
I stood in the shadow of the Cyclops. The
creature's glare penetrated my very being.
The fax machine carried the monster's
message loud and clear. I am going to
destroy you. You never should have come back
to Booth. Your soul is mine.
     When Tom reached over his desk and
handed me my fake Georgia driver's license,
I decided to take care of the Cyclops for
```

```
good. At that moment, it was clear I had
become Odysseus.
     I said to myself, "I will kill the
Cyclops. It's him or me. Destroying the
photograph will not satiate my vengeance.
I'm going for the monster Friday night. Then
I will scour Ithaca of the suitors on Sunday
and be free of this place."
```

Based on the length of this particular recording, we also know that Ronald Reagan went straight from Tom Canada's office to attack the Cyclops. We are even more fortunate to have a full accounting of this event, which appears to have been written either during a moment of clarity during Ronald Reagan's bender, or at a later date as he revised his manuscript. It is a scene that Bob and I have come to refer to as "Bravely into the Cyclops' Lair."

UNTITLED JOURNAL ENTRY

This morning I woke up under the fence by the pig farm near the jail. Confused by the pale blue sky and the disorienting stench of pig shit. I sat up and smoked a cigarette and tried to piece together Friday night.

From the other side of the fence a pig trotted over and nuzzled me while I smoked and looked around for my backpack, which I found covered in mud, two posts down next to a trash bag with the Cyclops head inside it.

Carrying these things, I limped down the access road to Rural Route 404, walking along the shoulder back to my writing den as the details of Friday night started to come back to me.

Columbus Day weekend game. Booth's Homecoming. The tenth anniversary of the Pirates' fourth straight title, a feat the school had not matched before or since Mooch graduated. During the second quarter, I left the stands and hid under the bleachers, where I mentally prepared myself.

At halftime the marching band played taps while they unveiled Justin's #1 jersey next to Mooch's #44 on the Guilford Prep Ring of Honor.

Mooch introduced Mrs. Haas, who would say a few words about her son, Justin, team manager for the Guilford Prep Pirates' all-time greatest team.

When the Cyclops walked out to midfield and stood between the podium and the purple-and-white-clad band, I pulled my thrift store ski mask from my pocket.

A frail short woman, Justin's mother wore a long purple skirt and a white blouse with big gold flowers scattered across it. Silver ribbon glinting under the lights. She stood behind the microphone affixed to a podium they wheeled in from the sidelines. The band stood at attention. Mrs. Haas cleared her throat and spoke about Justin's death at the hands of the Werewolf Killer. She talked about Justin taking-in Mooch and securing him a free ride to Prep. Words poured out in tearful reminiscence. She told the whole sob story about Justin having no friends, struggling to find his place in high school.

"He always said he was a one-man team, until he started managing for the Pirates."

Mrs. Haas collected herself. Mooch put his hand on her shoulder. The mascot bowed its bulbous foam head in reverence.

I moved to the front of the bleachers. How many of these people knew about all the uppers and painkillers Justin gave to the team? How many would care?

"Let us remember Justin and celebrate his life by being more kind to our team managers, and those students who might not be as gifted athletically as others."

I thought about Mooch's OxyContin habit and eventual heroin addiction, the rampant drug abuse among most of the high school athletes I knew. Justin perpetuated this cycle to make friends and got in way over his head. He was gutted for it.

I put on the ski mask.

Projected onto the tower in the south end zone behind Mrs. Haas: a highlight reel to the tune of "Like a Rock." On the highlight reel: Justin filling water bottles, gathering the team's laundry, cheering for the Pirates on the sidelines.

I slid under the railing and snuck up behind the chain crew, who, like the rest of the crowd, stoically fixed their gaze on Mrs. Haas as she buried her face in Mooch's broad chest, unable to watch the highlights.

Mooch leaned toward the microphone.

"Let's have a moment of silence."

Heads bowed. My chance.

I pivoted and grabbed one of the first down markers. Sweat pooled in my ski mask. I ran past the band. Using the yard marker as a lance, I charged the Cyclops and hit him in the eye. My nemesis momentarily stunned, I swiped the monster's legs and jumped on his chest.

Standing over him, I tore off his head. "You will never take my soul. Not this time. Not ever." I spoke quietly. "I'm Ronald Reagan fucking Middleton."

I held aloft the head triumphantly and broke for the opening between the tower and the bleachers. I was well on my way before anyone fully grasped the situation. The crowd might have thought it was part of the halftime show.

In vanquishing my foe I felt the wonderful sense of pride and relief that accompanies a grand act of self-preservation.

From the parking lot, I cut through the woods to avoid being followed or spotted on the open road. But I must have misjudged my latitude, because I came out of the forest by the old pig farm near the county jail. I leaned against the fence to rest and smoke a victory joint. I was all out of meth, and once again found myself among the pigs.

THE PARADE

Tormented by the image of the Guilford Prep Pirate and all that it represented to him, Ronald Reagan's only recourse was to eliminate his enemy. But this was not a random act of violence committed by a deranged meth addict. The defeat of the Cyclops was only one element of a larger premeditated plot, proof that Ronald Reagan had not given up. I would feel remiss in my duties as an educator and academic if I did not attempt to piece together the ending of our hero's story.

Out of necessity, I constructed the following scene using various found footage from the internet, security cameras, police reports, Ronald Reagan's recordings, and firsthand accounts from several witnesses.

Ronald Reagan waited behind a pile of pallets in the alley between a store that sold clothing for house cats and the old methadone clinic (which now dispenses Nedvedol). Drinking from a Pepsi bottle full of whiskey to settle his nerves, he prepared for battle. Mind and body readied for the upcoming tests of skill, strength, and intelligence. "Subversion," he said to himself. "Odysseus."

Sweat seeped into the lining of Ronald Reagan's blazer. He had duct-taped his notebooks around his torso like armor, tape recorder similarly secured to his chest. The Nedvedol had likely kicked in, bringing with it the faint allusion to LSD and speed, activating his serotonin receptors (effects we are now familiar with from the initial public trials); his brain focused solely on the task at hand. Due to the construction of the pirate head, his peripheral vision was limited, but he could hear the parade approaching. When the parade passed the alley, Ronald Reagan waited for the right moment and inserted himself into the group of citizens walking behind three floats, replicas of the boats on Columbus' journey to America.

Ronald Reagan's mask allowed him to assimilate reasonably well with the high school students dressed as sailors and Native Americans. Whiskey fumes swirled inside the oversized head and the smell of sweat grew oppressive. Ronald Reagan adjusted the mascot head and tried to befriend one of his fellow sailors. "Hello, good sir," he said. "I was late due to the inhibiting nature of my costume."

"I don't remember you from dress rehearsal."

"You'll remember me after this."

"What?"

"Whiskey?" Ronald Reagan held out the Pepsi bottle. A peace offering.

It is worth noting the Homeric parallels of this scene. In *The Odyssey*, Polyphemus drinks wine procured by Odysseus, allowing Odysseus to tie his men to the underside of the monster's sheep in order to escape. Perhaps Ronald Reagan's belief in wine (or other controlled substances) as a source of comfort also factored in to his plan.

Police, National Guardsmen, and reporters lined the streets. The vigil for the Werewolf Killer's victims had grown so large that it now spread past Sophie's house and around the corner. To make matters worse, thousands of protesters had traveled from all over the state to use the Booth Columbus Day parade as a platform for their message of anti-imperialism and disgust at the sexist, racist and classist policies enacted at the state and national level. The Preacher and his followers had also come out in droves to support the anti-anti-Columbus protesters. Overlapping chants for and against the celebration of Columbus grew louder and the air took on a surreal feeling as the parade neared Sophie's block.

"You sure you don't want a drink?" Ronald Reagan said.

"It's ten in the morning," the sailor replied.

"You're too good to drink my whiskey?"

The sailor moved quickly ahead of Ronald Reagan and climbed

onto the float in front of them.

The parade headed down Sophie's street, the final stretch of the route. Trailers and tents and news vans covered Sophie's front yard. Wires ran in thick bundles like veins over the trampled grass. A mass of reporters and television personalities waited and watched. Geoff Sanderson lurked across the street, handing out flyers for the Gryphon's Den. Bruce and Maggie wore headsets and paced on Sophie's front lawn, arguing over the best course of action; side-stepping the candles and pictures of murdered drug addicts that lined the sidewalk at the edge of the grass, it looked as though they were dancing as their discussion grew more animated.

From the midst of the protesters, Cindy and her students lit flares and hurled them at the police officers. Unable to distinguish the source of the smoke, police turned their batons on the Preacher's followers, who in turn attacked the college students holding pro-Native American placards, some of which compared Christopher Columbus to the Werewolf Killer.

Ronald Reagan diverged from the parade as it passed Sophie's house.

Adjusting the pirate head, he charged the media on Sophie's lawn. While removing the stolen discus from his pants, he tripped on a wire and hit his head on a tree stump. It appeared his neck was broken until Ronald Reagan stood up, removed the false head, and spit before re-donning the disguise. He hurled the discus at Bruce, who ducked. The discus smashed the windshield of a green Prius and rolled into the vigil, scattering candles.

The candles served as an incendiary mechanism, lighting the photographs and flowers set out for the victims. The pyre reached for the heavens, flames like fingers searching for purchase. Protesters and pro-Columbus supporters battled the smoke and each other. National Guardsmen launched tear gas and shot rubber bullets indiscriminately into the crowd.

Bruce picked up his headset and pleaded, "Ronald Reagan, please, let us help. Time takes time."

"Time is one thing I don't have, Bruce." He steadied the pirate head. Bruce paused and looked to the heavens.

Ronald Reagan picked up a discarded placard and swung it at Bruce, landing a direct blow to the sternum. "Guess I owe you an amends for that," he said.

Clearly in pain, Bruce smiled. "We don't have to live like this anymore!"

Armed with a protest sign, Ronald Reagan barreled toward the house, swinging the placard wildly to allow himself passage through the clot of humanity, but when he tried to enter the screened-in porch, the mascot head stuck in the door frame. Ronald Reagan then dropped his weapon, and ducked out of the head. He stood on the porch between two doors. On one side, the screen door jammed with the head of the Cyclops, on the other, the front door to Sophie's home.

The god Janus presided over the beginning and ending of conflicts, the very space which Ronald Reagan inhabited at that moment. Janus also controlled doors and transitions, trading and traveling, gates and dualities. His depiction was often that of a two-faced human. The duality of Janus (common in drug addicts and TV executives) makes me wonder if he wasn't looking over Ronald Reagan when Sophie answered his knocking and pulled him into the kitchen, away from the violence, and toward a new beginning.

"Sophie, Jesus," Ronald Reagan said, "I'm so sorry for all this."

"Don't hug me."

Ronald Reagan limped inside. Sophie walked from the front door to the edge of the porch where Bruce and Maggie pried at the head with a rake.

"Hey," Sophie shouted, "if you leave now, you can have this. Ronald Reagan wrote this in jail. It's the story of his life." She reached through the opening between the screen door frame and the mascot head and held up a ratty manuscript titled *The True Story of Ronald Reagan Middleton*. She slid the document through a small space below the obstruction. "Now get the fuck off my lawn."

"I'm so proud he stuck with his journaling!" Bruce said.

Maggie dropped the rake. "The profits. Bruce, think of the profits. We can run a special: 'The True Story of Ronald Reagan Middleton.' Reenactment with voiceover narration," she said. "It will help so many people."

Bruce grabbed the papers, and he and Maggie ran for the Prius. The remaining reporters appeared confused and continued pushing forward against the oversized mask, further wedging it into the doorframe while, all around them, the isolated scuffles merged into a riot.

Once inside, the public, and therefore myself, lost track of Ronald Reagan. The lone witness to his final, post-parade time in Booth was his mentor and teacher, Sophia Trent.

CONFRONTING THE MISSING MANUSCRIPT PAGES: MY LAST INTERACTION WITH RONALD REAGAN

BY SOPHIA TRENT

I hadn't been staying at home very much. But with the protest happening that day, and the announcement that the National Guard had been called in, I figured I should be around in case I could open my home to anyone who needed help or somewhere to hide. I definitely wasn't expecting Ronald Reagan to show up, but when he did, I knew what he was after.

When Maggie and Bruce left, I walked in from the porch and saw Ronald Reagan rummaging through the fridge. "What did you give them?" he asked.

"Gator's poems."

"Fantastic." Ronald Reagan emerged with a can of beer.

"Your stuff is in the basement." I pointed at the door covered in peeling blue paint.

"Sorry again. About the circumstances," Ronald Reagan said. "I've been hard at work."

We descended into my basement office and I poured us coffee in a couple Mason jars. The walls shook. Dust jumped out of the cracks in the mortar. Ronald Reagan looked around at the place like he was trying to figure out if it was what he should expect from my workspace.

"This is terrible," he said, and set the jar down in favor of his beer. "Look, Sophie, I've filled almost five notebooks, here." He winced when he ripped the duct tape off his body and passed me the dog-eared stack of notebooks he had taped to his stomach. "I needed to show you this. To get it all together like you said. I swear, I've been… Shit. I don't, I mean, I can't keep it together in my head anymore."

Ronald Reagan ran his hand along the basement ceiling and looked out the window at a series of frantic ankles.

I set the notebooks down on the coffee table. "Boundaries are important. I'll help you because I said I would, but you can't come here again. For any reason."

I felt a sadness blow through the room, followed by an abrupt silence, and then a blood curdling scream from outside. Someone said, "God will eat the souls of the wicked and send them to hell for eternal damnation." A series of small explosions and a swell of indiscernible chanting echoed around the house. A helicopter took off, a siren wailed.

Stepping over a box full of office supplies, I opened my filing cabinet. "This is what you wrote in my class. You were a great student." I held up a manila folder containing his work from jail. The story of his childhood.

"Hey," he raised his voice and I held the folder close to my chest. At that moment I felt certain he was capable of anything, that I'd let my guard down, broken a rule I'd set for myself, and would pay for being so naïve. For all I knew he was the Werewolf Killer. "Listen," he said, "I'm leaving anyway, so you won't have to worry about seeing me anymore. I won't even write you. Not one postcard."

My fear dissipated when I saw he was near tears, and I tried to say, "it's all right," but I'm not sure if words came out.

"I've written about everything up to yesterday," he said, "starting from jail and I just..." He backed up from the space under the window, softly pressing the beer can to his cheek before taking another long pull. "I feel if I can, like, spread it all out and look at it, I'll be able to revise and really illuminate the connections and elicit themes and stuff," he said. "We could maybe do it now, before I go?"

His early work spoke of a small house in coastal Georgia, tucked into a cut in the shoreline. He wrote about looking up at things, from a young boy's perspective. His parents smiled in these chapters. Ronald Reagan and his father fished off the deck and collected driftwood spit up by the tide, smooth and worn. His family life was happy.

I handed him the folder. Ten typed pages in total.

I flipped through Ronald Reagan's notebooks while he sat in a lawn chair and read what he'd written. The town roared outside. He wiped his face with the crook of his arm, and placed the pages by his feet as he finished them.

He took a long purposeful drink, rattled the beer can by his ear, and tossed it in the corner. Lights flickered in the basement and the house shook. I watched him read the last page. When he dropped it, the paper flipped and somersaulted toward a cigarette burn on the rug. All that he could recall of his youth lay fanned out on the floor.

We lit cigarettes simultaneously, and I opened a beer.

"I don't know what any of it means," he said, "none of it." He gathered the text. "I don't want this." He picked up a metal wastebasket in the corner, dumped its contents on the floor, then put his childhood story in the can and stared at the end of his cigarette. From his pack of Camels Ronald Reagan dug out a roach and lit it with the end of his cigarette. "Nobody needs to read this."

"It doesn't need to mean anything," I said. "But you do what you want with it."

Ronald Reagan removed the recorder taped to his chest and dropped it next to the stack of notebooks on the desk. "Keep it," he said.

When the roach was finished, I offered to let him stay until things calmed down outside, and we spent the rest of the day discussing the work he'd done since leaving jail. He said he planned to send the manuscript to his brother at boarding school. When it was dark enough, and the riots had subsided, we snuck out the back and I drove him to meet his friend Cindy, who had a car waiting.

That was the last I saw of him.

There was something about that shitty jail ink holding all those sacred times that he couldn't reconcile.

LOOSE ENDS

After the ugly scene outside Sophie's home in Booth, Maggie and Bruce returned to New Jersey, where they discovered the contents of the manuscript they obtained were, in fact, poems written by Ted "Gator" Williams. While they were initially disappointed to discover they did not have the story of Ronald Reagan's childhood, they did find a publisher for the work. A poem entitled "Hemingway" was selected to appear in that year's *Best American Poetry*, and, upon his release, Gator will be teaching a poetry class on *Clean Time: Greensboro*.

According to Maggie, there is still a small team of field reporters assigned to locating Ronald Reagan Middleton. Progress has been minimal. National interest has increased with the upcoming release of *Werewolf Hunter! The Movie II!!!*, which is loosely based on Ronald Reagan Middleton and his encounters with the alleged killer. Teasers and trailers indicate the film will be a bit "meta" for good taste, but I suppose the fourth wall was made to be broken.

•

After our interview, Bob and I bid Maggie farewell and graciously accepted her parting gift of *Clean Time* sweatpants and Ronald Reagan Middleton Sleeveless Blazers by Jordache$Fitch. "This has all been very unfortunate," Maggie told us. "The murders and the riots that leveled parts of GSU campus. Such a terrible turn of events we could not have foreseen. Please note that as my official stance."

Perhaps the most disturbing revelation that occurred during my trip with Bob was that of the motives and identity of the Werewolf Killer, who was arrested shortly after our interview with Maggie. The killer was apprehended when Geoff Sanderson saw "Easy" Edward Phelps (or, as Ronald Reagan called him, "the Preacher") accosting a dancer outside the Gryphon's Den. Sanderson alerted local police, and when officers arrived they found a werewolf mask and the weapon used in multiple murders in Phelps' car. This is not entirely surprising. However, I was struck by the alleged conspiracy theory regarding the motivation of the murders that has gained popularity in various corners of the internet. The theory purports that the killing spree was not simply the act of a deranged right-wing sociopath who sought to "purge the vermin from the south," as it were, but the result of a ploy far more sinister and difficult to process.

During our discussion with Maggie, I had sent Bob away to cool off, at which point, without my knowledge, he snuck into Maggie's office. The urge to snoop, according to Bob, came from his general distrust of Maggie. Had he known then about the identity of the Werewolf Killer, he might have thought to save what he'd found. While rummaging through Maggie's office, Bob stumbled upon a thick folder of memos referencing a person or entity named "E.P." Also in this folder were bank statements indicating an "E.P. Inc." was paid handsomely for undisclosed services. These large sums of money had been transferred into an offshore account and each transfer, to the best of Bob's recollection, occurred within days of a reported murder.

When we returned from our trip, Bob was inspired to travel back to New Jersey for a weekend in search of more proof. He searched his father's office, however, if Bob Senior was in fact involved, he was much more careful than Maggie.

Bob returned to Booth empty-handed and continued preparing the manuscript. I hesitate to say his work suffered, but Bob did spend every spare moment pursuing his detective work. I'm afraid he became a bit obsessed by it, to the point where, sadly, all his leads dead-ended in speculation and conspiracy, his theories held together by evidence found while sifting the forums of Reddit and 32-Chan.

The most popular theory, which is beginning to make its way

into the conventional wisdom, goes as follows: Edward Phelps was paid by Philson & Jackson Co. to follow Ronald Reagan and murder addicts and dealers, preferably Ronald Reagan's known associates, who would, as one document reads, "not be missed due to their criminal histories and troubles with substance abuse." Initially, this directive was proposed by Mr. Middleton in an attempt to scare his son straight and force him into rehab at Rose-Thorn, hence the murder of Justin Haas.

Not lost on Mr. Middleton was the positive effect the murders would have as a means to promote the television series and movie upon which said killings were based. When *Clean Time* turned Ronald Reagan into a star, the murders intensified. The Preacher was then directed away from Ronald Reagan's friends in Booth and toward the other cast members on *Clean Time*, with whom the public already had an existing relationship, in order to promote the upcoming release of *Werewolf Hunter!: The Movie I!!*. Some circles allege the Preacher was ordered to kill Ronald Reagan the day before the premier in order to increase the buzz on opening night. We do not know if Mr. Middleton was consulted about the final phase of this plan, or if it was ever enacted.

•

There is a natural feeling of emptiness after the completion of a project of this magnitude. So when Sophia Trent contacted me and volunteered to fill some gaps toward the end of Ronald Reagan's story (her telling appears as the previous chapter, as noted in the header), I was struck with a pang of excitement and nostalgia for the time Bob and I had spent traveling the state earlier that summer. I welcomed her input and agreed to meet again at the same café in Booth.

I held out hope that the missing manuscript pages might accompany her chapter detailing Ronald Reagan's last day in Booth prior to his disappearance. Such first-hand accounts are invaluable to research projects and, while I considered summarizing her work and folding it into the denouement in my own words, Bob professed a desire for another voice and perspective on his brother, and I agreed to include the work, as is, as part of the mosaic that is Ronald Reagan's life. In the same spirit, I agreed to let Bob write the afterword. Who better to conclude such a story than Ronald Reagan's own brother? Additionally, Bob shared with me the letter Ronald Reagan sent along with the manuscript, which he says motivated him to take the notebooks to Booth:

Bob,

Enclosed is a money order for $689 and a Ken Griffey, Jr. rookie card in Bad to Poor condition. At the moment, this is the best I can do to cover the CDs.

Find Dr. Blank at GSU. He's the only person I trust, and I want him to see all the work I've done. Meet him in person. Mom and Dad's place is under surveillance. All the phones are tapped. When I come home we'll get Mets tickets.

Goodnight,

RR

Naturally, we had a good laugh at Professor Blank's expense. Bob and I had bonded over the course of our work together. He had spent the summer in Booth, living in the dorms and assisting me with the edits, and we both met Sophie once again on a balmy evening.

In the café, after dinner and discussion and several bottles of wine, Sophie's recounting of Ronald Reagan's last day in Booth left me hungry for the chance to see my old student again.

Bob looked over his shoulder and poured himself another glass of wine. We were the only patrons left on the café patio when I reached my hand across the table, placed it on Sophie's, and asked, "May I have a copy of the first chapters of Ronald Reagan's story, the chapters detailing his childhood?"

Sophie leaned toward me, her teeth dark and wine-stained. She smelled of cigarettes and faintly of orange peels; her lips opened slightly, as if she had a secret to tell or a kiss to give, and I felt her breath on my neck and waited for what might follow.

"No," she said. "If I give you the stuff he wrote in jail without his permission, I'm as bad as they are."

I told Sophie I understood.

Resigned to the reality that this was one piece of the story I would have to surrender, I consoled myself for this failure. Regardless of the consequences I would face for my inability to obtain the completed manuscript, I let it go. Almost immediately upon my decision, my standing with the university seemed less important than it had when I started this journey. I couldn't figure out how or why exactly, but I knew Ronald Reagan had changed me.

CONCLUSION

If Homer were alive today, perhaps he would pen odes to meth dealers and heroin addicts struggling with their inner demons and tragic character flaws. The hero's journey of Odysseus resonates not in spite of his flaws, after all, but because of his ability to identify and overcome these flaws during his journey. Much as the Greeks used mythology and storytelling to better explain the social climate of the era, and to represent the values they held dear as evidenced by the heroes of their time, so too has Ronald Reagan's story shed light on contemporary American culture. Ronald Reagan's battle with addiction and subsequent rise to fame peeled back the veneer of a divided, celebrity-obsessed culture at its worst. The isolation, detachment, and disillusionment pervading large segments of a country falling deeper into addiction and celebrity-worship had been distilled into this young man. Contemporary mythology, told through the experiences of Ronald Reagan Middleton, provides the foundation for the start of a new canonical archetype.

We are a country without the wherewithal to act heroically, so we look outward for a hero. In looking outward, we find Ronald Reagan Middleton. But I dare say, his story should teach us to instead look inward, to find Ronald Reagan's strength within ourselves. To embody Ronald Reagan Middleton, with all his imperfections, is to be undeniably and unapologetically American.

AFTERWORD

BY BOB MIDDLETON

Let me preface this by telling you what a ball player my brother was, because he'll never talk about it.

Baseball gave Ronald Reagan a way to process everything. "Baseball is fair," he told me once. "You have twenty-seven outs to score more than the other team. There's no time limit."

As a high school sophomore, Ronald Reagan Middleton hit .650 and got the attention of some big baseball schools and pro scouts (Mom kept a big pile of letters from colleges on her dresser next to a scrapbook of newspaper clippings from all his games). He threw right-handed, but hit lefty, and everyone compared his swing to Ken Griffey Jr.'s. He once hit a 516-foot homer. If you could've seen him run, man. He stole home six times one season. In four years of high school ball, he struck out twice (once looking, once swinging, both as a freshman). The Mets drafted my brother in the thirteenth round out of high school, but Ronald Reagan had plans to go to USC and be a Trojan. He wasn't in a rush.

Every night before dinner, Dad would get out his tennis racquet and can of balls and hit us pop-ups in the back yard. I was seven or eight years old and my brother was a freshman, and I never really cared for the activity itself, but Ronald Reagan loved it. He'd come home after practice, wait for Dad to get home from work, and go out back and shag flies. Nothing fell. Ronald Reagan wouldn't allow it. I just enjoyed watching him track the fuzzy green balls that flew and drifted up over everything. My brother told me all the time, "You don't get anything for letting it hit the ground."

I was ten when he played his last game, a state semifinal for

Hope Township American Legion Post 933, the summer after his senior year. Down in Camden on a field where the outfield went for miles and ended in a point where a waist-high, chain-link fence surrounding a playground met a brick school building with barred windows.

With Hope up one run in the bottom of the ninth, there was one out and a guy on second for Camden. Ronald Reagan always played shallow. Camden's three-hitter got into one, a hanging slider, and ripped it to straight away center. I mean, this ball was heading for Philly. Ronald Reagan turned and ran. The runner on second took off.

At the last second, when there was no way he had enough room to get this ball, Ronald Reagan grabbed it. I'd never seen anyone jump that high. Then he took another step, flipped over the fence, and landed on the concrete playground, right on his throwing arm. He held up his glove and kind of rolled himself back over the fence and jogged toward the infield. The batter was already past second, and the runner from second had already crossed the plate and was on his way to the dugout when Ronald Reagan stepped on second base and recorded the only unassisted double play by an outfielder in New Jersey American Legion playoff history.

But when he crossed the mound and neared the dugout you could see the pain in his face. Not just that he'd hurt himself, but that his whole means of processing the world was about to disappear and things were about to change—like on some level he knew it. His hand almost reached to his shin. Blood dripped down his sleeve. That night, while his teammates celebrated a trip to regionals, Ronald Reagan had the first of three shoulder surgeries.

It should have been routine, but his arm never healed right. Dad thought he was doing Ronald Reagan a favor by getting him all these top of the line, non-FDA approved painkillers. At this point we can all see that was a bad idea. Until then I'd only ever seen him drink a few beers now and again, mostly out of social obligation. After the injury, I don't think I saw him sober.

He lost his scholarship, enrolled in GSU and tried to walk on, but he failed his physical. We were still keeping in touch with weekly phone calls then. Baseball was no longer a topic of conversation unless he was a special kind of drunk. "Bobby," he'd say, "Bobby, I will never be one of those sad fucks who does nothing but talk about how good he was at high school sports. Fuck all that."

Wherever my brother is, I find it helpful to remember him in the back yard, looking up at a tennis ball arcing higher than anything my eight-year-old head could comprehend, then breaking backward, whipping his neck around, and cradling the ball before it hit the ground while the next one was already on its way up.

After almost ten years, I'd like to think Ronald Reagan has made his peace with all of it. But it's hard to tell. As far as I know, our family never had a house in Georgia.

WEIGHT

BY RONALD REAGAN MIDDLETON

We spiraled down the ramp and the highway turned into Washington Avenue in the middle of the projects. I sat in the back between Cindy and a pile of Justin's dress shirts. Jacky rode shotgun. One of us had to wait near the corner of Eighth and Washington while Mooch picked up his man who would take him to *his* man a few blocks down. Later on we'd head to All-Nite Cleaners where the third-shift manager let us deal out of the back. Since we lost our connection up north, this is how it went. No one ever wanted to wait at home. We didn't trust each other enough.

They let me out at the 24-Hour McDonald's. On the far side of Washington, there was a vacant lot that held a bunch of construction equipment—machines bent like sleeping monsters in the shadows. The air smelled sickly sweet, like fruit about to go bad. I walked around the corner to Eighth and the bus-stop bench where I usually sat, across the street from the empty Baby World. I shook a few Vicodin from a bottle I'd swiped from Justin earlier and stared at an advertisement for strollers.

I picked a dandelion out of a crack in the sidewalk and threw it toward the curb. A man pushing a shopping cart emerged from the alley next to Baby World. He limped around a fire hydrant and stopped by the back of a Mercury sedan. We made eye contact, and the man nodded in my direction, holding up a brown bag as if to offer me a drink, or an explanation.

I waved and said, "I'm good, thanks," but couldn't tell if I'd whispered or shouted at him and figured he didn't offer me any anyway.

He got into the back of the car. The glow of a cigarette looped around in the rear window, then went dark.

For fifteen minutes I sat there chain smoking and ripping random weeds out of the sidewalk. Knowing Mooch, it could be another half hour, longer maybe. Bass from a passing car hummed through my chest and down my arms. A siren blaring in the distance suddenly went quiet. My spine started to itch from the pills, and the night took on an anxious feeling, like the sky might rumble to life and crush me. Gradually the city sounds faded into the background, but the sense of panic didn't dissipate. I sensed it under the surface of every building and passerby, every bolt in the expandable steel gate drawn across the Baby World storefront, every broken chunk of cement. It bled out into the air and seeped into my skin. I decided to get a milkshake.

My bare arms radiated yellow under the McDonald's sign. While I stood out front, finishing my cigarette, a young couple came out of the restaurant and tried to sell me a greasy bag of food.

"Please, please, please," the kid held the *ease* in the last *please* until he ran out of breath and gasped for air. The girl next to him looked up at me with a face so sad it had to be practiced. They were the only other white people anywhere. "Please," he explained, "I need money for a pair of socks. This lady, God bless her, I told this lady, I need money for socks, and she got me this value meal instead."

True, he wasn't wearing socks. He had on cargo shorts and a battered pair of Jordans. His white t-shirt was turned inside out, and I noticed streaks of black marker bleeding through but couldn't make out what had been written there.

"Sorry," I said, "I'm broke." I had two hundred dollars in fifties rolled up in the pill bottle in my pocket.

He grabbed my arm and I pulled it away.

"Hey. Hey, man," he said. "You can fuck my girlfriend for fifty bucks." He nodded at the girl, and she put on a slightly different, pouty face. "She'll do anything." At this he winked, as if we had some kind of inside joke about the meaning of anything.

I said, "I'm cool."

He said, "How about twenty?"

The girl stood, twirled around in her miniskirt and torn stockings. Her body looked good, all things considered. Her black eyes shimmered beneath the light falling off the golden arches.

"Twenty? Really?" I took a long pull off my cigarette. "Sorry. My girlfriend is coming back for me soon. Good luck with the socks."

"Please." He was crying again. "For fifteen I'll let you drag me into that abandoned lot and beat the shit out of me. I won't even fight back, but no hits to the face. Then you can piss all over me." He reached for my arm. "She'll watch, or help. Whatever you want."

"Don't fucking touch me."

I pulled away and stepped into the McDonald's, swaying slightly, still unable to scratch the spot in the middle of my back.

On my way to the counter, I passed two grade-school kids wearing brand new high tops and a woman sleeping in a booth. While I waited in line, a man in a suit left McDonald's and wandered into the shadows of the vacant lot with the girl. I ordered a strawberry shake from a skinny cashier with green barrettes who smiled as she passed my change through the slot in the bulletproof glass.

Back on my bench again and it felt even hotter outside. I took my shirt halfway off, then reconsidered, pulled it down. There was so much condensation on my cup I thought it might disintegrate. A cigarette burned in one corner of my mouth while the ineffective bendy straw chortled in the other.

At the light, a horn blared, and I squeezed the cup so hard the shake erupted out of the top and ran all over my fist and mucked up my arm hair. I wiped my hands on my jeans. Lightheaded and sticky, pink smears on my thighs, I tossed the cup at an overflowing trashcan. Where the fuck was Mooch?

I ate another Vicodin.

The girl and her boyfriend walked around the corner. She held his hand as they weaved down the sidewalk. Between the crests of two streetlights they stood and smoked crack, and I wondered how anyone wound up in a situation this fucked. So I figured I'd ask them.

I approached the couple, offered them each a cigarette.

"Where do you stay?" I asked.

"Around," the guy said. "You want to hit this?"

Not one to turn down drugs, I considered it. And I would have if Mooch hadn't assured me his guy was automatic. We never came into the city if it wasn't automatic, never dealt with the kids dealing in the McDonald's unless it was a last resort. We came down here to buy weight. We weren't like these people who offered their girlfriends, their bags of cold fries.

"I'm straight," I said.

"Suit yourself."

"So," I said, "how'd you get to be staying around instead of somewhere?"

"I don't know." When his girl hit the pipe, he knelt and ran a hand over her thigh, rested his head on her hip. "We used to be in with this kid who knew a guy, or maybe he was the guy, and we had it pretty good—a room out by the airport, weekly rent. Sometimes he'd front us and we'd work for him, but..." he stood up and looked me over, focused on the burning cigarette in my hand still stained with milkshake. "Hey. Why the fuck do you care?"

"Curious is all."

"It's not so bad," the girl said and pushed her hair behind her ear.

"My ride's coming soon." I looked at my wrist, as if I wore a watch, then put my hand in my back pocket.

"Hey man," the guy said. "Give me another cigarette and I won't cut you."

"Cut me with what?" I tossed a few cigarettes at his feet and walked back to my bench.

The couple crossed the street and sat on the Mercury where the crippled shopping-cart man slept, leaning in like they were holding each other up. They stayed like that for a while, draped in each other's arms, in love and almost beautiful. A twinge of jealousy struck me out of nowhere and stung until they started arguing. The guy banged his palms on the trunk, his Jordans off the rear bumper. The girl covered her eyes while he yelled.

When he slapped her it was at one of those odd times when everything goes completely quiet for a second, and the sound jolted me upright. The girl bawled something about loving him, got on her knees and popped the hubcap off one of the rear wheels. "Two bucks a piece, easy," she said, and gave it to her boyfriend.

"Lot doesn't open for four hours. You're so fucking stupid." He took the hubcap and held it in front of him like a steering wheel while he paced to the end of the block and back. "Four fucking hours," he yelled, and the girl raised her hand like he was about to hit her again before she crawled ahead and started on the next hubcap.

I threw another dandelion in the street. The crippled man stumbled out of his car, gained his footing and let go an arc of piss against the front of Baby World.

The couple stopped what they were doing.

"Hey." The boyfriend walked over to the homeless man and started beating on him with the hubcap.

The girl started pulling shit out of the car.

I walked back to the McDonald's, lit a cigarette and stared into the vacant lot. Wondered what they would possibly build there, and what had already been torn down.

When they came around the corner, the guy was pushing his girl in the shopping cart. In the cart: hub caps, several feet of thin metal pipe, a cheap stereo, spark plugs, and some still-in-the-package children's toys. She held up a pack of cigarettes over her head for her boyfriend as they labored past. Her skirt rode up above her hips. They were laughing and smiling as they crossed the street. By the way they were talking you'd have thought they were a couple of newlyweds out for a stroll, deciding what to do with their Friday night out. I wanted a car to hit them, but didn't see another vehicle till Mooch picked me up.

Jacky leaned out the front window to kiss me real quick, and I got in the back. I traced the cigarette burns in the leather seats while we headed to the cleaners. Watching Cindy move a razorblade through powder on a cafeteria tray, I marveled at how focused she was. How intricate the process. The distorted reflection caught in her glasses. When we pulled back on the highway, I started to say something about what I'd seen, but swallowed it. Mooch had the music up loud, and no one would have known what I was talking about anyway.

ENDNOTES

[1] Technically the manuscript was bound for Dr. Blank, RR's mentor and the professor under which I was a teaching assistant. However, Dr. Blank had been let go due to budget cuts.

[2] The running joke in the department is that my office *is* the department. We'd been under strenuous budgetary restrictions, and the President, Dr. Penny Evergreen, promised she would "allow me to pursue other academic opportunities if [I] did not change the prudent nature of [my] productivity." While I asserted that quality publications and research take time, she stood fast in her demands that I publish quickly. Despite my insistence that inter-institutional politics stood in the way of publication, she only granted me four semesters to produce a work that would put Guilford State back in the discussion of the top liberal arts college and universities. Unfortunately, this led to a fog of depression, which I was unable to cure, that prevented me from doing little else but spend nights in my office with my ancient television and count down the days until my termination. I had hit bottom. But when Bob Middleton Jr. arrived with his brother's memoir, I was offered a way out.

[3] According to Bob, this behavior was somewhat out of character for his brother. As RR's addiction accelerated during his college years, his thought patterns and actions became increasingly erratic and unpredictable; this incident exemplifies RR at his worst.

[4] In this entry, RR establishes the inspirational foundation of his work. This so rarely happens—that an addict sets a goal and sees it through to the end. RR's ability to accomplish this goal without coming out of hiding to take credit shows great spiritual and emotional strength, the development of which, in drug addicts especially, takes decades if it happens at all. The Ego and inherent fear of judgment lie at the heart of the addict's problem. RR's ability to shed his Ego and lay bare his soul in his writing, to follow through and complete his task, then to let his words see the light of day, is a phenomenon.

[5] It is unclear whether RR is eliciting the two-headed hellhound Orthrus, or perhaps the serpent Hydra, who, when one of her heads was injured, grew two in its place. As the memoir progresses and RR, who goes in search of its lost pages, begins to take his journaling more seriously (perhaps realizing it is also an important part of his story), we'll discover more and more references to mythology emerge. As for Orthrus and Hyrda, Hercules killed both of these monsters.

[6] Tragic hero Achilles' only vulnerability was his heel. He was killed when Paris shot him with an arrow in his lone weak spot. RR's reference to his Achilles heel at this point in the text is perhaps a subliminal call to his inability to stay clean and maintain healthy relationships with women.

[7] I tracked down Dr. Blank at the Shakespeare on Film Conference in Connecticut a few months before Bob and I set out on our fact-checking journey. Primarily, Dr. Blank remembers RR's enthusiasm and fondness for marijuana. He described the screenplay in question as quite good, but RR as difficult to work with. I pried at the circumstances surrounding the end of his working relationship with RR, but Dr. Blank was not forthright. To change the subject, I told him I had climbed out of the basement over at State, and, ironically, occupied his old office. Laughter ensued. Over pinot noir, the Doctor and I reminisced of our days together at Guilford State. Surprisingly, a request by Dr. Blank to assist Bob and I with our project was not offered.

[8] Notice how the influence of mythology has extended beyond the screenplay and seeped into RR's jail journals. Here, RR alludes to the myth of Icarus. Flying too close to the sun is certainly an apt metaphor for the highs and lows of a drug addict, both in his day-to-day existence, and in the macro spectrum in which he must hit bottom in order to recover.

[9] After two bottles of wine, Dr. Blank offered his curt but vague description of the events leading up to the loss of the screenplay: RR went through a spell in which he'd been rather concerned about the ability of the Department Head (ironically, this was Penny Evergreen, who had been head of Classics before her abrupt promotion during the budget restructurings) and the state of North Carolina to spy on him via his computer and thus made extreme efforts to go "paper-only." Dr. Blank assumes it was during this time that the hard copy was misfiled or recycled. RR had destroyed all digital backups. Dr. Blank periodically searches his home (I myself have rummaged through the University offices thoroughly for the document), and assured us he would follow up should the screenplay's whereabouts become known.

[10] Drew "Mooch" Perry ended his career at Guilford Prep as the all-time leading tackler in NCISPAL high school football and is still regarded as the best middle linebacker in the history of North Carolina high school football. Unfortunately, his college career ended before it started. Shortly after Mr. Perry took a demolition job in West Booth, the summer before his freshman year at Clemson, a Canada Construction bulldozer ran over both his feet during the initial stages of the controversial Section 8 Relocation and Renovation project, which included funds for the 33/77 bypass. The construction of this bypass ultimately led to the re-routing of the bus RR and Jacky attempted to take to Georgia.

[11] Traditionally Greek ideals, the acceptance and practice of homosexuality are represented by RR's description of "Mooch" and Justin. RR inserts Mooch into this tale as a tragic hero, given the circumstance of the end of Mooch's football career—football serving as the modern equivalent of battle, Olympic triumph, and social standing in contemporary society. This is also referenced later when RR alludes to the tale of Apollo and Hyacinth.

[12] When Bob and I came upon the late Nancy Crane's Pontiac at her old home, the license plates had been removed. After crudely using a coat hanger to open the door, Bob discovered that the contents of the center console and glove box had been rummaged through, and all the papers were missing. The spare tire in the trunk was absent, as was the jack. Finding this puzzling, we searched the garage and found two bright yellow license plates buried among the gardening tools and bags of fertilizer. It was in this manner we also discovered the trap door to Nancy's LSD lab. Based on my admittedly limited knowledge of the subject, as derived from television and cinema, it looked as if she had the foundations to also produce Methamphetamine.

[13] The reference to the Minotaur, which we could not confirm as a direct quote from Cindy, is clearly a moment of foreshadowing by RR. In the story of the Minotaur, the Minotaur was seen as a shameful creature and banished to the labyrinth, similar to the way addicts are treated in modern society. However, this metaphor falls short, as the monster itself was the product of an extra-marital affair with a bull, and no such parallel exists in the text.

[14] At this point in the text, RR described the climactic scene of his capture, which appears at the start of this book. I changed the verb tense from past to present in order to heighten the urgency and dramatic effect of his near-escape from Booth.

[15] The Ferris wheel may have originated in seventeenth-century Bulgaria. RR's inclusion of a ride commonly associated with children and county fairs shows his desire to find his youth, as well as his desire to "get off the ride" on which he currently finds himself. It is a keen symbol. The circular motion of the Ferris wheel represents the cycle of self-destructive behavior common in addicts. Perhaps this allusion was also meant to imply Sisyphus, who was forced to push a boulder up a hill for all eternity as punishment for betraying Zeus. Sisyphus was allegedly the most cunning mortal; he plotted to live forever by trapping Hades on earth so he could not bring souls to the Underworld. Perhaps RR's desire to return to a simpler childhood time, as symbolized by the Ferris wheel, parallels Sisyphus' desire for immortality. However, Sisyphus was a murderous king who sought to rule with an iron fist, so perhaps the murders he committed in order to maintain control of his kingdom relate to the way

drug dealers and addicts murder themselves with drugs, violence, and lifestyle choices. If so, this could also be read as an expression of guilt by RR.

[16] According to Bob, RR was conceived on the day President Reagan's head was blasted into Mount Rushmore. The Middletons have a shrine on their mantel in honor of the Great Communicator.

[17] Not coincidentally, in Homer's *Odyssey*, Odysseus' men were turned into pigs by the beautiful witch-goddess Circe on the isle of Aeaea. In the myth, Hermes came to Odysseus' aid. He gave Odysseus the drug, moly, to counter the effects of Circe's own drug, which she had used to turn his men into swine. When Odysseus repelled her attack, Circe lamented and returned his crew to their human forms. Shortly thereafter, Odysseus and Circe became lovers, and he and his crew stayed on Aeaea for one year, living a life of luxury. RR's own life certainly includes a wide range of love affairs and drugs, and he repeatedly falls under the "spell" of different women on his voyage. He even references molly (MDMA) when describing the drugs that changed Justin from a friend to an enemy. The presence of drug use as both RR's problem and solution is exemplified in Hermes' gift. Certainly the obvious notion that men turn into pigs is also present in RR's work, specifically in the way they treat women, but also in the way they revert to animal instincts when under the influence of controlled substances.

[18] We were unable to recover RR's workbook.

[19] Two years prior to RR's incarceration, Jackson Entertainment (which created The Recovery Channel) merged with Philson Pharmaceuticals, where RR's father worked as Executive VP in charge of Marketing Development and Promotional Materials. Neither Mr. Middleton nor Philson & Jackson Co. not be reached for comment regarding the events that led to Nedvedol's circulation as a street drug in Booth.

[20] Situated on an island somewhere in the Mediterranean, Sirens had the bodies of birds, and could enchant and charm with the power of their song. They tried to capture Odysseus, but Circe advised he and his crew to put wax in their ears, thus preventing the Sirens' spell from taking effect. Here, RR subtly acknowledges the Sirens as they relate to his tendency to become obsessed with women at the expense of other matters in his life.

[21] For reference, I've gone through and compared the script with the pilot episode and noted the Viewer Approval Ratings as they appeared during the voting. The ratings that appear in the script are my addition. This information allows us to observe how the public responded to RR during his first week of rehab as it was presented on television.

[22] RR's entry for Day 3 was ripped from his recovery journal. It appears to have been several pages. Based on a note in the margin that was not completely torn off, the entry appears to consist of RR's thoughts about Jacky and his misgivings about the relationship as one of his triggers. "Bruce keeps saying we have to change old relationships. Maybe he's right?" is a quote I was able to attribute to Day 3 by repeated close viewings of the pilot episode. I then found a torn section of one of the missing pages folded over and stuck to the side of the box containing the rest of RR's notebooks, tapes, etc. A partial entry for what is most likely Day 3 of RR's rehab reads: "I just wrote like ten pages about Jacky, but it's all redundant bullshit that I've already been over. I don't feel good about this Althea situation, but I don't know if I have a choice. I'm just not going to worry about Jacky so much right now. This guilt is killing me, but I'll work it out with her later, if there is a later."

[23] RR continues to take on the traits of the Greek hero Odysseus. In his interactions with Dolph, we see his deftness and cunning, along with the characteristic manipulation common among addicts. A likely side effect of studying *The Odyssey* in such great depth, RR draws inspiration from the text and comes to the understanding that he must use all of his abilities to get home safely. Many disguises are necessary. RR adapts to his surroundings, carefully deliberates on a course of action, and sets his plans in motion.

[24] The letter in question was stapled into RR's journal. I've transposed it for clarity.

[25] The phenomenon of "prayer bottling" is common among low-bottom methamphetamine addicts. Named for the position in which the addict finds his or herself—kneeling by the side of the road drinking with both hands—and is described in the documentary *American Meth*.

[26] When I came upon it, this journal entry below Bob's letter had been erased, though it was still legible. It is unclear if RR erased this immediately after he wrote it, or later on, when he knew these journals would be part of what he would publish. Perhaps at first RR did not foresee including these journal entries as part of his memoir, and later erased them to hide his crass understanding of his own fame. The line "the public loves me" is a bit of a gloat, when viewed in a certain light. He also may have wanted to hide his explicit intention of writing a memoir. It is possible RR erased these words to manipulate his image. The idea of putting on a different face for different situations (a disguise, if you will) is a recurring theme among addicts who, by nature and out of necessity, are able to manipulate others in order to maintain their lifestyle—for instance, to keep an addiction hidden, or to befriend whomever might get them high at a given time. Not only is it physically draining to keep up such charades,

the emotional and psychological toil can weigh heavily as well. Or, perhaps this self-censorship was more impulsive than premeditated. In this light, the entry shows how RR was having trouble coming to grips with the idea of being a writer, and how his success might be dependant upon how well he was received by the viewing public. RR might have been worried that anything he wrote would be published solely on the merit of his fame. Such a reading signals RR's maturity and growing self-awareness. But it is difficult to arrive at a precise interpretation. This entry, after all, is not the strongest paragraph in American literature.

[27] The Governor ran on a platform of expanding New Jersey's prison system at the expense of social programs and public schools. Before he was caught with Bruce and the Nedvedol, and before his subsequent resignation, the Governor's last official act was signing legislation that re-zoned the original Montclair Wellness Home, which allowed Jackson Entertainment to purchase the land and remodel and rebrand the house as the Rose-Thorn Recovery Center, which is technically zoned for commercial use. In addition, the US Senate passed a budget bill containing a rider that, in effect, deregulated pharmaceutical companies' production of behavior modification drugs, including Nedvedol, a highly experimental drug only legal in Norway until this year, allowing it to be tested on anyone who signed a legally binding waiver. The New Jersey Senator that originally introduced the legislation happens to be the Governor's brother-in-law. Both men are avid *Clean Time* fans; and both men first met Bruce at the Rose-Thorn ribbon cutting ceremony.

[28] Adrenaline and fear appear to prompt Althea to evoke the music of Robert Johnson, specifically this indirect reference to Johnson's "Hellhound Blues." Isolation and the inevitable drive to find comfort in a complex and frightening society—prospects especially terrifying to an addict—are ideas found in much of Johnson's work. The mythology surrounding Johnson and his famed deal with the devil (a version of the Faustian myth) is the foundation of Althea's scholarly work. Here we see how her immersion in blues mythology presents itself in a manner similar to RR's love of Greek mythology and *The Odyssey*. Their shared interest in mythology is perhaps the unifying principle that draws them together on their impending journey. Both studied these fields during high points in their lives, prior to their respective descents into addiction.

[29] See endnote 16.

[30] Years ago, in order to meet the conditions of court mandated probation in the state of North Carolina, the guilty party was required to meet with his or her probation officer, present meeting slips signed by a 12-Step group's chairperson on a weekly basis, pass random urine screenings, refrain from associating with known criminals, and

obey all local, state, and federal laws. Since the government restructuring, the social services department has been cut in half and the workload has doubled. Essentially, all the drug addiction, mental health, and social services in the state are handled by three people and a fax machine. The terms of RR and Althea's probation required twenty-four meetings in thirty days. While this probably implied six meetings a week for four weeks, the court did not specify the frequency of meeting attendance, only the total number of meetings attended. One fax with twenty-four signatures would suffice. Conversely, if either of them were found in violation of their probation, they would be treated as repeat offenders and sentenced accordingly.

[31] Taurus (Latin for "bull") is one of the oldest constellations. When Odysseus encountered the cyclops, Polyphemus, the sun was in Taurus, the constellation of the spring equinox. As we will see, the cyclops plays a large role in RR's story and, in retrospect, it is very fitting that RR's travels occur in such an aptly named vehicle.

[32] In Greek mythology, Gryphons are considered noble, majestic, and almost saintly. It is no surprise that RR would be drawn to imagery of this creature.

[33] One wonders RR's motivation for telling Althea this story, and what that might indicate about his state of mind. Though his written account is expressed more fluidly, and thus included here, Althea may not have been aware that the tape was rolling, but it appears clear, after several conversations about Jacky, all of them instigated by RR, that Althea was not particularly interested in hearing about her. In the most notable conversation, while traveling from Montclair to Booth, RR gave Althea a version of the night of his last trip into the city with Jacky and Mooch, which appears in prose form in this book as the chapter titled, "Weight." Despite moments of tenderness throughout their road trip, Althea's romantic feelings for RR remain ambiguous.

[34] Owls are considered a symbol of good fortune in ancient Greece, and associated with Athena, goddess of wisdom and war, who assisted Odysseus in *The Odyssey*. Associating the owl with Althea is apt; her wisdom and vision are clearly prominent traits, as is her complicated relationship with birds. However, Matt the security guard helping RR in the rest stop serves as a competing analogy, as his actions echo the scenes in which Athena disguised herself as Mentor in order to help Odysseus along the way. Though tempting, any further association between Athena and Althea, despite their similar names, would be academically reckless.

[35] Philson & Jackson Co. effectively outsourced much of the reporting footwork to several disreputable tabloids, as well as the entertainment sections of *USA Today*, the *Washington Post*, and the *Wall Street Journal*, who were already entrenched in their

coverage of the Werewolf Murders. It was a simple trade off. The resources of the various news outlets were pooled and directed by The Recovery Channel under the watchful eye of Maggie Turner in return for cross-promotion and advertising. The Recovery Channel shared their information on RR and the victims, and the mainstream outlets allowed The Recovery Channel access to their mobile television editing studios. As RR gained a popularity that transcended demographics, bloggers and freelancers jumped on the proverbial bandwagon and, from a legal standpoint, complicated things tremendously with regard to intellectual property rights.

[36] The "house" Kevin refers to is called Serenity House, a sober living facility. Both the Serenity House and Alano Club, located on the outskirts of Booth, have long been on the radar of local authorities and the IRS. The two institutions are suspected tax shelters for Tom Canada, who, despite making no public appearances and his involvement in the drug trade, goes to great pains to promote himself as a man trying to help the town of Booth deal with issues of addiction, mental illness, and the resulting stresses placed upon society by these issues.

[37] Cindy's play, *The Firm*, was first performed by a small theater group in Brelyn, Georgia, and opened to wide critical acclaim. Her story was that of a man named Elton Ontario, a trafficker of blemished blue jeans and narcotics throughout the Southeast. Elton takes a high school football star, Windsor, under his wing. Windsor, who had lost his arm in a tragic fire and his closeted gay lover to a serial killer, longs to move up the ladder of the drug trade, which forces him to make decisions that lead to tragedy and a wonderful twist of dark comedy. Hailed as "Richard III meets the Bad News Bears" at the time of this book's publication, *The Firm* is enjoying a year-long run on Peachtree St. in Atlanta, the Broadway of The South.

[38] Here RR begins losing his identity as it is packaged for public consumption and rendered as entertainment, similar to the way addicts lose their identity at the hands of illicit substances. In order to fend off this double-assault, I find it likely RR is once again calling on the theme of cunning over strength by donning a disguise in order to preserve his sense of self and avoid falling into relapse. With internal and external pressures building, we see RR's actions become increasingly informed by his past as a student of Greek mythology, the study of which occurred during a much simpler time in RR's life.

[39] The discus, an iconic piece of Greek sporting equipment, offers RR comfort while he's trapped in the supply closet. During this chaotic time, RR finds himself longing for the structure and simplicity of sport.

[40] Thematically, the importance of home is evident throughout *The Odyssey*. It is the foundation upon which the entire epic poem was written. RR looking in on his old home as Maggie rummages through his belongings parallels the homesickness felt by Odysseus throughout his journey. In this scene, RR not only longs for the security and comfort of his home on Frederick Street, but also for his childhood home in New Jersey. Having to constantly redefine home, RR places his hopes in escaping to the family vacation home in Georgia.

[41] Here RR provides an example of the importance of storytelling. In 12-Step circles, telling one's story is vital to the recovery process. Storytelling is similarly important in *The Odyssey*, as it is the means by which the reader learns of Odysseus' heroic deeds. RR upholds both these traditions by sharing the stories of other addicts with the reader. By associating recovery with heroism, RR sets the foundation for the creation of a new heroic archetype.

[42] RR's hesitance to embrace the Christ-centric nature of the Preacher's recovery philosophy is likely due to his immersion in Greek mythology, in which a polytheistic belief system was the norm.

[43] Serendipity, which simply means good fortune, is often incorrectly personified as a kind of goddess. Serendipity plays no role in *The Odyssey* or RR's story. During Odysseus' travels, it was The Fates that ensured his return home. Just as The Fates delivered RR's manuscript to me, so too did they oversee the events that allowed RR to elude his captors for so long. (Tyche is the Greek goddess of good fortune.)

[44] The story is included in this book under the chapter titled "Weight."

[45] This poem was first published in *Dark Hour Review* and is reprinted here with permission from the author.

[46] Here we see RR eliciting the myth of Prometheus. After stealing fire from the Gods, Prometheus was chained to a cliff while an eagle ate his liver every day for eternity. RR once again finds himself chained up in county jail, seemingly doomed to the cyclical punishment of the life of an addict (which often leads to liver damage… Though I feel the liver damage may be coincidental, it is the punishment that is most relevant, regardless of the specifics). Prometheus was martyred for bringing light to humanity, which is certainly pertinent to the story of RR given the way he was subjected to various punishments, as mentioned above, while bringing a great deal of joy to the American people. Adding further relevance to this comparison is the way Prometheus influenced future works of art well into the twentieth and twenty-first centuries, including Mary Shelly's *Frankenstein* and the *Alien* movie franchise.

[47] Here we see RR evoking the story of Narcissus, who, upon seeing his reflection, fell in love with himself and stared at his own face until he died. This scene represents the death of RR's TV persona and the moment he begins to accept his true self.

[48] Here Tom Canada displays the omnipotence of Zeus, a constant deterrent to Odysseus.

[49] This brings to mind the myth of Eurydice and Orpheus. Orpheus loved his wife, Eurydice. When Eurydice died, Orpheus traveled into the Underworld and begged his great uncle Hades to allow his wife to return to earth. Hades agreed on one condition: he would allow Eurydice to follow her husband back to earth and life, but, during the trip, Orpheus had to promise not to look back until both he and his wife were safe, back on earth. Orpheus worried. He was afraid his wife might need his help returning to the surface. He worried Hades would recant and not send her. To ensure that all was well, he risked a quick look behind him and lost his wife forever. I believe the parallel between these two couples is clear and does not need further commentary.

ABOUT THE AUTHOR

Ben Gwin's writing has appeared in *The Normal School*, *Mary: a Journal of New Writing*, *Bridge Eight*, *Thin Noon*, *Belt Magazine* and others. He's taught creative writing to inmates in the Allegheny County Jail, and to veterans in the Pittsburgh VA. He lives in Pittsburgh with his daughter.

ACKNOWLEDGEMENTS

Ryan Rivas, thank you. Ronald Reagan and I were lucky to have such a patient, hard working, and talented editor. Thanks also to the rest of the Burrow crew, especially Tina Craig, Iljeen Jo and Karis Moyers. *Clean Time* found the perfect home.

Thanks to everyone involved with Words Without Walls for the opportunity to teach, and for being nothing like the outreach program in this book.

Thanks to Sherrie Flick and Marc Nieson for your invaluable encouragement and direction when this was just a vague idea for an overly complicated graduate thesis.

From Pitt: Cathy Day for letting me write the unwieldy mess that started this whole thing, and Michael Byers for not letting me give up on myself. From the 90s: Blair Thompson, Holly Jones, and Jake Rashkind for instilling a curiosity about Ronald Reagan and a desire to write. Also, Josh Barkan, Lori Jakiela, and Dave Newman for the help with query letters and submissions.

Derek Green, I could not ask for a better mentor. Yes, I'm working on the next one.

Geoff Greer for your insight into reality TV, Bryan Takacs for the real Independence Way, and Hugh Lippincott for your continued support.

Jenna Wetmore, you have helped me and Rosie and this book in more ways than I could possibly write here.

TC Jones, Matt Bohn, Rob Swanger, and Leah Brennan for your stories and your honest, smart feedback over the years. Matt Pease, Michelle Payanzo, and Andrew Emig for reading early drafts. Celine Roberts and Taylor Grieshober for White Reggie's poetry.

Special thanks to Sarah Shotland and Claire Cunningham.

Rich Gegick, you've been reading this book for twelve years, I hope it was worth the wait.

Mom, Dad, Liz, and Rach, thank you for supporting my creative endeavors without judgment. I do not deserve such a great family.

Most importantly, Rosalie. You are the inspiration behind everything good I will ever do. I hope you're proud of your dad. Don't read this book until you're 30.

Finally, thanks to all the night owls on West Carson Street. I couldn't have done it without you.

Subscribe

We thrive on the direct support of enthusiastic readers like you. Your generous support has helped Burrow, since our founding in 2010, provide over 1,000 opportunities for writers to publish and share their work.

Burrow publishes four, carefully selected books each year, offered in an annual subscription package for a mere $60 (which is like $5/month, $0.20/day, or 1 night at the bar). Subscribers are recognized by name in the back of our books, and are inducted into our not-so-secret society: the illiterati.

Glance to your right to view our 2018 line-up. Since you've already (presumably) read *this* book, enter code **CLEAN25** at checkout to knock 25% off this year's subscriber rate:

BURROWPRESS.COM/SUBSCRIBE

Second Wife
stories by Rita Ciresi
978-1-941681-89-3

Linked fictional snapshots of feminine lust, loss and estrangement by the Flannery O'Connor Award-winning author of *Mother Rocket.*

Clean Time: the True Story of
Ronald Reagan Middleton
a novel by Ben Gwin
978-1-941681-70-1

A darkly comic satire of academia, celebrity worship, and recovery memoirs set in a near-future America ravaged by addiction.

Worm Fiddling Nocturne in the Key
of a Broken Heart
stories by Kimberly Lojewski
978-1-941681-71-8

Fabulist, folkloric and whimsical stories featuring an itinerant marionette, a camp counselor haunted by her dead best friend, and a juvenile delinquent languishing in a bootcamp run by authoritarian grandmas… to name a few.

Space Heart
a memoir by Linda Buckmaster
978-1-941681-73-2

The story of growing up in 1960s Space-Coast Florida with a heart condition and an alcoholic, NASA engineer father.

the illiterati

Florida isn't known as a bastion of literature. Being one of the few literary publishers in the state, we embrace this misperception with good humor. That's why we refer to our subscribers as "the illiterati," and recognize them each year in our print books and online.

To follow a specific publishing house, just as you might follow a record label, requires a certain level of trust. Trust that you're going to like what we publish, even if our tastes are eclectic and unpredictable. Which they are. And even if our tastes challenge your own. Which they might.

Subscribers support our dual mission of publishing a lasting body of literature and fostering literary community in Florida. If you're an adventurous reader, consider joining our cult—er, cause, and becoming one of us...

One of us! One of us! One of us!

2017-18 illiterati

Emily Dziuban

John Henry Fleming

Nathan Andrew Deuel

Dina Mack

Abigail Craig

Teresa Carmody

Spencer Rhodes

Stephen Cagnina

Letter & Spears

Matthew Lang

David Rego

Rita Sotolongo

Michael Wheaton

Thomas M. Bunting Projects

Michael Cuglietta

Christie Hill

Alison Townsend

Rick Gwin & Peggy Uzmack

Michael Gualandri

Hunter Choate

Nathan and Heather Holic

Rita Ciresi

Lauren Salzman

Drew Hoffmann

Joanna Hoffmann

Dustin Bowersett

Stacey Matrazzo

pete !

H Blaine Strickland

Karen Price

Leslie Salas

Jessica Penza

Randi Brooks

To a Certain Degree

Yana Keyzerman

Erica McCay

A.G. Asendorf

Sarah Taitt

Winston Taitt

Lauren Zimmerman

Martha Brenckle

Nikki Fragala Barnes

Michael Barnes

Matthew Broffman

Shaina Anderson

Secret Society Goods

Stephanie Rizzo

Patrick Rushin

2017-18 illiterati

Stacy Barton

Marcella Benton

Roberta Alfonso Malone

Catherine Carson

Lora Waring

Naomi Butterfield

Nayma Russi

Nathan Holic

Mary Nesler

Dowell Bethea

Sarah Wildeman

Ginger Duggan

Ashley French

Lauren Groff

Susan Fallows

Sean Walsh

Liesl Swogger

Shawn McKee

Shane Hinton

Janna Benge

John Upperco

Peter Bacopoulos

Mike Cabrera

Sara Isaac

Kevin Craig

Lisa Roney

Joyce Sharman

Amy Parker

Martha Brenckle

Denise Gottshalk

Sarah Curley

Jonathan Kosik

Pat Greene

Susan Frith

Benjamin Noel

Matthew Lang

David Poissant

Erin Hartigan

Isabel Arias

Erika Friedlander

Amy Sindler

Kirsten Holz

Dan Reiter

Alexander Lenhoff

Rebecca Fortes

Giti Khalsa

Nikki Barnes

Jeremy Bassetti

Mira Tanna

Chuck Dinkins

2017-18 illiterati

Stuart Buchanan
Rich Wahl
Tyler Koon
Bob Lipscomb
Craig Ustler
Laura Albert
Emily Willix
Danielle Kessinger
Elisabeth Dang
Vicki Nelson
Camile Araujo
Leslie Salas
Cindy Simmons
Lauren Mitchell
Peter Knocke
Lauren Georgia
Susan Lilley
Jeffrey Shuster
Susan Pascalar
Jessica Horton
Jason Katz
Kim Robinson
Delila Smalley
Christine Daniel
Karen Rigsby

Tod Caviness
Terri Ackley
Terry Thaxton
Danita Berg
Karen Roby
Jesse Bradley
JT Taylor
Ben Comer
Grace Fiandaca
Aaron Harriss
Jonathan Miller
Pamela Gilbert
Nylda Dieppa-Aldarondo
Leeann M. Lee
Gerry Wolfson-Grande

We Can't Help It If We're From Florida
ed. Shane Hinton
978-1-941681-87-9

"As hot and wild and dangerous as our beloved (or is it bedeviled?) state, itself."
–Lauren Groff, *Fates & Furies*

"As weird and funny and beautiful and unnerving as you might expect from some of our state's best writers." –Karen Russell, *Swamplandia!*

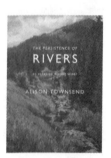

The Persistence of Rivers: an essay on moving water, by Alison Townsend
978-1-941681-83-1

In the vein of Thoreau and Dillard, Townsend considers the impact of rivers at pivotal moments in her life, examining issues of landscape, loss, memory, healing, and the search for home.

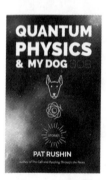

Quantum Physics & My Dog Bob
stories by Pat Rushin
978-1-941681-81-7

Each darkly funny story is like a parallel universe where everyday characters find themselves in a reality slightly askew from the one we know.

The Call: a virtual parable
by Pat Rushin
978-1-941681-90-9

"Pat Rushin is out of his fucking mind. I like that in a writer; that and his daredevil usage of the semi-colon and asterisk make *The Call* unputdownable."
–Terry Gilliam, director of *The Zero Theorem*

Pinkies: stories
by Shane Hinton
978-1-941681-92-3

"If Kafka got it on with Flannery O' Connor,
Pinkies would be their love child."
– Lidia Yuknavitch, *The Small Backs of Children*

Songs for the Deaf: stories
by John Henry Fleming
978-0-9849538-5-1

"Songs for the Deaf is a joyful, deranged, endlessly
surprising book. Fleming's prose is glorious music; his
rhythms will get into your bloodstream, and his images
will sink into your dreams."
– Karen Russell, *Swamplandia!*

Train Shots: stories
by Vanessa Blakeslee
978-0-9849538-4-4

"Train Shots is more than a promising first collection
by a formidably talented writer; it is a haunting story
collection
of the first order."
– John Dufresne, *No Regrets, Coyote*

15 Views of Miami
edited by Jaquira Díaz
978-0-9849538-3-7

A loosely linked literary portrait of the Magic City.
Named one of the 7 best books about Miami by
the *Miami New Times.*

Forty Martyrs
by Philip F. Deaver
978-1-941681-94-7

"I could hardly stop reading, from first to last."
– Ann Beattie, *The State We're In*

If you have any information regarding the whereabouts of Ronald Reagan Middleton, please visit: WhereIsRRMiddleton.com or email: Harold.Swanger@gmail.com